EX LIBRIS

VINTAGE CLASSICS

JULIO CORTÁZAR

Julio Cortázar lived in Buenos Aires for the first thirty years of his life, and, after that, in Paris. His stories, written under the dual influence of the English masters of the uncanny and of French surrealism, are extraordinary inventions, just this side of nightmare. In later life, Cortázar became a passionate advocate for human rights and a persistent critic of the military dictatorships in Latin America. He died in 1984.

ALSO BY JULIO CORTÁZAR

A Certain Lucas

A Change of Light and Other Stories

All Fires the Fire

A Manual for Manuel

Bestiary

Around the Day in Eighty Worlds

Autonauts of the Cosmoroute

Blow-Up and Other Stories

Cronopios and Famas

Diary of Andrés Fava

Divertimento

Fantomas Versus the Multinational Vampires

From the Observatory

Hopscotch

Literature Class, Berkeley 1980

Nicaraguan Sketches

Save Twilight

62: A Model Kit

Someone Walking Around

The Winners

Unreasonable Hours

We Love Glenda So Much and Other Tales

JULIO CORTÁZAR
FINAL EXAM

TRANSLATED FROM THE SPANISH AND WITH AN
INTRODUCTION BY
Alfred Mac Adam

VINTAGE CLASSICS

1 3 5 7 9 10 8 6 4 2

Vintage Classics is part of the Penguin Random House group of companies

Vintage, Penguin Random House UK, One Embassy Gardens,
8 Viaduct Gardens, London SW11 7BW

penguin.co.uk/vintage-classics
global.penguinrandomhouse.com

Copyright © Julio Cortázar and Heirs of Julio Cortázar, 1986
Translation © Alfred Mac Adam, 2000

The moral right of the author has been asserted

First published in Spanish by Sudamericana in 1986
First published in the United States of America by New Directions in 2000
This paperback first published in Vintage Classics in 2025

Penguin Random House values and supports copyright. Copyright fuels creativity, encourages diverse voices, promotes freedom of expression and supports a vibrant culture. Thank you for purchasing an authorised edition of this book and for respecting intellectual property laws by not reproducing, scanning or distributing any part of it by any means without permission. You are supporting authors and enabling Penguin Random House to continue to publish books for everyone. No part of this book may be used or reproduced in any manner for the purpose of training artificial intelligence technologies or systems. In accordance with Article 4(3) of the DSM Directive 2019/790, Penguin Random House expressly reserves this work from the text and data mining exception.

A CIP catalogue record for this book is available from the British Library

ISBN 9781529956757

Typeset in 11/13pt Bembo Book MT Pro by Six Red Marbles UK, Thetford, Norfolk
Printed and bound in Great Britain by Clays Ltd, Elcograf S.p.A.

The authorised representative in the EEA is Penguin Random House Ireland,
Morrison Chambers, 32 Nassau Street, Dublin D02 YH68

Penguin Random House is committed to a sustainable future
for our business, our readers and our planet. This book is made
from Forest Stewardship Council® certified paper.

Introduction

The brilliant Spanish American novelists of the sixties – Gabriel García Márquez, Carlos Fuentes, Mario Vargas Llosa, José Donoso, Guillermo Cabrera Infante, Alejo Carpentier – all admired Julio Cortázar's *Hopscotch* (1963). It was the quintessence of what had come to be known as the Boom, a new kind of novel from Spanish America: experimental, highly intellectual, hilarious, and irreverent. And it seemed to come out of nowhere: while Cortázar's first novel, *The Winners* (1960), does have some avant-garde touches, it really presents the situation of post-Perón Argentina as a ship-of-fools allegory.

Before 1960, Cortázar was famous as a writer of short stories, which he first published in 1949 in Jorge Luis Borges' magazine *Los Anales de Buenos Aires*. Until 1960, most of his readers assumed that Cortázar would follow in Borges' foot steps, in the sense of being an all-around man of letters – short-story writer, essayist, and translator. Invisibly, slowly, Cortázar (1914–1984) was developing into a writer very different from Borges. As a young man, he aspired to be a poet, because in Spanish America, poetry was considered the supreme literary art form. His first book, *Presencia (Presence)*, published in 1938 under the name Julio Denis, was a collection of Mallarmé-inspired sonnets. It is now rarer than the Gutenberg Bible.

Cortázar finished the manuscript of *Final Exam* in 1950. A few friends read it, but for political and personal reasons, the book would not appear until 1986. So if we were to ask 1950 Buenos Aires literati who Cortázar was, they would probably answer that he was an essayist and, occasionally, a translator. It is in his essays, beginning with his 1946 Symbolist reading of Keats, 'The Grecian Urn in the Poetry of John Keats,' where Cortázar tries to define the nature of literature and to determine how it should be written. These articles, published in a variety of Buenos Aires literary magazines, constitute a kind of literary autobiography, the intellectual foundation of his artistic career.

The principal tension in Cortázar's esthetics is between art-for-art's sake, which derives from his reading of Mallarmé and other French Symbolist poets, and art as provocation, which he discovered in Surrealism. French Existentialism is yet another presence in Cortázar's intellectual development, though in his case its effects would have more to do with art than politics. In fact — and *Final Exam* bears this out — Cortázar is remarkably apolitical until the sixties, when, inspired by the Cuban Revolution, he becomes a man of the left. Politics, usually from a moral rather than a rigorously ideological point of view, becomes his second career during the sixties, eventually eclipsing his literary production.

But in the forties, Cortázar is a man searching for a method, a writer trying to decide what kind of fiction to produce before taking the first step. So the major theme of his essays is the novel, which for him is the product of Europe or North America, since he rarely refers to Latin American literature during those years. It is a genre in need of rejuvenation. How to do it? One way, he suggests, is to make novels more like poems in the sense that novels should be stripped of explanatory passages that help the reader along. This means that characters would be shorn of psychology: the reader is responsible for creating them through interpretation. In this we also see the didactic element in Cortázar, who as a young man trained to be a teacher.

Cortázar never abandons the esthetic principles he discovers during the forties. They constitute the intellectual foundation of his major fiction, *Hopscotch*, and reappear in the gnomic utterances about literature made by one of its characters Morelli, a dying avant-garde writer. But to see these ideas in their purest form, the reader must turn to *Final Exam*, which summarizes all of Cortázar's thinking during the forties.

Unlike *Hopscotch*, *Final Exam* deals with a totally Argentine, actually Buenos Aires (*porteño*), world. The story is simple even if the novel itself is quite dense: Juan and Clara are about to take their final university examinations: they are to appear before a committee and answer a question chosen lottery style by a professor. They are nervous and over-prepared, so they decide to stay up all night and walk around Buenos Aires with three friends; a couple: Andrés, an intellectual dropout who prefigures Horacio Oliveira in *Hopscotch*, and his not overly bright girlfriend Stella; and a newspaper reporter referred to simply as 'the chronicler.'

The Buenos Aires they inhabit is filled with a mysterious fog. Public services like subways and trolleys are on the verge of total breakdown; the streets are caving in, and there is a bizarre ritual taking place in Plaza de Mayo, the political heart of the Argentine nation. Thousands of people from all over the republic are visiting a small bone on display in a huge tent. The visitors are treated to speeches, music, and various mysterious rites. The friends who read Cortázar's manuscript in 1950 began to regard him as a prophet in 1952, when Eva Perón died and her cadaver became an object of veneration.

Juan and Clara are also being stalked by a former friend, Abel, now insane, who seems to have been (like Andrés) one of Clara's lovers. There is, then, a double frame around the action: social anxiety on one hand and revenge on the other, the collective and the personal. It is tempting to read the novel as Cortázar's autobiography, but that is inaccurate, even though he infuses many of his literary and esthetic beliefs into Juan and Andrés. For example, Andrés, like Cortázar himself, is dazzled by Jean Cocteau's *Opium*, which opens the door to Surrealism.

Above all, *Final Exam* is a novel about Buenos Aires, but it is Buenos Aires transformed into a Kafkaesque nightmare. Other writers, the Argentine Roberto Arlt and the Uruguayan Juan Carlos Onetti, had seen the city through a distorted, Expressionist optic, but Cortázar, as he does in his best fantastic stories, walks a very fine line between realism and hallucination.

We must take into account the Argentina in which Cortázar

grew up. When he was two years old, Hipólito Yrigoyen, last of the old-style, nineteenth-century political bosses, became president of Argentina. When Cortázar was sixteen, in 1930, Yrigoyen was swept out of office by General Uriburu in a military coup. Between 1930 and 1943, a combination of military men and civilians bumbled along until the next military coup, which takes place on June 14, 1943. This marks the advent of Juan Perón and his wife Evita Duarte.

Cortázar witnessed a great deal of political unrest and violence before his definitive departure for Paris in 1951, when he took a position with UNESCO as a translator. This too is relevant to *Final Exam*, which juxtaposes the crises of personal life (broken relationships, jealousy) with the perpetual crisis of Argentine civil society. The main characters love being Argentine – they refer to the tango even in their most heated literary debates – but they view the nation as pure façade, a fraud. This phoniness appears in the novel's pseudo-climax, the final examination, which turns out to be nothing more than a hoax.

Not surprisingly, Cortázar's characters constantly wonder how it is possible to write under such circumstances. They have no real answers and can only fall back on the solutions they find in the Western tradition, which are not totally relevant to Argentine reality. In many ways then, *Final Exam* is Cortázar's farewell to Argentina, the country he loved but had to leave to become the kind of novelist he hoped to be.

Often to the dismay of younger readers, *Final Exam* is also a summary of Cortázar's readings during the forties, from the forgotten detective novels of Nigel Balchin to the almost forgotten Existentialist novels of André Malraux. The presence of Edgar Allan Poe, whose prose works Cortázar translated into Spanish, is also a strong one here, not because Cortázar was especially fascinated with nineteenth-century American literature, but because Poe, translated by Baudelaire, was part of the internationalized French culture that permeates the novel. There are many writers, public figures (the boxer Primo Carnera for example), or literary characters (Balzac's Eugenie Grandet) who may well be unknown to today's general reader. Not to worry! Cortázar's depiction of social disintegration and the vicissitudes of love are so powerful that a few enigmatic allusions will not prevent the reader from understanding the action. Leave the archeological investigation for a second reading!

Alfred Mac Adam

A Note on the Translation

In *Final Exam*, Cortázar employs a technique he uses throughout his career, the mixture of very vulgar Argentine street Spanish with high-flown esthetic concepts. This generates irony and humor, but is virtually impossible to replicate in English, where regional dialects lead inevitably to caricature. There is a great deal of Italian mixed in as well, because there were (and are) so many Italians living in Buenos Aires.

Author's Note

I wrote *Final Exam* midway through 1950 in a Buenos Aires where the imagination only had to add the slightest touch to history to obtain the results the reader will soon see.

It was impossible to publish the book then, so only a few friends read it. Later on and from very far away, I learned that those same friends believed they saw in certain episodes a portent of the events that illuminated our annals during 1952 and 1953. Scoring that necrological and governmental bulls-eye brought me no joy. In point of fact, it was too easy: the Argentine future so insistently repeats the present that exercises in prophecy have no merit whatsoever.

I publish this old tale today because I irremediably enjoy its free language, its fable devoid of moralizing, its Buenos Aires melancholy, and also because the nightmare from which it was born is still awake and prowling the streets.

J.C.

I

'Il Y A Terriblement D'années, Je M'en Allais chasser le gibier d'eau dans les marais de l'Ouest – et comme il n'y avait pas alors de chemins de fer dans le pays où il me fallait voyager, je prenais la diligence . . .'* *You have a good time, and I hope you bag many, many partridges*, thought Clara, walking away from the classroom door. She could no longer hear the voice of the Reader. How wonderfully isolated the rooms in the House were, all you had to do was step back a few yards to re-enter the mildly buzzing silence of the gallery. She walked toward the stairway, but, undecided, stopped when she came to another hallway. From there, she could hear clearly the Readers in Section A, Modern English Novel. But it was unlikely Juan would be in one of those classrooms. *The annoying thing is that with him you just never know*. Then she decided to go look and find out for sure, angrily squeezing her notebook. She turned left, though it didn't matter which way she went. '"Was there a husband?" "Yes. Husband died of anthrax." "Anthrax?" "Yes, there were a lot of cheap shaving brushes on the market just then . . ."'

Nothing wrong with stopping for a second to see if Juan –

'"some of them infected. There was a regular scandal about it." "Convenient," suggested Poirot.' – but he wasn't there. 7:40, and Juan said he'd meet her at 7:30. The jerk! He was probably in one of the classrooms, mixed in with the parasites of the House – listening without hearing. Other times, they'd met on the ground floor next to the stairway, but Juan had probably gone up to the

---

*A terrible number of years ago, I set out to hunt wild fowl in the Western swamps – and since there were no railroads in the land in which I was to travel, I hired a carriage . . .

second floor. *What a jerk! Unless, he's late, unless . . . Maybe the other gallery, he's probably there someplace . . .*

'dans les mélodies nous l'avons vu, les emprunts et les échanges s'effectuent très souvent par- . . .'

But no, he wasn't there. *This Reader has a good voice*, she told herself, stopping near the door. The room was brightly lit, and she could see the little sign announcing the title of the book: *Le Livre Des Chansons, ou Introduction à la Chanson Populaire Française (Henry Davenson). Chapter II. Reader: Mr Roberto Chaves.*

This must be the man who read La Bruyère last year, thought Clara. A light voice devoid of emphasis, well able to withstand the five-hour stretch of reading. Just then, the Reader paused, dropping a silence as if it were a spoonful of tapioca pudding. The length of the silence told the listeners if it was a full stop or a footnote. *A footnote*, thought Clara. The Reader went on: 'Voir là-dessus la seconde partie de la thèse de C. Brouwer *Das Volklied in Deutschland, Frankreich* . . .' *A good Reader, one of the best. I couldn't do it, I get distracted, and then I run on like a dog. And that nervous yawning after reading aloud for a while*, she remembered that in fifth grade, Miss Capello made her read passages from *Marianela*. For the first few pages, everything went fine, but then came the yawning, the slow tightening slowly but surely taking control of her throat and mouth, and Miss Capello with her angelic face, listening in ecstasy. The forced pause to control the yawn — she seemed to feel it all over again, transferred it to the Reader, and regretted it for his sake, poor devil — and again reading until the next yawn, no, she most certainly was not suitable for the House. *There's Juan! Here he comes, happy as a lark, his head in the clouds as usual.*

But it wasn't Juan, only a fellow who looked like him. Clara was livid and stalked over to the other side of the gallery where there were no readings in progress, but she could smell Ramiro's coffee. *I'll ask Ramiro for a cup to drown my rage.* She was annoyed that she'd confused Juan with another man. That fatso Herlick would have said, 'See? Tricks of the *gestalt*: three lines given, use your imagination to complete the picture. Given: a rather skinny

4

body, chestnut-colored hair, and a certain way of walking – as if he were dragging a Buenos-Aires idleness along with him – and you see Juan.' The *gestalt* could . . . *Ramiro, Ramiro, how I could go for a cup of his coffee, but it's only for the Readers and for Dr Menta.* The House: coffee and readings. And now it's 7:45.

Two young women left a classroom almost running. They exchanged phrases the way birds exchange pecks and didn't even see Clara in their haste to get to the stairs. *The kind who run and listen to another chapter of another book, as if they were switching the dial from a tango to Lohengrin, to the stock-market report, ads for refrigerators, Ella Fitzgerald . . . The House ought to prohibit that kind of promiscuity. One at a time, dear members of the radio audience, you don't take up Stendhal until you finish Zogoibi.*

But it was Dr Menta, slave to culture, who ruled the House. Read books and you'll find yourself. Believe in the printed word, in the voice of the Reader. Accept the spiritual bread. *Those two are the kind who'd go up to listen to some Russian novel read by Menghi or Spanish poetry recited so nicely by Miss Rodríguez. They swallow everything without chewing, and when they leave they eat a sandwich in the House snack bar so they won't lose time – and then off they go to a film or a concert. They're so cultured, they're just divine. Never in my life have I seen pedantry raised to so high a degree of excellence . . .* Because it would have been useless to ask one of those girls what she thought about things going on in the city, the provinces, the country, the hemisphere, in the entire blessed world. Information? All you want: Archimedes, a famous mathematician; Lorenzo de' Medici, the son of Giovanni; 'Puss 'n Boots,' a charming tale by Perrault, and so on . . . She was in the first gallery again. Some doors were closed, an annoying buzz, the Reader. *Les Temps Modernes, Number 50, December, 1949. Reader: Mr Osmán Caravazzi.*

I should try out this idea of listening to magazines, thought Clara. *It could be fun. First one subject and then another, like a continuous show at the movies: the reading begins whenever you arrive.* She felt tired and walked over to where the gallery opened onto the patio below. There were stars and lights. Clara sat down on one of the cold benches and felt for her chocolate bar, a Dolca with almonds. From a window above, came a dry, clear voice. Moyano, or perhaps Dr Bergmann, who'd read all of Balzac in three years. Unless it was Bustamante ... That was probably Dr Wolff up on the fourth floor, all nasal with her *Wolfnaselgang Goethenasal*; and from somewhere else little Mary Robbins, Reader of Nigel Balchin.

Clara felt her compassion aroused by the chocolate, she was no longer angry with her husband. 8:00, and she wasn't annoyed by the bell tolling from the huge clock on the corner. After all, it was her fault for coming to the House; the readings didn't matter a bit to Juan, damn him. These days it was difficult to find interesting courses, or original lectures – the House served the purpose of keeping the spiritual bread hot. [Sic.] What it was really good for was to meet with some friend and chat in a low voice while the grand program of useful works created by Dr Menta and the Dean of the Faculty was simultaneously put into practice.

She could just hear them: 'Of course, doctor, but of course: young people are always young people, they never study at home. On the other hand, if you make them *listen* to the works, recited by our first-rate Readers.' (Those horns of plenty were paid professorial salaries, you know.) 'You'll find you can attract more bees with honey than with vinegar. Isn't that the case, Dr Menta? Dr Menta, ...' *But if I keep on reconstructing each and every one of his crimes*, thought Clara, *I'll end up believing in the House. I'd rather bite right through my Dolca bar*. The House wasn't so bad after all. Under the pretext of passing on world culture, Dr Menta had given jobs to dozens of Readers; the Readers read and the girls (especially those who were always such good little students and so attentive to the grand program of useful works) listened. Something would remain of all that, even if nothing more than Nigel Balchin.

'Tomorrow night,' explained Juan over the phone. 'The final examination. Yes, but of course we're going to have lunch. And go to the concert, for sure. The exam's at night, there's time for everything.'

When he hung up, furious that the telephone connection had been so bad and that he'd barely been able to hear his father-in-law, furious about how late it was, he saw Abel walking into the bar through the door on Carlos Pellegrini Street. Wearing blue, Abel was extremely pale and thin; as usual, he looked no one in the eye and made his way crabwise, avoiding faces even more than tables.

'Abelito,' whispered Juan, leaning on the bar. 'Abelito!'

But Abel settled into a corner and stared at the wall without seeing him or, more likely, without wanting to see him. Juan stirred his coffee, not wanting to drink it. He'd ordered it out of habit. He never liked making telephone calls from bars without first ordering something. Seen from the back, Abel seemed even thinner, his shoulders were stooped. How long it had been since they'd seen each other. In the old days, Abelito never wore anything as nice as that blue suit. *He's got money*, thought Juan. The most natural thing would have been for them to wave to each other even if from a distance, not to shake hands. They'd never had a falling out. How could you fight with Abel? He vaguely remembered the creeps who would sometimes appear in the bathroom of the house where they lived – he'd come back late in his student days. Poor Abelito, really, it was too much to compare him with . . . He gulped down the tepid, overly sweet coffee, stared tenderly at his shopping bag with the cauliflower in it. (As soon as he came in, he'd put the bag near him on the bar near the telephone, so no one would put a hand or elbow, on it.) Now a blond man in shirt sleeves was shouting into the telephone. Juan glanced once more at Abel, who was sitting at the other end of the café, then paid, and walked out carrying the bag very carefully.

He walked along Cangallo, making his way through the scurrying passersby. The evening was hot; it was crowded, the cafés on the corners were overflowing. *But what the fuck are all these people doing here at this hour?* thought Juan. *What lives, what deaths are they plotting? Well, how about me, what business do I have in the House? I would have been better off going up to Abel, asking him why he was walking around with a fresh-pressed face . . .* Seeing him in the café, he was beginning to suspect that perhaps Abelito . . . But the fact was no one liked Abelito; which was more than sufficient reason to run into him in cafés. Poor Abel, so alone, so looking for something.

If he were really looking for us, he'd have found us by now, thought Juan.

He crossed Libertad, crossed Talcahuano. The House had turned on the extra lights for Thursdays. *Not one classroom empty! Six thousand listeners they pack in in sections of a thousand each. How Menta must regret not having Kavanagh . . . And he's probably in his office, wearing a dark blue or black suit, checking over forms, taking care of the public, filled with good intentions: We think the Dostoyevsky course should be given again, and the one on Ricardo Güiraldes. We waste too much time with Central American magazines. When will the cinematheque open? Dr Menta is terribly sorry, but in classroom 31, they still have enough material for six more weeks with Pérez Galdós. It's not easy running the House*, thought Juan. He went up the stairs two at a time and almost ran into pug-nose Gómez, who was running out.

'You should warn people if you're running away from the cops.'

'Worse than that, Juan, I'm escaping from that pudgy Maers,' said pug nose. 'Every time she corners me, she starts explaining Darwin and anthropoid behavior.'

'Holy Mother,' said Juan.

'And *her* mother too, because she's always talking about her family and a sister she's got out in Ramos Mejía. See you later. Everything okay?'

'Yeah, everything's okay. What about you?'

'I'm in the Interest on Earnings course,' said pug nose, and he went his lugubrious way.

Juan crossed the gallery and went to the patio, where with all certainty Clara was in a fury. He sneaked up behind her and tickled her.

'You're odious,' said Clara, handing him the last of the Dolca bar.

'You smell like a birthday. You've got the air of the victim, of the laboratory subject. Dr Menta regrets.'

8

'Disgusting man.'

'And you receive me with the charm associated with fountains, with hills.'

'It's 8:20.'

'Indeed it is. Time's marched on and passed us by.

            Time, like a child
            led by the hand
            who looks back . . . I wrote that haiku two years ago, imagine . . . Clara, in this bag you see here I have a prodigious cauliflower.'

'Eat it and, if you like, puke it. Besides, you're supposed to say "cauliflower" not "colleyflower."'

'It isn't meant for eating,' explained Juan. 'This cauliflower is for carrying around in a bag to admire it from time to time. I think the present moment is propitious for the admiration of the cauliflower. So . . .'

'I'd rather not see it,' said Clara, proud of herself.

'Just for a second, so you get to know it. It cost me 1.90 in the Plata Market. I couldn't resist its beauty, so I went in and they wrapped it up for me. It was more beautiful than an early Flemish painting, and you know how I . . . Just take a good look at it . . .'

'It's pretty. I can see it just fine that way. No need to take it all the way out.'

'There's something of an insect's eye to it magnified thousands of times,' said Juan, allowing his finger to pass over the tightly bunched, grayish surface. 'Just think: it's a flower, the enormous flower of the cabbage family – a *cau-li*-flower. But, you know, it's got something of a vegetable brain to it. O, cauliflower, what are you thinking about?'

'You were late because of that thing?'

'Yes. Also because I called your Dad, who's inviting us to lunch tomorrow; and I was looking at Abel.'

'You certainly know how to waste time,' said Clara. 'Abel and Dad . . . I'd opt for the cauliflower.'

'Besides, I was counting on your forgiveness, dear,' said Juan. 'Moreover, we've still got time to listen to Moyano for a while. And I know how much you like Moyano's voice. The great acoustic fondler, the telephonic rapist.'

'Jerk.'

'But he's just fine! The guy reads with such a degree of perfection, it doesn't matter what he's reading. And I like the three blondes who sit in the first row to drink it all in. The poor man, the superheterodyne lover! Hold on while I fix up the wrapping, someone could damage the colossus, the colossal cauliflower – the brilliant cauliflory, the caulicle.'

From a room on the left, where the gallery began, came a psalmody muffled by the glass doors. *They're reading Balmes*, thought Clara, *or it could be Javier de Viana* . . . A couple came running in and separated to read the little signs on the doors; they exchanged angry glances. Bam, headfirst, into the *Ballad of the Wolves*, Galiano Sifredi reader. A boy with huge eyeglasses was diligently reading the motto of the House written in gold letters on the wall:

> *L'art de la lecture doit laisser l'imagination de*
> *l'auditeur, sinon tout à fait libre, du moins pouvant*
> *croire à sa liberté.* – Stendhal

(Everyone knew it was Gide who really said it, that Dr Menta had swallowed the attribution to Stendhal.)

Just invent an apocryphal intellectual structure, thought Clara. *Make a founding father say what he should have said and didn't; modify stupid temporality, render unto Caesar what should have been rendered unto him, but what was something actually said by Frederick II or President Yrigoyen* . . .

'Let's go,' said Juan. 'I hope there's a place to sit.'

Halfway up the stairs, they paused to examine the bust of Caracalla. Clara liked the domineering gesture in his eyebrows, which closed over the eyes like drawbridges. She always caressed the bust as she passed, deploring the crack in the nose that made him look wicked.

'One of these days, he's going to bite your hand, Clara. Caracalla was like that.'

'Caesars don't bite. And with a name as sweet as that, Caracalla, lord of the Romans.'

'It's not a sweet name,' said Juan. 'It snaps like the whips of his charioteers.'

'You're mixing him up with Caligula.'

'No, *he* sounds like some bitter root. Two grains of caligula in a glass of honey. Or how about this: The sky is caligulated, who will discaligulate it? Oh, good-bye, Dr Romero.'

'Good night, youngsters,' she said, firmly grasping the banister.

'Hurry up, Juan, Moyano probably started reading twenty minutes ago.'

'You were the one who stopped to jerk off that poor Caesar.'

'So what? He deserves it, he's good to me. And no one stops to look at him — he who was once so looked at.'

'Caracalla's caracoles,' said Juan. 'The Romans were like that. Dr Romero's turned into an elephant by the way. She turned around and contemplated my package. She smelled the cauliflower.'

'Are you really going to carry that thing into the room?' asked Clara. 'You're going to make noise rustling the paper bag and disturb everybody.'

'If I could only put it in my buttonhole, how about that? A caracallesque caprice. But you do think it's pretty, right? You just can't get cauliflower like this anymore.'

'It's okay. In my house, they bought bigger ones.'

'Your famous house,' said Juan.

The Reader made his end-of-chapter pause. Before beginning the next one, he allowed time for coughs, the manifestation of handkerchiefs, quick comments. Like a veteran pianist, he permitted a few seconds of relaxation, but not too many, so as not to lose that fluid yet tense substance adhering his voice to the people, his reading to attentions not always easily attracted.

Making a small bow:

Moise prenait de l'âge, mais aussi de l'apparence. Les banquiers ses contemporains, qu'il avait dépassés à trente ans en influence, à quarante en fortune . . .

'Let me put the package between us,' whispered Juan. 'This fat guy on my left is fully capable of flattening the cauliflower.'

'Give it to me,' said Clara, grabbing the paper bag which rustled, causing Andrés Fava to turn his face toward them and grimace. In the finally ensuing silence, the Reader's voice dropped effortlessly from its preceding discrete volume. Clara suddenly remembered:

'What was he doing?'

'Who?'

'Abelito. What was he doing in the café?'

'I don't know. Looking for you, maybe.'

'Hmm. But looking for me in the exact place I'm not.'

'That might explain,' said Juan, 'why he's looking for you.'

'Be quiet, both of you,' grumbled Andrés. 'You two walk in, and everything falls apart. I lose my concentration, see? Then I lose my mind.'

Abelito, thought Clara, staring in a friendly way at Andrés' slightly skinny neck, examining critically the vulgar permanent ruining Stella's appearance – Stella, naturally, was sitting next to Andrés. *Yes, he looks for me in the exact place I'm not, where I never was. Poor Abelito.*

Stella slowly slipped her hand into Andrés' pocket. Slowly Stella slipped her hand. Stella, into Andrés' pocket, slipped her hand, slowly. It's no easy thing to slip a hand (your own, that is) into the trouser pocket of a seated man. Andrés played dumb and watched her out of the corner of his eye. The funny thing was that his handkerchief was in his other pocket.

'You're tickling me.'

'Give me your handkerchief, I'm going to sneeze.'

'Let's at least cry together, sweetheart, because I don't have one.'

'You most certainly do have a handkerchief.'

'Yes, I most certainly have a handkerchief, but not for you.'

'Hateful thing.'

'Germ bearer.'

'You're the one demanding silence,' whispered Juan, 'and now you start a riot over a handkerchief. How about some respect for culture, buddy? Let the rest of us hear.'

'That's right,' said another fat man sitting to Stella's right. 'Show a little respect.'

'Right,' said Juan. 'That's just what I say, sir: more respect.'

'That's right,' said the fat guy.

Clara was listening to *Eglantine*:

Eglantine entrait, et redonnait subitement leur réalité, pour les yeux de Moise ému, au taupé et au Transvaal . . .

And she was appreciating the Reader's talent for reading with a minimum of gestures. *I'd be flapping my hands every which way*, thought Clara. *Juan is perfectly capable of falling over backwards in his chair just reading me some article in 'Crítica.'* Completely distracted, incapable of focusing on *Eglantine* (she intended to read it on her own, as she did so many books she never ended up reading), she again stared at Andrés' back, at Stella's hair, at the Reader's indifferent face. She was surprised to find herself using her fingers to explore the contents of the package, moving along like an insect over the cold, wrinkled surface of the cauliflower. She brought her fingers up to her nose: they had a weak scent of moist bran, a rainy season in a room with a piano and furniture draped with slipcovers, of a set-aside copy of *Para Ti*.

Juan allowed her to keep holding the package. He took advantage of the next pause in the reading to move to Andrés' left. Now they could talk without annoying the fat man – he was chatting with a lady who was probably retired, and wearing a violet dress.

'One day the true contents of a pocket will be revealed,' said Juan, 'and it will be seen they have very little to do with Charles Morgan.'

'The *introspection* of you,' said Andrés. 'So what's happening, man?'

'Everything's the same, my friend. And you? Stella's as pretty as ever.'

'You're always the same,' said Stella. 'All Andrés' friends are the same, a bunch of liars and scoundrels!'

'Charming young lady,' said Juan to Andrés. 'You've got a treasure in your own house and you probably don't even realize it.'

'How wrong you are,' said Andrés. 'I'm the first to appreciate Stella's merits and delights. I've already filled several notebooks with praise, and posterity will one day know what the city with Stella in it meant to me.'

'Do you write, young fellow?' asked Juan, initiating one of their pseudo interviews. 'Amazing. How promising.'

'And you, lad? Don't you write? It would be a sad thing if you didn't, believe me when I say it.'

'Calm down, young man. I also write. All of us, all of us in our intelligent set write. As for you, I've heard rumors that you keep up a kind of day book I'd someday like to get a squint at, if that would be acceptable to you.'

'You're asking for it,' said Andrés. 'But it isn't a day book, it's a night book.'

'Did you hear that?' asked Stella. 'It sounded like a siren.'

'It was a siren,' said Clara. 'Loud enough to penetrate the insulated armor walls of our holy House.'

'Rude reality ends up coinciding with mythology,' said Andrés. 'My personal opinion is that we should go somewhere where we can use our vocal cords to the full. Stella, darling, you won't be angry if we interrupt your intimate colloquy with literature, will you?'

'But there are only five minutes left,' complained Stella, who easily confused attendance with time well spent.

'Five minutes, what nonsense,' said Andrés. 'Anyway, Clara doesn't even allow us to hear with all that rustling of paper. Man, the devotion some people have to fine writing is incredible. One night at the boxing matches I spotted a guy reading a couple of pages of Karl Jaspers between fights.'

'I'm not bothering you with the paper in the slightest,' said Clara. 'He's the guilty party: he bought the cauliflower, and then handed it over to me for safekeeping.'

'I don't want anyone to bruise it,' said Juan. 'As I was saying before we were so rudely interrupted, I wouldn't mind at all if you were to let me read your recent essays. I hold your prose in high esteem, and besides, I humbly respect my destiny, which consists of reading the lives and opinions of others. It was the same with Abelito. And with Clara it's even worse: she informs me orally – she's the factory, and I'm the consumer. Intimacy: just think of it. Her mother had four false teeth, her brother collects Frank Sinatra records . . . Why did we come to the House? The best things to hear are outside.'

'Five before nine,' said Stella. 'Gosh, today I was so inattentive . . .'

'Don't take it so hard, sweety,' said Andrés. 'Next time, I'll take you to hear a reading of Vicki Baum.'

'You're mean. You don't see that what I want to do is practice my French. It's because of all of you that I lose track of things. What a pain you all are.'

Clara ran her hand through Stella's hair, moved by her words. *Is she an idiot, or does she play at being one?* she thought. *Poor Andrés, but it seems he chose her.* Stella's thick hair allowed itself to be invaded by fingers slipping smoothly through it. It made a kind of halo though which Clara saw the Reader close his book and get up. The chairs began to creak and squeak – as if they too had begun to comment on the reading. *What the poor things must know*, thought Clara. *One book after another, week in, week out.* The lights blinked twice, went out, then came on again: one of Dr Menta's ideas to empty out the House rapidly at 9:00 P.M.

Andrés walked out next to Clara and felt the package.

'Nice vegetable you've got there,' he said. 'But you're looking a little thin.'

'Guard duty. Tomorrow's the final exam,' said Clara. 'Why do you come here, Andrés?'

'Actually I bring Stella so she can practice phonetics. It's all the same to me whether I'm here or not. A habit I must have picked up when I studied at the University; and besides I always run into some friend or other. For instance tonight – I was lucky.'

'The truth is we've been seeing very little of each other recently,' said Clara. 'What a stupid life.'

'Please don't be redundant. Anyway, the House is amusing, and Stella thinks it does both of us good. Personally what I like most about it are the sandwiches in the café. Especially the pâté.'

Clara glanced at him out of the corner of her eye. The unusual, habitual, elusive four-eyed roach. And he suddenly laughed, out of happiness.

'Poor you, so you're studying hard! Why are you wasting your time here?'

'It's the best thing to do. We couldn't study anymore,' said Juan. 'Light entertainment on the eve of battle. Clara's going to pass, for sure. As for me, I don't know. Sometimes they ask the damndest things . . .'

'How right you are,' said Stella. 'It's like the quiz shows. I bite my nails and get so nervous . . .'

(Stella:

> *'Now, miss, this question's worth fifty pesos. Will you take a chance?'*
>
> *'Well . . .'*
>
> *'Very well, miss. You're a brave young woman. Let's see now. Okay. Who discovered the principle of flotation in bodies?'*)

'You've got to resort to trickery,' said Andrés. 'A stupid question deserves an absolutely absurd answer. Then the three guys asking the questions are left wondering if you're teasing them or if you actually have a brain. Time runs out, they get bored, and they pass you.'

'It looks easy to you,' said Juan, 'but a final exam is no joke. Especially for me, because I'm paying the price for my rather disorganized autodidactic methods. You'd have to be an idiot to think you learn something in the sacred halls of higher Argentine learning.'

'Clara must know a lot,' said Stella. 'I bet she studied like mad.'

'I knew the entire curriculum,' said Clara with a sigh. 'But it's like a well: I look down to the bottom and see only myself, with a washed face.'

'She's scared out of her wits,' Juan explained. 'But she's going to pass. So where are you going now?'

'To watch the night pass and have a drink with Stella.'

'And with us.'

'Okay.'

'We'll talk about black masks,' said Clara.

'And the paintings of Antonio Berni,' said Stella, who admired Antonio Berni.

Andrés and Juan brought up the rear. The women walked arm in arm, mixing in with the people coming out of the other lecture halls. They heard the voice of Lorenzo Wahrens, who was hurriedly finishing up a chapter. While many listeners clogged the door, walking out on tiptoe with a slightly mortified air.

'Poor author!' said Andrés. 'Look at them running for it before Wahrens finishes.'

'What do you expect, man? He's reading *La Nouvelle Héloïse*,' said Juan.

'Good point, but can you explain this anxiety people have about leaving places? It's the same at the movies; half an hour on line waiting to get in and then there's no time to lose at the end . . . Superficial forms of anxiety, I suppose. I also suppose it's the same everywhere. I say that because around here we've got myriad pseudo sociologists who think they recognize *specifically* Argentine forms of behavior when they are only *specific* forms of behavior. All that crap people have been saying about our solitude, our escapism . . .'

'The truth is people here are always anxious,' said Juan. 'Unfortunately, the things that cause their anxiety are usually things like the teakettle – "Go see if it's boiling, hurry up, I'm sure it's boiling, my God, you can't take your eye off it for a minute! . . ."'

'Wait: if they're boiling water to make *maté*, then there's good reason,' said Andrés.

'Or the fear of missing the train, even if there's another one in ten minutes. Look, once I subscribed to a series of string-quartet recitals. The woman who sat next to me left every concert before the last movement! Since we were already friends, she explained to me after the third time that she'd have to wait twenty minutes at Constitución Station if she missed the train to Lomas de Zamora. Imagine, missing the end of Ravel's *Assez vif et rhythmé* to save twenty minutes.'

'Worse things have been exchanged for a bowl of pottage,' said Andrés. 'One way or another, people always repeat the same basic crimes. One day you're Ixion, and the next you're an office-model Macbeth. And to think, we have the nerve after all that to ask for a good-conduct award.'

'Maybe that's why I'm always afraid when I go into a police station,' said Juan. 'Nobody's record is spotless.'

'Who knows if the things we take to be disasters or sicknesses are simply penalties,' said Andrés. 'I imagine that old man Freud would say pretty much the same thing. Take baldness, for example. Doesn't it seem to you it might just be that bald men have fallen for a Delilah of the unconscious? Or arthritics turned to look at something they shouldn't have? Once I dreamt I was sentenced to capital punishment. By which, of course, I don't mean death: to the contrary. The punishment was capital because it consisted in living on the other side of the dream, constantly remembering that I'd forgotten it. The punishment was just that, having forgotten it.'

'Abel talked like that sometimes,' said Juan. 'His own name put him in the club of "juicy victims". Maybe that's why he's always turning over papers, plays the bad guy with mirrors.'

Andrés said nothing. They began walking down Cangallo, feeling the heat on their faces.

'Be careful with the package,' said Juan, moving ahead. 'Even better, give it to me, Clarita, darling. When you walk down the street you turn into a calamity.'

He dropped back next to Andrés. Stella suggested they walk through the market and eat something in a grill. So they walked up to take the 86 streetcar at Sarmiento Avenue. Clara wanted to call home, so they waited for her on the corner. Andrés was casting a calculating eye over Juan.

'You're quite a guy. Shouldn't you study a little?'

'I'd rather have some white wine and a chat with you. You know we see very little of each other, almost as if we were intimate friends.'

'God save us from that, and may He save you from more bad paradoxes. Don't you feel there's something in the air?'

'Fog, dearest,' said Stella. 'Right around now the fog rolls in.'

'Baloney, sweetheart. Right around now it's only whores and dancers that do that. But you're right, fog is what it is.'

'It's humid downtown, too,' said Juan uselessly.

'Your clothes stick to your skin,' said Stella. 'This morning when I woke up I thought the sheets were wet.'

'When you wake up,
the alarm clock starts to bleed.
When you wake up,
it's almost time to sup.
Love, moist sheets,
when you wake up,' said Andrés. 'I offer these bolero lyrics to you as a gift, to console that immoral little heart of yours.'

Stella pinched his ear and shook him to her heart's content.

'When I wake up,' said Juan, 'the first thing I think of as an emergency measure is to go back to sleep.'

'What we would call turning your back on reality,' said Andrés. 'Now listen to this, this is important. You talk about going back to sleep, and you try to do it. But you're mistaken if you think that's how you're going to sink back into yourself, that you're going to take cover behind something that will protect you from your day. Sleeping is nothing more than getting lost. When you try to go back to sleep, you're trying to find an escape again.'

'I know, I know, it's a light little death devoid of consequences,' said Juan. 'But, that's the great prestige, the perfection, of it. Vacation from your self – not seeing, and not seeing yourself. Perfect.'

'Maybe. Anyway, we cling so much like barnacles to

ourselves – even when we're half-asleep, it's hard to shake off. For instance, sometimes I get up at four in the morning to pee – inevitable consequence of having stayed up late drinking *maté*. When I get back into bed, I can tell that my body, on its own' ('I feel a warm spot!' shouted Stella) 'exactly, sweetheart – it seeks out the warm spot, its copy, its living imprint. The feet in the toasty little corner, the man in his protected niche . . . Nothing to be done about it, old man, not in vain do we believe that A is A.'

'The only part that looks for a cool spot is the head,' said Juan, 'which proves it's the thinking part of the person. Here comes Clara, and I think that's the 86 pulling in.'

The streetcar was hanging on to itself, like a woman stumbling along weighed down with packages. Juan ended up in a corner, a window seat (thanks to one of those odd roulette-wheel swirls
    that occur in all conflicts among wills
    that are almost always resolved by chance
    that leave you standing – thought Clara – while that enormous loafer happily sits down).

Juan liked the fog on the windows, the lights like swift tigers (but how pretty it is, how pretty) running across the dripping windows. As always, whenever he sat down on a trolley, he was taken over by a renunciation, a satisfactory abandonment. He deferred to the trolley – allowing a fragment of the city to pass slowly by him, with curves, stops, and sudden accelerations. The fog helped him to feel passive, slip deeper and deeper into a small, fifteen-minute nirvana – ten blocks in length because the good citizens of Buenos Aires never walk if they can avoid it. Buddha's bo tree was named 86. Cabalistically – 86: two even numbers, one number divisible by two, 43. And in his pocket, he had precisely that: a pack of 43's. But the sign said NO SMOKING NO SPITTING. Beneath the bo tree.

A man can be happy with so little, he thought. *Without even a kiss. So little. The cup of tea prepared with its minimal liturgy, an insect asleep on a book, an old perfume. Yes, almost the nothingness . . .* As long as you accept abandoning yourself to the shade of the bo tree, settling for being happy a few blocks on a bit of streetcar.

A numerous and hyperactive family got off at the second stop. Stella made the moves necessary to block access to a seat and let Clara sit next to the window. The two women looked at each other with the smiling joy of all those who manage to get seats on a crowded trolley (a theme for moralists). They tried to see something of the street, but the fog didn't allow them much.

'Wow, I thought those old ladies would never get off,' said Stella. 'I'm too tired to stand, even if it's only for ten blocks. And to think someone offered Andrés a Morris five years ago for four grand and I told him to wait. I told him that cheaper cars would come later from the United States.'

'Big mistake, dearie. That's what you get for having ideas in this country.'

'Everyone said it was going to happen.'

'That's a better reason to doubt it. But Andrés would have gotten fed up with the Morris. Or the two of you would have been squashed by a tractor-trailer. I can just see him letting go of the steering wheel to make a little picture in the moisture on the windshield.'

'Andrés' mother says the same thing. But you've got to try things.'

Clara looked at her out of the corner of her eye. Stella was like that – her thoughts were like the trolley: fixed route. Andrés was Auguste Dupin: all of Stella's ideas known beforehand. *What economy*, thought Clara, amused. She did like Stella: she was easy to handle. Women of her kind *think* they can take the initiative (that's the worst thing about them); but Stella hung back, like the peasant girl on the maté box. At most she kept up. *In any case, Andrés, what a sad situation. Having to put up with an airhead like that, poor guy.* At the same time, the fact Andrés had made such a choice made her indignant – even if Stella always ended up moving her to compassion.

'How dark downtown is,' said Stella. 'I don't like it this dark. Hey, look at that shop window with the jodhpurs, how strange it should be lit up like that.'

'Pretty wools,' said Clara, interested. 'What's that bell ringing?'

'Some car coming out of an underground parking lot.'

'No, it must be that the sweepers are getting on.'

Stella refused to believe it and insisted on opening the window. A hot breeze swept over them, so wet with fog that it soaked them. Standing in the aisle, almost next to Juan, Andrés whistled dryly at them to close the window.

'He's right, because then I catch cold, and he gets furious,' said Stella. 'Yes, I think it is the street cleaners. But the wools were nice, weren't they? You really like to knit Clara, isn't that so?'

'Only when I'm completely swamped in readings or before an examination.'

'It's very soothing. Like bitter *maté*, which I find disgusting, by the way. Andrés says it's so soothing. You should see him drinking *maté* at night.'

'Does he write at night?'

'Yes, he writes at night. He puts on his old jacket, asks me to keep quiet, and brews his *maté*.'

One of the sweepers appeared at the forward door – Clara was surprised to see the doors spread apart, apparently without anyone touching them. When the driver opened them to say something to the conductor it was always the same; surprise – like a disappointment – not just because it was the same man with his mole-like face, his big feet. *A bit like the idea of a theater curtain*, she thought, amused. *The curtain parts and bang, nothing. You were hoping for Edwige Feuillère and what you get is a municipal inspector – peering wearily at the people squashed together in the aisle.* When the door closed, he skillfully

> slipped in his body and the broom first, leaving the door
> open
> at his back:
> and then with a rapid flutter of his hands behind him

like a magician (because now the broom and a
                    dust bin with a handle were
leaning against one of the door panels),
he closed the door with a dry, unpleasant sound, a snap
like the snapping of a skinny dog.

Ah, how bored they must get, thought Andrés, seeing the street sweeper's pale face. He knew that boredom (as he conceived it) is the punishment for perfectionism; but all the same it grieved him to project onto the sweeper the possibility of ennui. He saw the other sweeper (because he was a tall man), where he was beginning to work from that side. He grabbed a handle when the trolley took the curve at 25 de Mayo and made its usual fishtail.

Juan had taken out a book and was reading. *Great, I write so someone can read me on the trolley.* He was just about to slap the book away from him, reach his hand along the back of a lady with packages and snatch it away, before Juan knew what was happening. *Oh well, oh well*, he thought, less irritated. *Come to think of it; at this stage of local sluttification, a streetcar is the perfect reading room. But we should nip that problem in the bud and write with that in mind – thinking about the circumstances in which we'll be read. Chapters for the café, for the trolley; and chapters for the weekend, when we put on our cologne and opt for a good armchair, a good pipe, and culture. It's just fine that way.* He saw Stella and Clara get up to allow the sweeper to clean the seat. The tall sweeper took charge of their seat, and the bored sweeper was passing his broom between Andrés' shoes. He raised one after another, and looked in turn at the boy next to him doing the same; the lady wearing sunglasses fearfully kept an eye on the movements of the broom handle and pushed herself harder and harder against a seat until she'd shoved her buttocks in the face of a man with a retired air to him; he lifted his copy of *La Razón Quinta* but wasn't brave enough to turn it completely into a screen between his face and the sunglass-wearing lady's ass.

'But can't you see I told you twice to get up,' protested the sweeper, and Juan, a bit flustered, closed the book and abandoned his seat muttering something that Andrés couldn't understand. The lady with the packages sighed at the height of Andrés' right nipple, and behind stood Juan, so taken by surprise in his reading, a finger stuck in the pages of his book, and foaming with rage.

'See, the poor author doesn't take these diversions into account,' Andrés informed him. 'And consider the word "diversion" in its other meaning. Look, the stylist pauses, modulates, orders, disposes, he accommodates the phrase, and then there you are reading him – and between two halves of a proposition you find yourself confronted by, of all things, a sweeper.'

'The son of a bitch,' said Juan, not really showing much respect for the lady with the packages.

Andrés winked at the girls, who were recovering their seat. In the center of the aisle, the confusion was deplorable. The two sweepers were moving toward the center from opposite ends of the trolley, and the passengers, wanting to make room for them, were packed closer and closer. The worst moment was when . . .

(by now Juan was seated again, *but what for*

– thought an ironical Andrés –

when they'd be getting off in three blocks)

when one of the sweepers bent over – after opening the dust bin with his foot, which he held in his left hand – picking up the lint, tickets, newspapers, buttons, threads, dust accumulated in a nucleus of spit, hairs, peanut shells, matchboxes, receipts for certified mail;

and when he did (he was bending over even if he didn't want to; the dust bin had a long handle, but with all the people and the terrible lighting at floor-level, there was a confused darkness), trying to see better;

the passengers

were pushed to one side by the bill of the sweeper's cap – a cap has a great deal of power when traveling inside on a head attentive to its obligations. On the other,

the other sweeper's ass moved along on a horizontal axis that corresponded exactly to his being bent over. And given that the two sweepers by now were about to meet at the center of the aisle – *Luckily*, thought Andrés, *they passed me by* – and were bent over the whole time, to get their dust bins to open, the space left to the passengers got smaller and smaller. The obvious result was that the passengers tried to avoid bumping against one another (and when two buttons touched, they made a dry noise) and whispered in low voices and made jokes to dissimulate the tension. *As long*, thought Juan, sticking his book in his pocket, *as they haven't mistreated my cauliflower*. He didn't want to look back where Clara was, fearful she'd understand his nervousness. *From now on, I'm going to carry the package*.

'Just look at 25 de Mayo,' Andrés said with an it-goes-without-saying wink. 'Remember?'

'Of course,' said Juan. 'They haven't left a single one. Thanks to the milk bars. Until someone discovers milk is obscene and eliminates the milk bars too.'

'Milk *is* obscene,' said Andrés. 'But not as obscene as phallic vanilla beans. Girls, we'll be getting off on the corner.'

'We're getting off,' said Clara. It was difficult for her to get out because Stella was . . . (*She says 'Excuse me' with the same voice an apprentice matador would use in a bullring. You've got to dominate people in streetcars with your voice if you don't have elbows.*) Over the head of one of the sweepers, she passed the package to Juan, and ended up exiting the streetcar with Stella by the rear door. By the time Juan reached the bottom step in the front, the trolley had started moving again, so he touched ground halfway through the streetcar's turn into Corrientes. Everything was brightly lit. There, the extremely proper city for families happily began two blocks from the poor, eradicated red-light district: the red cap on the mailbox of the little café, the *Jousten*; and the dumb trolley that takes you to the Amusement Park and offers lots of fights for lots of pesos.

The chronicler was listening to 'London Again' and remembering so many, so many pleasant and beloved things, like a perfumed lotion, like Eric Coates' melodies. The Wurlitzer, an eschatological object, threatened him with its *sambas* and its *machichas* – which is why the chronicler prefered to sit next to the speaker even if his ears exploded and feed the Wurlitzer more and more coins so only 'London Again' played and afterwards a little tango:

> *Remember, honey pie, you were*
> *the cutest dolly in Chiclana*

with the counterpoint, surreptitious entries of accordions, the dry interventions of the piano, the precise cuts; and the chronicler waved a finger to answer the distant greeting of Andrés Fava, who was coming in with his girlfriend and another couple (but, of course, it was Juan and Clara) while he meditated the style of Juan D'Arienzo, vindication of the pianola, the canary, the wind-up nightingale,

And the emperor was going to die. (It was the nightingale's fault, yes sir, it was.)

'Give me change for a peso in twenty centavo coins,' said the chronicler. If that guy with dirty eyes got anywhere near the Wurlitzer, he'd play *chamamés* for sure. (There were three on the Wurlitzer's list, and an ocean of *chacareras* and *gatos*.) *I detest folk songs*, he declared to himself. *I only like other people's folk songs – that is, folklore that's free and gratuitous, not what my blood imposes on me. The impositions of the blood are vomitatious in general. Now they'll come over to chat as soon as they've had their drink. If only it was Andrés – that woman is horrible. Now what should I play?* The list on the machine was long and in double columns. He chose a record by the Metronome All Star Band: 'One O'Clock Jump.' Then Juan and Clara came over.

Eating french fries at the counter Andrés and Stella looked over to where the chronicler was bestowing his greeting and bringing over chairs. Clara was amusing herself studying the inner workings of the Wurlitzer.

The Moloch of the cafés, thought Andrés. *A sacrifice of coins to the potbellied, strident little god. Baal, Melkarth – obscene bug, a musical fish. And the chronicler, a lamentable version of a magistrate from antiquity, a Carthaginian suffete perhaps*. He was very fond of the chronicler – a good buddy for boxing nights, late-night cafés, dialogues on love, essays, and miscellanies;

the chronicler, a tranquil guy with his little apartment on Alsina Street (the address was in the 400's) and his Buenos Aires habits: a good example of 'live and let live,' and 'I don't give a damn,' of . . .

Poor country, you're on the right track

for the next election (a little tango they whistled together, when they had hung around together more – before Stella, before the fall into the present. *Watch out*, thought Andrés, *don't rely so heavily on glib lines. We were always already fallen into the present, man.*).

'Come on, honey, let's go chat with the chronicler.'

'You go. These french fries are so good I'm going to finish them,' said Stella.

When he reached the table, the three of them were already seated; and the Wurlitzer was silent but dangerous.

'Look at this guy,' said the chronicler squeezing his hand as if he had it in a monkey wrench. 'Come on now, are you ashamed to say hello? Lost man, may your vest be covered with pockets, and in each one may you have a wet cigarette, a counterfeit bank note, and a leaky ballpoint pen –

the horror of our time.'

'The same to you,' said Andrés. They looked each other over, happy. Clara and Juan were having fun just watching them.

'And when are you all having dinner?' asked the chronicler.

'Right now. But we stopped off to moisten our appetites. It's a special night, see, tomorrow great things are happening.'

'Great things never happen,' said the chronicler, who knew how to be blasé when the occasion called for it.

'Yes they do,' said Andrés. 'Except they never happen to us. Tomorrow Clara and Juan are taking their final exams. At 9:00 P.M.'

'I don't see it as such a great thing,' said Clara.

'Of course, because it's happening to you,' said Andrés. 'But for me and the chronicler it's a real event. It isn't everyone who goes around with friends suffering preexam anxiety, people about to take their final examination. You have to hype the event so it becomes great in historical terms! How about this headline: *CATASTROPHE IN EGYPT: TWENTY WOMEN BURNED ALIVE*. People read it and say it's really a horrible catastrophe. Meanwhile, ten thousand women have died in other places, and the world couldn't care less. Ask the chronicler, he knows about these things.'

But Juan was showing a tiny piece of the cauliflower to the chronicler, using two fingers to pull back some of the wrapping. Clara took the package away from him and put it on top of the Wurlitzer, but the bartender waved furiously, and Clara retrieved it and put it on her lap. *The things I do for this idiot. For me he wouldn't even carry an aspirin in his pocket, not even if I asked him*. She pet the package – the great white face covered with eyes beneath the paper. Andrés and the chronicler talked and talked, happy to have run into each other.

'Today I went out at eight,' said the chronicler. 'I went out at eight and came to listen to "London Again," It's incredible how much I like it. Man, why don't we go have dinner?'

'But it's just a lot of crap,' said Andrés.

'Okay, okay, I'm not saying it isn't. You know we all have a sentimental spot somewhere inside us. My sentimental spot knows English, that's all. So I played "London Again," and was thinking of playing it again when you all came in. But let's get something to eat.'

'Stella wanted a grill.'

'We all want a grill. And to talk a lot.'

'Yeah, about Abel,' said Stella incongruently.

'You're perfect,' said Juan, not at all content. 'We'll give you a double portion of sweetbreads. I think it's a great idea that the chronicler come with us! His presence will break up our even number, which is always stupid, and also add his personal qualities.'

'And perhaps he'll pick up the check,' said Andrés, elbowing the chronicler, who was looking at him tenderly. 'The chronicler has recently returned from Europe and bears wisdom in his words.

Prepare to drink it in with each glass of white wine. Besides, the chronicler reads my essays or did read them in the old days.'

'As far as I'm concerned,' said the chronicler, 'I'd still be reading them, *volontièri*, but you're one of those guys who disappears for six months, and no one sees hide nor hair of you. Stella, do you keep him locked up?'

'If only I could,' said Stella. 'The truth is he writes a lot and spends his time drinking *maté*. I keep telling him so much studying is going to hurt him someday.'

'Just look,' said Andrés. 'They're painting me as the perfect anchorite, *maté* included.'

'So why is it no one can find out what you're writing?' asked Juan. 'In this country people at least write for their friends – our publishers are too worried about leaves-in-the-storm themes and detective novels.'

'Look, you gather up your material, then you've got to go over it, then you've got to make a clean copy ... And besides, why do people have to read so much?' said Andrés, furious. 'You're all talking about what a person does as if it were an absolute necessity. Yes, I keep a day book. So what? It's really more a night book. Who cares? Let's be reasonable; with all there is to read out there ...'

'You know very well that people read their friends for other reasons,' said Clara.

'Okay, you win, but when a crowd starts to gather, as if it were a car accident,

then things start to smell like a funeral, the kind with speeches and twenty-one gun salutes.'

'But we love cliques in Buenos Aires,' said Clara. 'In these parts, we know our obligations. You write something, and five or six relatives or friends read it. The next week, the order changes: Juan writes a story, you and I read it ... It works very well, Andrés, don't tell me it doesn't. Sometimes I laugh thinking there must be hundreds of cliques in the House that know nothing of one another. Tons of people writing for three, eight, twenty readers.'

'Your description just turned my stomach,' said Andrés.

'Never before dinner, man,' said an alarmed chronicler.

'Let's get going because I'm dying of hunger.'

'The fog is thicker,' said Clara, sniffing the street.

'It's not fog, it's smoke,' said Stella.

The chronicler made a dubious gesture.

'So what is it?'

'No one knows,' he said. 'Tonight people were talking about it at the city desk. That's just the point: no one knows. They were making analyses.'

Since Juan had gone ahead, talking with Stella and the chronicler, Andrés took Clara by the arm and they fell behind. Clara let herself be led, half closing her eyes.

'Are you afraid of the exam?' he asked.

'No, I'm actually rather curious. Usually in life, you know how things are going to happen. You can imagine even in great detail things like what the dentist is going to do to you, what you're going to eat at your aunt's house . . . But this is different: it's a kind of abyss, the perfect enigma.'

'You're right, it's going to be a bad half hour. Maybe I'll go with you tomorrow. I don't know if you like seeing people in situations like that. Sometimes it's worse, like in wakes.'

'No, it's fine. I think it would be a good idea. That way, no matter how it turns out for us, we'll all end up drinking somewhere. Don't you feel hot and something like vertigo?' said Clara confusedly, clutching Andrés' arm. 'How weird this street is, this fog.'

'Sticky.'

'I can't bear this heat tonight. Juan laughs at me when I tell him that all I have to do is think of coolness and I feel it. It's true, I always go around surrounded by a climate that's just for me, but tonight it's failing me. Probably it's nerves,' she added with humility.

'And Juan's calm?'

'He says he is, but just look at him, waving his arms around.

And he's been writing like a madman these past nights. Halfway through a note card, he starts writing poetry. He's angry at everything, Buenos Aires pains him, I pain him, he doesn't eat, he yawns.'

'Nice picture you paint.'

'You know that everything affects him in a particular way,' said Clara. 'It's not easy to find the right soup for Juan. You give him tapioca, and it turns out he's in the mood for *pastina*. He's not even in the mood for me sometimes.'

'As long as you get along at night . . .' said Andrés, stating things in shocking terms.

'Oh, that's the easiest part of all. With Juan, the problems start when we wake up. Ask him to read you the poems he's written over these past weeks, you'll see. I have to insist we go out — I make him go out for a walk, take me around. I think he needs it. Last night, half-asleep, he said to me: "The house is falling down." Then he was quiet, but I know he was awake. But why am I telling you these things? . . .'

'No good reason, which is how things ought to be told. Where are these people taking us? Oh, the restaurant opposite the stadium. Poems, poems, everything ends up with poems.'

'Everything begins with poems,' said Clara intelligently.

'I didn't mean what I said before. But look: tonight and every night, all we ever do is talk about what we write and what we read.'

'But that's okay.'

'You think so? Do you really think we have a right?'

'What do you mean? I don't follow you.'

'The explanation's going to be more literary than the question,' said Andrés sadly. 'Especially because I don't really know what the question is. Part of it has to do with an intellectual's rage against his colleagues and himself. His horrible suspicion of parasites and superfluity.'

'Don't talk like some resentful gaucho,' Clara joked.

'Let me make myself clear. I'm not denying your right or your reason to be intellectual. Juan's poetry is fine, my day book and my essays are fine too. But look, Clara, think about it; when it comes down to it, he and I and everyone else show off too much. *I write*. It makes you want to answer with the shortest and most insolent retort in the English language: *So what?*'

'But you can't just say that,' said Clara. 'What matters is knowing that people do it. The right to assert comes afterward. I don't know, a Valéry could say *I write*. Would it have bothered you to hear him say it?'

'No,' said Andrés meekly. 'I suppose that's the problem. But all this talk, this passing around of papers, these café tables where books and books and books and openings and galleries . . . Look there's a lot of sleight of hand here, betrayal.'

'All you've got to do is say "betrayal of reality, life, action," and wear the words on a button on your lapel – then you're ready to launch any career.'

'Of course, words again. But I was trying to say something else. It's the nature of our intellectualism that concerns me. There's something damp about it, like the air down at the docks.'

'But you write your day book,' said Clara, defending Juan.

'And the day book smells of fog. Look, what we're doing is swallowing this dirty air and fixing it on paper. My day book is flypaper, a disgusting honey filled with dying little animals.'

'Well, at least you know it,' said Clara, consoling him; she had wanted to be a nurse when she was a girl.

Andrés shrugged his shoulders, squeezed her arm, felt vaguely happy. That night he was easy to console.

'I don't agree,' said the chronicler. 'Yes, Stella, I'm going to order an antipasto, and I suggest you do likewise. They serve an entomological antipasto here – fascinating mélange of things.'

'The Yellow Nineties,' said Juan in English. 'Ham for me. So in that case you do agree.'

'No. I think there are few of us here and that we are of little use. Intelligence chooses its zones, and Argentina is not among them.'

'A simple case of being blinded by your profession,' said Juan. 'Since you're what my father-in-law calls a man of letters, you forget about the numbers men. Here, intelligence chooses the scientific. We all sit around denying the creative potential of Argentines without seeing that our way of seeing is just one of many, and that other people may be working and doing their own things. A good biologist would have to laugh listening to us sniveling. We don't even shout; we screech, like rats. I'll have half a grapefruit.'

'My dear boy,' said the chronicler, 'neither you nor I is in the opposite camp! We don't know enough biology to be able to present an informed opinion about whether things in that field are going well anyway – though what I manage to see doesn't look out of this world. But, giving you credit for the question you raised, I insist that this is a country of plain and simple observers – nosey bodies who entrust what they see and hear to their precarious memories. Fifty-thousand guys watching Labruna make a goal: Argentina! Incidentally, that gives you the possible ratio between those who are useless and those who create. You're going to tell me we've got great poets in these parts, and that's true. I've said before that writing poetry isn't some great human merit but a fatality people suffer. Around here we've got a good stock of men infected with poetry; but I invite you to give me a list of the active, by which I mean, *intelligent* creators.'

'You paint a pretty sad picture,' said Juan. 'But why all this sudden enthusiasm for intelligence? What does that have to do with it? The Argentines, I mean the good citizens of Buenos Aires – the people I know, with whom I live and interact – are always intelligent. Creation is born from *morality*, chronicler, not intelligence.'

'Mmm,' said Clara. 'So what we are is softies.'

'That's it, softies – no rigor. A common trait of people from Buenos Aires is that they have brilliant ideas, but the ideas are disconnected – I mean, with no context, no real point to them. On the other hand, in a well-ordered mind, one idea tends to agglutinate another, completing the picture. Excuse this vocabulary, but it's really clearer than using other metaphors. What I mean is that we lack a spirit of system (even if that system is freedom or for freedom) – and that is a moral defect worse than any other kind. We waste tons of subjects, shooting them off in isolated skyrockets that any old professor from Lyon or Birmingham would organize coherently in a few weeks, simply by taking notes on himself and everyone else.'

'So, we *are* basically on the same page,' said the chronicler. 'When I said we lack intelligence, I really meant the creative results of intelligence, rather than its gratuitous manifestation. Now, examining things at closer range, we should look at the *causes* of this . . . this status. Man, what expressions I use.'

'If they could only be published in the paper, right?' said Stella, completely happy thinking about the flan with whipped cream she was going to have for dessert.

Andrés was listening and looking at Clara. Without knowing why, he found himself thinking of Curzio Malaparte. 'Everyone knows how egoistic the dead are. There's no one but them in the world. No one else counts. They are colossi – envious: they forgive the living everything except being alive . . .' He wondered if the dead might be arguing somewhere the way Juan and the chronicler were – if among them there might be one who'd look, as he was looking, at Clara (and Stella was looking at him, amused but not knowing why). For an instant, the position each of them was sitting in around the table with its tablecloth and food, the reflection from a knife flashing in his eyes – all of it seemed inconceivable. Thinking something, knowing it, but not taking the step to fix it with some mental reference. They talked and talked: bread and butter, Clara, Stella, the fog, the night; you know that what we have here is a borrowed culture, the groups coming in, the strange creaking of the door, the acid smell of grapefruit juice. *They forgive the living everything except being alive.* He took a deep breath, to put the brakes on an up-and-down pressure that suddenly anguished him. If it were possible . . .

But he never finished the idea (which had no basis and could be stopped just like that, halfway: dissolved in nothingness, in that black thing without blackness inside, that sensation of an interior without space) and he continued to look at Clara, trying to find relief in her immobile face as she listened to the dialogue of her friends.

'I concede the point – we don't have a great deal to say,' admitted Juan, 'because in reality we Argentines spend our time avoiding committing ourselves individually to the human adventure. We're part of our mud and our river – those elements devoid of history, or whose history belongs to others. We're tired beforehand of not having anything true that would whip us up into a frenzy. We're so free, we live tied down only so slightly by a past or future. It's an *ineffable* quality that would seem our most authentic way of being. Think of a book making the rounds in 1930: the *Complete Works of Hipólito Yrigoyen*. You open it up, and all the pages are blank. That also explains why our stationery stores are more inviting than our bookstores.'

'This guy cranks up his machine, and he's a happy man,' said the chronicler, offended. 'Look here, if it's true we don't have much to say, we should at least shut up, or, what would be more fitting for people like us,

> victims of Ardolafath, the demon of language, the powerful one –

commit the act of pure creation, the absolute *ex nihilo* : A bit the way Buenos Aires rises up between the two plains of water and grass.'

'You're wrong. There is no such thing as *pure creation* without a morality of creation,' said Juan. 'You can't write without personal dignity. You can be contemptible in your personal life, but passing from that contemptible state to a work of art – the chronicle of that contemptible state you're in – requires morality, by that I mean you're safe from compromises and transactions, the Argentine Society of Writers, and the photo section of the Sunday paper. You've got to have both feet on the ground even if you're a son of a bitch. And now lend me your ear for a little while longer. Around here, what you call pure creation – which might be a great way of getting around determinism and creating something, even if you weren't given the bricks to do it – still seems to me, even today, a disgusting escapism. I myself, *me first*, chronicler. I write poems, and I know why I write them. I'm a traitor. And if I talk about furies and widowhood in my poems, it's that I'm seeing myself with exploded eyes, I'm following myself down the street, and I spit on my shadow so others will realize what kind of a swine I am.'

'You're always blaming yourself,' said Stella, distressed. 'Let's eat first, and above all don't get your bile flowing. We all have a bad image of ourselves because in fact we're really better than lots of people.'

'Surprising,' said the chronicler, staring at her in praise.

Clara shrugged her shoulders and bit into the juicy meat. She was used to Juan, his vocabulary, his boxes of puzzles. Next to her, on the chair, the bag containing the cauliflower rustled every time the floor shook. Through one of the windows it was possible to see the fog over Bouchard. For a while it would thicken, and then suddenly rise as if it were going to lift; the street and the cars became visible. Clara imagined herself on the street, walking through the fog. The words around her became distant and higher pitched, as if she were hearing them over the telephone. She thought, without fear, almost without expectation, about the examination. Andrés was looking at her, slowly breaking into a smile. Oh, she'd been hard on him a little while before. To defend Juan, she always had to hurt others. Abel, Andrés. Everything being said was absurd, innocent: college students having an intellectual discussion, Aristotle's idea of pleasant conversation: *eutrapely* – just innocent fun.

'The word *eutrapely* smells of a heliotrope,' she said to Andrés in a low voice. 'It's a shame, don't you think, that we have to live in such a metaphysical age? Literarily speaking, of course.'

'Of course I don't understand you.'

'Me neither,' said a wide-eyed Stella.

How dense they are. 'Listen: these guys – and just look at the way they wear themselves out – they base their arguments on whether man as man, man as flesh and destiny, is embodied in writing. You're completely Frenchified, as you see, but I'm telling you that Malraux is *metaphysics*: Behind the 170 or so pounds each of you weighs is a destiny, and your destiny is your reason for being, or the other way around. Your reason for being leads you back to your self like a root or a point of departure, and that's metaphysics.'

'Oh Clarita,' said Juan, sadly caressing her cheek.

'On the other hand, if *eutrapely* smells of a heliotrope: that's concrete, a problem of the sort Mallarmé and his age liked. Just look how we always end up referring to Mallarmé. But in this case it's appropriate.

> I would prefer to hear them,
> let's say hear us,

talking about something more concrete and not so metaphysical – as the elucidation of why the word *eutrapely* puts a heliotrope in my nose. Philology, analogy, semantics, symbolism, now these are beautiful things! How well we would live with them! But no, Juan has to save himself from elegance like that, he has to find in himself a reason for being. That's what he calls making a work, or the basis of a work, concrete. I call it bringing a lighted match to the fuse of a skyrocket

and up she goes, whizz' – Clara *dixit*.

'Astounding,' conceded the chronicler. 'What's already gone by during this century can just retire. *Eutrapely*. Shit!'

'Coffee,' said Andrés. 'No, sweetheart, I don't want flan with whipped cream on it. No, dearest.'

'I'll have flan with whipped cream on it,' said Stella.

Abel, thought Clara, fatigued. *Poor Abelito. He would have turned to stone if he'd heard me perorating like that. And tomorrow . . . No, Andrés, it's too late for you to be looking at me that way. It's always too late,*

Andrés. Always. The waiter dropped a glass, and the noise made Stella laugh. Then the waiter explained to her that the glass had slipped, and Stella stopped laughing to show she was very interested in the explanation.

'Occupational hazards,' said the waiter, intelligently kicking the chunks of glass towards the wall. 'Every day three or four get broken. The boss gets pissed off, but what can you do? It's just part of the job.'

'And then there's the question of helping the guy who makes the glasses turn a profit,' said Stella.

'Eat your flan,' ordered Clara, still looking at Andrés out of the corner of her eye. His eyes he'd closed. He seemed to be awaiting either an electric shock or a miracle. The horrible screeching of a newsboy rattled all of them. The kid ran in, threaded his way around the tables, and shouted the name of his paper, though in a lower voice. The chronicler watched him leave and made a gesture of fatigue. 'I write it, and he sells it. You all read it, and the trinity becomes complete – the paper Juggernaut, and all. Okay, let's go.'

It's so absurd to talk just for the sake of talking, thought Juan as they walked out, *listening to oneself talk and knowing that you're never very right. That's another of our cowardly traits, perhaps the worst. Those of us around here who are worth something aren't sure of anything by now. You've got to be an animal to have convictions.*

'Let's walk down Leandro Alem to Plaza de Mayo,' said Stella. 'I want to see what's going on.'

'If we can actually see anything,' complained the chronicler, sniffing the fog.

They passed by the Mail and Telecommunications building, feeling sticky, not wanting to talk. A sudden clamor from the Amusement Park reached them. The noise became louder, shriller, until it faded into something like a bland fall, a loss.

'Something's down for the count,' said the chronicler. 'Juancito, boxers are so happy, they sock each other around so enthusiastically, they're the music of life.'

'Lysippos' statue of the athlete is singing,' said Juan. 'But no one's singing around here tonight. Listen to this, chronicler: a present from me to you, still fresh and uncorrected. I think it will be called "Fauna and Flora of the River."'

> This river leaves the sky and settles in in order to last,
> pulling the sheets up to its neck, and sleeping
> right in front of us who come and go.
> The river of silver is this thing that by day
> soaks us with wind and gelatin; and it is
> the renunciation of the east, because the world
> ends with the lanterns of the Costanera.
> Don't argue the point closer to us, read these things
> in cafés preferentially; a tune of coins,
> where you take refuge from the outside, from the next workday,
> harassed by dreams, by the river's spittle.
> Almost nothing's left; yes, shameful love
> entering mailboxes to weep or walking
> alone on street corners (but being seen just the same)
> putting away his sweet objects, his photos and watch chains
> and hankies
> storing them in the region of shame,
> the zone of the pocket, where a small night whispers
> amid bits of fuzz and small change.
>
> For some people everything is the same, but I
> don't like Rácing, I don't like
> aspirin, I resent
> the return of days, I tear myself apart in hopes,
> I curse sometimes, and people say to me
> what's the problem, friend?
> North wind, damn it.

      'I like it,' Andrés said, simply
          (because they'd all fallen silent, surrounding Juan, whose eyes where shining and who suddenly ran the back of his hand over his face and turned around so they wouldn't see him).

★

When they crossed the parking lot of the Automobile Club, they saw all the papers. A gust of wind lofted them over the parked cars, where they condensed in a filthy copy of a snowstorm, draping themselves over door handles, slipping over the soaped roofs of Chevrolets and Pontiacs. The entire lot was covered with pieces of newsprint, clumps of cardboard, marbleized paper, envelopes, cigarette packs torn into five or ten pieces, onionskin paper, old carbon copies, rough drafts. The gust of wind had bunched them together between cars, on sidewalks, in the gutters.

Juan was walking ahead. When he saw the sea of dirty paper he wanted to make a detour, to go down to the market, and continue from there. The others were commenting

they'd begun talking in lower voices

the kind that lingers at the end of a sonata or a thunderclap;

and Juan was walking ahead, squeezing the cauliflower, wondering how they were going to pass the hours left before the examination. The examination seemed a fixed boundary to him, a buoy towards which he could advance. Fixed boundaries, examinations are good things. Above all, a fixed boundary is like a pencil mark on a ruler: it delineates what comes before, marks a distance

        here a time   a space of time   an impulse   that at a certain moment stops

    like resetting a watch by calculating it will stop at

                      7:15

    and at 7:10 the watch begins to tick slowly,

                getting lazy,

    drifting on until
    7:18   most   painfully
    a heartbeat   a heartbeat
    nothing more than a heartbeat

    a thing shrunken become cold without reason face up;

    schedule, toothpick; minute hand, toothpick; second hand, toothpick.

From Bartolomé Mitre (there were no more papers), they saw the violent light of Plaza de Mayo. Casa Rosada, the presidential palace, grew in the air of fog, appearing in shreds with lights on its balconies and doors. *A reception*, thought Juan. *Or a change of cabinet*. But that last possibility was absurd, they wouldn't turn on extra lights for a little thing like that. Probably the illumination of Plaza de Mayo was reflecting onto the nearby buildings. From far off came metallic-sounding music – that abjection of music, even if it's bad, when broadcast from rows of loudspeakers – the degradation of something beautiful. Antinous tied to a garbage truck, or a lark in a shoe. *Or a lark in a shoe*, repeated Juan.

Clara came up alongside him and peered at him over his eyes. 'Give me the package if you're getting tired.' 'No, I want to carry it myself.' 'Suit yourself.' 'I have no idea why we're going to Plaza de Mayo.' 'Stella always liked it,' said Clara. 'It looks as though they're still going on with the ceremonies.'

The chronicler joined them. He walked with his hands in his trouser pockets, and since he hadn't unbuttoned his jacket it bulged out on both sides like two fins.

'All of Buenos Aires is coming to see the bone,' he said. 'Last night, a train from Tucumán pulled in with 1,500 workers – they're having a dance in front of Town Hall. Hey, look! They're rerouting traffic at the corner. We're going to be in incredible heat.'

They walked up the slope on the side of the government offices. From above (now they were all in line, and no one was talking), they saw people flow toward the other side of the plaza, moving along Rivadavia and Yrigoyen. But at the center, the multitude was almost immobile, swaying barely back and forth in enormous waves that could only be seen from a distance.

'They constructed the Sanctuary using the pyramid as one of its supports,' explained the chronicler. 'The rest is nothing but burlap.'

'You were there?' asked Juan.

'In my professional capacity,' said the chronicler. 'I wrote a terrific article.'

'Ergo, it was you who sanctified the pilgrimage. Don't look at me that way, because it's the truth. They put up the canvas, and your newspaper brings in the people, at twenty centavos per jerk.'

'Don't say that,' said Andrés, very seriously. 'People don't come only because of the paper. No publicity campaign can explain certain furors and enthusiasms. I've been told the rituals in the square are spontaneous. Every so often new ones are invented.'

'Rituals aren't invented,' said the chronicler. 'They're either remembered or discovered. They've been there for all time.'

'Let's go into the plaza,' said Stella. 'We can't see anything here.'

Behind them a siren howled, obliging them to turn around. Two ambulances were racing south along Alem followed by motorcycles, behind which came a third ambulance.

They crossed the plaza under the balconies of the Government Building. There the fog gave way to the heat of lights and people – the other, dark fog at street level. Thousands of men and women, all dressed alike in blue, tobacco, mouse-gray, and sometimes dark green moleskin. The ground had been muddy ever since they'd removed the wide sidewalks in order to clear the plaza, although nothing was helped by doing that, the chronicler declared, and he furiously stamped the ground. They had to make their way carefully, from time to time grabbing the elbow or shoulder of someone on a firmer piece of that shapeless field, where the only thing that looked solid was the Pyramid.

Andrés saw Clara stumble and caught her by the arm. Juan had raised the package containing the cauliflower to his chest to protect it. They moved forward that way a few yards, trying to get a better view of the Sanctuary.

'You should be in bed, Clara, strengthening yourself for tomorrow,' said Andrés.

'I wouldn't be able to sleep,' she said. 'It's better to be tired for exams, your phosphorescence is greater. Maybe they'll ask me about crowd psychology; I'll tell them about this, and that will be that.'

'Well, that's certainly something to tell them about,' said Andrés, forcing his way through so she could get a good view. But getting a good view was a matter of elbows and shoves and watch your manners, you'd think you didn't know how to walk down a street properly,

tell your little brother not to get so far ahead, forgodssake, the kid is really the living end!

Stop your shoving, sonny, you're driving me nuts!

in a confusing proliferation of bodies and necks with handkerchiefs tied around them, breaking like waves against a barrier of silent men who seemed to be waiting for something. Jammed up against Andrés, Clara could peer through a crack between two black jackets and stare into the magic circle,

it was a circle, the men had their arms locked and were surrounding the woman dressed in white. She was wearing a tunic somewhere between a schoolteacher's apron and something from an allegory about the homeland never trampled by any tyrant; her extremely blond hair was a mess, cascading down to her breasts. And at the center of it all, two or three lean men dressed in black, with reddish complexions – Clara saw they were acting as officiants, serving in the ceremony with movements like those in some ill-timed quadrille. She thought about Prilidiano Pueyrredón, about glazed pumpkin. She sniffed the soapy air, as if this would help her see better. One of the men in black went over to the woman and put his hand on her shoulder.

'She is good,' he said. 'She is very good.'

'She is good,' the others repeated.

'She comes from Lincoln, from Curuzú Cuatiá, and Presidente Roca,' said the man.

'She is coming,' repeated the others.

'She is coming from Formosa, from Covunco, from Nogoyá and from Chapadmalal.'

'She is coming.'

'She is good,' said the man.

'She is good.'

The woman did not move, but Clara could see her hands pressed tightly to her thighs. She was opening and closing her fingers as if in a hysteria suddenly about to explode. Clara felt afraid, as well as the disgust of realizing

that how had she been able, how

had she been able

(and now there is no going back – all speeds of takeoff, things are as *IRREVERSIBLE* as the time-that-bears-them-away)

but how could she, finally, whisper with the others, 'She is good'? She heard herself with the other side of her hearing, the true part, that hears the voice as it is being born, in the very throat

(as a little girl she liked to cover her ears and sing or breathe deeply; and, when she had bronchitis, to hear the wheezes, the whistles like little frogs or owls, and after coughing hard, the whole orchestra would put itself back together little by little, different themes, charming, because she was

good).

'Let's go,' she said, clinging to Andrés, terrified.

He looked at her, but said nothing. Juan and Stella veered off to the right, the chronicler steering them like a tugboat. They followed with difficulty because everyone was fighting to see the woman who was good, who came from Chapadmalal. Clara squeezed closer to Andrés, walked with her eyes closed, panting. 'I sang with them, I prayed with them, I've signed, I've signed.' It was stupid but something in her

a part of her inside herself, freeing itself for a moment from the rest, had partaken in the ritual, had swallowed the host, consented.

'I'm afraid, Andrés,' she said in a very low voice.

He saw her point of view, but was above all that.

Armageddon, he thought. *O pallid plain, o ending of things*.

'Careful with that little guy on the left there, he looks like a crook,' said the chronicler elbowing Juan. 'You're walking along here as if you were totally bewildered. You and your package. I wish shorty would grab it. Since we have purse snatchers, we should also have cauliflower snatchers. Ah, this is what I like:

After you, ma'am.

Finding pretty words.
What was all that about *eutrapely*? But you know —
Sure, kid, the Sanctuary
is THERE.
— that the Editor hates style. He thinks it's, well, he thinks, that it's the *eutrapely* of journalism. He believes in headlines that take over the whole page. He won't let me write well. I tell you, the prospects are gloomy.'

'I wonder what it is you call "writing well,"' said Juan. 'Besides, stop trying to distract us with all that. We came to look at this thing, and we're damned well going to. Stella, slip between those two stout Paraguayan maidens. Just stylize yourself kid, no Editor is going to say a word to you.'

'You're bad as a friend,' said the chronicler. 'But do remind me later to explain what I think about style.'

By then they could see the poles holding up the canvas of the Sanctuary. They still had to get through the most crowded space: the passive cadres of hundreds of women standing there like posts sharing the wait, leaning against one another, and the thick smell, the murmuring. Andrés pointed toward a spot and right then a child began screaming. They made their way through, guided by the shriek, until they could see. There was a little bench where a boy about eight years old was seated. Two kneeling men held him in place by the shoulders and the waist. A peasant with eyes like slits and a brutal face was standing a yard in front of the kid, aiming an upholsterer's needle at his face. Little by little, he came closer, pointing the needle first at the boy's mouth, then at an eye, then at his nose. The boy pleaded, shouted in terror; on his light-colored shorts the urine stains of terror were clearly visible. Then the peasant stepped back, impassive, and the people standing around murmured something that Andrés — the only one of the group who'd gone forward to get a look at the scene — didn't understand. Something like

in the middle/ the middle/ the middle/ the middle —
unless it were —

Enemies/ enemies/ enemies/ enemies —

Suspecting something, Juan and the chronicler held the ladies' arms, not letting them move forward.

'What bastards sons of bitches,' said Andrés grabbing hold of Clara and starting to walk toward the Sanctuary.

'You're as white as a sheet!' said Stella.

'What kind of sheet,' said Andrés without looking at her. 'There are bed sheets, sheets of paper . . .'

'This guy will be a philologist till the day he dies,' said the chronicler. 'But just listen to the music.'

A curtain of solid shoulders — Blue black blue red green black — stopped them fifteen feet from the Sanctuary;

and nothing worked, not pushing, not excuse me miss, not even make way for the police.

'It's all so confusing,' whispered Juan. 'So devoid of style.'

'Style's dead,' said Andrés.

'Long live style!' said the chronicler. 'But just listen to this music.'

What you'd call listen to it they did, having no other choice. POET AND SMALL TOWN MAAAAN. *Son of a bitch, thought the chronicler. How right Juan is. So void of style. How can anyone understand the combination of all these short-haired black women here with that von Suppée apple sauce in the background? Would you expect to find a Frigidaire in a country store? What are we doing here?*

'Those are the most diarrheic violins I've ever smelled in my life,' said Juan. 'For God's sake, this is crazy. Why don't they just play tangos?'

'Because they like this,' said the chronicler. 'Don't you see that poor people have discovered music because of movies? Don't you think that disgusting mess called "Unforgettable Song" had something to do with it? The bone of Tchaikovsky, man — pizza and Rachmaninoff.'

'Let's just get inside and be done with it,' said Clara. 'I hope you don't think I'll be able to stand much more of this. With each step I take I'm sinking deeper into the mud, and I'm dying of thirst.'

'Dying of thirst at the foot of the pyramid,' said the chronicler. 'My, what a delicate theme.'

'Dying of thirst at the foot of the pyramid!' said Juan.

'*Ecco*: the very image of the Fatherland!'

'Just Egypt will do,' said Andrés. 'Ma'am, if you don't mind, we'll just pass through.'

'As far as I'm concerned, just go right on ahead,' said the lady. 'No one said you couldn't.'

'True enough. I never heard anything truer than that,' said Andrés.

'What's that you said?'

'Nothing, ma'am. *Just a little tune*
          lookin' at the moon
          catapoom, catapoom.

'There's always got to be a wise guy,' said the lady.

After that they ran into a pair of Slavs – man and wife – going their way; but they managed things so well, they gave the impression they were going in the opposite direction. And after that – oh, successions, oh A, B, C, of things! – it turned out that they missed the Sanctuary and ended up at the canvas wall that faced toward Rivadavia, so that the entrance

– as with piles of records

boxes of tools

portfolios filled with papers –

was on the other side, on the pyramid side –

WHERE FROM ON HIGH TWENTY CENTURIES DO NOT CONTEMPLATE YOU;

it opened onto the nearby and crowded horizon of Hipólito Yrigoyen.

'They screwed up my cauliflower,' Juan said to Stella, who was ecstatic with joy. 'It's a shame, because if you'd seen it when it was fresh out of the market, it would certainly have refreshed your soul.'

'You can buy another tomorrow,' said Stella.

'Sure. As Cocteau said to Orpheus: Kill Eurydice. You'll feel much better afterward.'

'Well,' said Stella. 'What I really meant to say . . .'

'Of course. But the fact is that it wasn't you who happened to be passing through the Plata market at the exact moment that a cauliflower like this was for sale. And just think of the thousands of factors that had a role in it. If my bus stops at that corner two minutes too late, I miss my chance to buy it. I know, because when I raised it in my arms —'

'Shitty maniflower,' an educated voice enunciated clearly somewhere in the crowd.

'I sing a lullaby to my cauli-

I sing a lullaby to my flower

Yes,

I really raised it in my arms — and just then a lady stood there staring at it with such envy—————so you see, there are thousands of factors.'

'Come on, push a little,' said the chronicler who was out of breath, puffing behind. 'What a night, kid. There I was in my café; and then you all turn up, and now this. I could have sworn we could get in on the Rivadavia side. I think I even said so in my article.'

They flanked the sanctuary

HUMMING A TANGO YOU STROLL THE STREEEEETS

and all of them managed to reach the high ground at the . . .

'Jacky baby! Where's it at?'

'Behina' pyramud!'

Gloriously unfading. Never tied to the jeep of any conqueror of the land; column of the free seat of honor, of the valiant.

AND THE FREEDOM FIGHTERS
TIED THEIR HORSES TO THE PYRAMID.

> Alzaga, to die
> Liniers, to die
> Dorrego, to die

> Facundo, to die
> Poor little dead guy
> Mista Kurtz, he dead.
> A penny for the old guy.
> Poor little shepherd girl
> who died in the fields.
> Crévons, crévons, qu'un sang impur.
> Abreuve nos fauteuils
> *PROVINCIAUX.*

'Sure, it must have been the buy of a lifetime,' said Stella.

A dog, almost invisible in the constantly shifting columns of trousers and stockings, sniffed Stella's shoes. Andrés and Clara had gone on ahead and were already looking back from one of the edges of the pyramid. *They've leveled the whole place here just so they could set up the Sanctuary*, thought Juan. *When all this is over, the plaza will look awful*. It was muddier here. Juan stumbled and had to rest his free hand on the pyramid. Then he saw Abel mixed in with the people on his left, but quite a ways behind. He only saw him because of one of those waves that crowds make (the same way a many-sided conversation will suddenly be broken by an instantaneous silence).

An angel's flying over, Grandma would say –

like an air pocket that lasts, that someone's got to burst by inventing the first word, the swerve that gets you out of the hole. *Here he is again*, thought Juan, not wanting to recognize the disquiet coming over him.

'At last,' said Stella. 'God, what heat! Inside it must be just horrible.'

'I think they only let in one small group at a time,' said Juan. 'Maybe they've installed air conditioning.'

He wanted to tell Andrés he'd just seen Abelito. He thought that perhaps he was mistaken; but that pale face, that slicked-down hair. And he was wearing the same suit in the café, with the pointy shoulder pads. *Poor Abelito, to think I have to knock the crap out of him the next time he pulls a fast one on me*. The canvas panels on the sanctuary trembled as if there were a flutter of wings inside.

Now all of them were part of a group that would enter in two or three more turns. The spotlights, hung on tall posts, were focused on the entrance, projecting light through the fog and smoke – yellow, tired shadows that were shining a dirty smudge on their faces.

'*Atenti al piato*,' warned the chronicler, indicating a political candidate who surged up from among the people, beyond the entrance to the sanctuary. They should have put him on top of a little table or a stool. He materialized out of nowhere, a white clown under the lights. He was surrounded by a silence in the heat, perforated by the shouts and songs coming from farther along, as well as the indifference of those who didn't see him.

'This is the moment when we must understand the way out,' said the candidate, whose rhetorical style was mechanical and whose voice sounded like a magpie. 'We've wasted our lives trying to explain the way in, the roads that lead to the entrance, the *requirements* for the entrance, the reason for the entrance.

IT WAS THE ANALYSIS OF THE ENTRANCE!

'You can rely on me. I return from the voyage like a mariner who scorns compasses,

because deep within his breast the stars of truth were showing him the way.'

'To Calcutta,' said Juan in a rather loud voice.

'For God's sake, shut up,' said Clara, pinching him so hard he jumped.

'Fellow citizens,' said the magpie,

'this is the moment for the way out.'   *Who killed Cock Robin?*

'Communion with the relic is over for you . . .'

(and suddenly they realized that the guy wasn't addressing them but the column that was leaving the Sanctuary and making its way toward the Cabildo)

'but you carry it away with you in your hearts.'

Hearts don't have bones. It would be a good thing if they did, thought Andrés. *Badly made for the life they stick us with. The skin and bones, poveretti. Bones, armor, chitin, and inside the skin, something like a lining of broken glass.*

'AND I ALSO MEAN ON THE ALTAR OF THE FATHERLAND!'

hiccup

' , ' , ' , ' , ' , ' , '(his voice like a car horn's)

'deposited here are our'

Hearts, again?

'our meek'

(*Theirs is the kingdom of heaven.*)

'sacrifices'

(*Now you put your foot in your mouth: your vanity's showing – that pointy little nose.*)

'ANDITWILLGIVEUSTHESTRENGTHTOGOFORWARDUNTILTHEEND!'

VIVAVIVAVIVA!!

'We are not worthy,' said the chronicler, 'of an oratory of such noble lineage, such profundity of concepts. As the Editor would put it: incommensurable.'

'There were some good moments,' said Clara. 'You don't really have to use Demosthenes as a standard to judge a man in the Plaza de Mayo – worn-out styles to new needs. I think Malraux was right when he said that there comes a moment when the arts would actually rather be taken as regressive, rather than continuing to copy blueprints bereft of vitality; and

that's what I intend to prove in detail during the exam, if I get – and I hope I do – question number 4.'

'All right, all right,' said the astonished chronicler. 'I don't believe in the need for metopes. But the guy didn't say anything! Of course, it would have been worse if he'd made us believe, with the help of *style,* that he *had* said something.'

THEN A PARTITA BY JOHANN SEBASTIAN BACH EMANATED FROM THE LOUDSPEAKERS, AND

FROM TIME TO TIME THE VIOLIN COULD BE
HEARD AMID THE COMMENTS AND THE VIVAS!

'How's that for a lesson in style?' said Andrés, laughing against his will. 'I'm not saying that in the old boy's time people would fall to their knees when they heard that music, and I think that most of us agree, all past time was not better. But what we try to understand as style – that, that ubiquitous thing, that perfect tuning of a violin whose strings sound, or should sound, different – that no longer exists. All we have left to us is a trunk filled with miscellaneous things, and it's time to get dressed and leave for the party.'

'You're not saying anything particularly new,' said Juan. 'After *The Waste Land*, I think all that's been said. The orator did a good job. He said nothing and was cheered. It was perfect. We're the ones who should say something, but we're standing here as you see, talking in low voices because we're afraid they'll beat the crap out of us. The orator fits in better than we do.'

'You're still crabby,' said the chronicler. 'Remember that later on I have to explain my 'Begriff' of style. Hey they let dogs in too?'

'I don't think so,' said Stella. 'They'd make a mess of the place.'

'But it's only right,' said Clara. 'Bones are for dogs.'

'Oh sweet, subtle, epigrammatic woman,' said Juan. 'Okay, I think our turn's about to come up. Now we'll find out if the chronicler's articles were a faithful portrait of the Sanctuary. It's not often you get a chance to compare journalism with reality.'

'Bah, all I changed were the important things,' said the chronicler. 'And I forgot to talk about the dogs. It's incredible how many there are near the Sanctuary. Look at that fox terrier, there, that bootlicker. I don't know why, I don't like seeing dogs mixed in with people. They lose status, they're reduced somehow.'

'They take on this imploring air that depresses you a little,' said Andrés. 'Careful, darling, you're up to your ankle in mud.' He closed his eyes and blinked in rage: the light fell on his face like hot semolina, and around the Sanctuary. Even the fog couldn't filter that attack of anger. He wondered if Juan had seen Abel making his furtive way behind a row of workers, who were organized in the joy of all the unions that take part in a MEETING OF HONOR.

'Just listen to that,' said the chronicler, snapping out of it delightedly. 'A friend of mine, a photographer, told me – listen carefully, because as a lesson in style it's of the highest quality: A cute little couple goes to be photographed and a week later comes back to see the proofs. They thought it over and finally chose one of the photos. But the girl says to the boy: "You don't seem to be completely okay about it." And the guy, a little embarrassed, says: "Well, the photo's pretty, and you look great: but it's a shame that you really can't see my party pin and ballpoint pen."'

'PAPER! PAPER! LATE EDITION!' screeched a newsboy, whose papers were sold out in every direction in a minute. Now they were standing in front of the entryway's canvas walls (one of them was spattered with something black – tar or glue), waiting, while other people in line amused themselves with the newspaper. A dog howled nearby. Everyone laughed at the same time. The lights blinked and then brightened again. The speakers were playing one of you-know-who's Hungarian Rhapsodies. 'It's odd that Abel would be around here,' Andrés said to himself looking over his shoulder. 'It was Abel, I'm sure of it. And Juan spotted him before we ate.'

Yesterday the two men, purportedly, went through their usual nighttime routine, returning home in a state of complete drunkenness. According to some neighbors, the violent argument started as soon as they'd entered their room. It quickly degenerated into a fist fight, during which Pérez picked up the knife he used to attack his assailant, managing to inflict ten fierce wounds on various parts of his body. As a result of the attack, the victim collapsed and died.

'How horrible,' said a lady. 'Just look at this, Estercita, the things that go on!'

'It's in the paper?' asked Estercita, who was cross-eyed.

'Every single gruesome detail. Poor man, no one's safe these days. If it weren't for God, we'd all be dead.'

'Listen to what they're playing,' said Estercita. 'That record Cuca has. Her boyfriend's brother gave it to her. The one with the record shop. Divine.'

'Yes, a classic,' said the lady. 'Like what the lady in Apartment 8 was playing Saturday, when we were at your aunt's house.'

'How divinely she played! How grand! If I had a hi-fi, all I'd do is listen to classical music. How divine! Just listen to the violin!'

'It's very grand,' said the lady. 'It sounds like the *Clair de lune*.'

'It does,' said Estercita. 'It's almost the same, except *Clair de lune* is more romantic.'

'Shit,' said the chronicler. 'And now in we go, children, it's our turn. Everybody hold on to everybody else, and make sure no dogs sneak into your pockets.'

They were entering when they heard yet another speaker bidding farewell to the column of people moving out. *I think he's speaking in verse*, thought Andrés. *This is getting to be ridiculous.*

The gods, thought Juan, and he remembered:

The gods walk among trampled things, holding up
the hems of their mantles, an expression of disgust
on their faces.
Among rotten cats, smashed larvae, accordions,
feeling the moisture of corrupt rags through their sandals –
the vomit of time.

They no longer dwell in their naked heaven, thrown
out of themselves by a pain, a turbid dream,
walking wounded by nightmares and slime, pausing
to recount their dead, the clouds face-down,
like dogs with their broken Assyrian tongues.

They lie without dreams, loving one another with the
expression of sleepwalkers,
mixed together in tombs and sponges, amid kisses
dark like weeping;

peering enviously into the abyss
where erect rats fight and squeal
over shreds of flag.

'Silence!'

'Okay, okay,' said the chronicler resentfully, and the guard stared hard at him: 'Less okay and more respect, mister. This is the house of adoration. Get into single file, form a line. Silence!'

In the half light, fearfully picking their way over the soft ground (as if the ground were given a different, almost menacing quality by the enclosed space), the fifteen members of their group lined up. It was almost impossible to see, but the guard showed the way, shining his flashlight on the ground. From outside came the noise of barking,

and the canvas trembled as if an enormous dog were scratching.

Voices, a kind of melopoeia. (*Now, on top of perorating in couplets, the son of a bitch is going to sing*, thought Andrés, enraged; but knowing that his anger was because of Abel, that he was transferring it to the orator – although, not even because of Abel but because he knew that Abel was nearby: actually,

a desire to have a reason for being angry – after all, Abel, so what? – and for something to do. *But that is the question, o Arjuna: to do something and why?*)

The beam from the guard's flashlight hit the ceiling. It was curious to observe how the white beam perforated the canvas, you could see the light go right through to the other side – and the searchlight outside illuminated the whole area with a weak column of light that copied the movements of the flashlight inside. The light from the flashlight smashed into a brilliant disk at a seam in the canvas; when the guard waved it around, it looked as if two enemy searchlights were looking for each other;

but the one outside was weaker.

On the plane of the canvas they joined ferociously, following one another, coupling, biting the cloth. From the inferior beam outside, there came a sufficient glow to see the figure of the guard, the line of those in the group, and a square black box on four legs, raised about five-and-a-half feet from the floor. It had a glass top (the tiny moon of the flashlight on the canvas, its course over the ceiling, was reflected weakly in the glass. It was extremely beautiful).

'You can move forward one at a time,' said the guard, suddenly lowering the flashlight (which ran like a whip along the body of the line) and shining the light on the interior of the box. 'Careful, the ground is slippery.'

Stella was the first to pass through, she had a right to be first. Juan was having fun seeing her stop when she got alongside (fun, without having fun – a *cutaneous* fun to pass the time), she was poking her tongue out, her purse held tightly to her bosom,

        on tiptoe

trembling, illuminated by the reflection on the glass –

darling, bone bearer, adorer without vocation, idle supplicant –

ogling by decree of nature.

       START COMING BACK, MISS.

There was some cotton; and the bone on top of it. The light from the flashlight got it to reflect some sparks, as if it were made of sugar. They all stared at it,

       COME ON BACK NOW, DON'T FALL
       ASLEEP THERE,

they could see the bone clearly, despite the fact that it was almost as white as the cotton; up against the cotton, the bone seemed almost pink, each end a very light yellow.

       ALL RIGHT, TELL US IF YOU PLAN TO
       SPEND THE NIGHT!

When the line turned, passing by the box, it proceeded straight out the exit, a flap of loosely hanging canvas. The chronicler, who brought up the rear, paused next to the bone, studying it slowly. Then the guard turned off his flashlight.

       YOUR TURN'S UP, MOVE ALONG.

So they had to leave, and ran into the others who had stopped in front of the speakers platform. The speaker they were assigned to was ruddy and potbellied, with a double-breasted vest and a gold chain. 'Well, let's hope he's a good speaker,' said Clara. 'We want to get the full effect of this experience.'

The line had collapsed when they moved out, and trapped them against the podium. A flood of light (the searchlights occasionally moving) cascaded down on them, pinning them in place like insects on a board. They reacted by forming a knot – Andrés and Stella, Clara and Juan, with the chronicler forming the center. A drum was beating some sixty feet from them, women were singing, and all of them had their eyes fixed on the orator, who was waiting for something.

'But I will not speak,' said the orator, standing on tiptoe (he was tiny and had a singsong voice). 'Instead,' pointing a little pink finger toward the Sanctuary, 'I'm going to ask for a moment of silence' – no one was speaking – 'as a tribute to the great' (indecisive pause) 'to the greatest of the' – still no one was speaking – 'to the unique, the unique!'

'This just had to happen to us,' said the chronicler. 'You expect a fiery sermon and look what you get.'

'Silence,' said a gentleman with a black tie.

'Silence,' said Andrés. 'Yes, a moment of silence, by the clock.'

'Would you please shut up,' begged Stella, looking all around.

The orator once again stood on tiptoe and waved his arms as if he were shooing away mosquitoes. *He counts the seconds like a referee at a boxing match*, thought Juan. Then he was opening and closing his mouth, his audience waited expectantly; but the strip of loose canvas was rising, and the group that had followed them in the Sanctuary began to flood in. The jam of people around the podium got tighter, there were mutterings of protest, instantly silenced by the orator with a terrible flutter of his arms. *This would be the perfect moment to kick over the podium and send this rosy-cheeked twit to hell*, thought Juan. He pushed Stella away so he could get a clear shot and was just getting ready to pretend he was being pushed by the people emerging from the Sanctuary – when the orator emitted something between a shriek and an entreaty, his eyes rolled back in their sockets, his hands stretched forward (his gold chain swinging back and forth on his belly).

'Hey, just a minute, everyone!' he shouted. 'A minute. What's a minute, when all the centuries combined wouldn't be enough time to silence and humble ourselves in the presence of this testimony . . .'

Listen here: do you think my feet are made of concrete?

'in the presence of which, ladies and gentlemen . . .'

'Let's get out of here,' said the chronicler. 'This is going to turn into a real speech, mark my words.'

'the grandeur of the greatest . . .'

Get that elbow out of there, I'm begging you in the name of God!

'the paternal authorities that over the course of history took on the supremacy and majesty – because this is the moment to say it; we ARGENTINES . . .'

'The little word that fixes everything,' said Andrés. 'Let's go, there's an opening over there. Follow that longhaired dog; he knows what he's doing.'

The dog got them out in a flash, and the thankful chronicler felt obliged to scratch his ear. The dog snapped at him but missed.

In the Bolívar Café, they liberated themselves from some of their mud and fatigue. The waiter, a frowning man from Galicia, talked about the fog as if it were a personal enemy. The mud was worse – they had to use a knife to scrape Stella's shoes; and Clara was ashamed to look at her stockings. The waiter was stupendous; for him the only topic was that thing, the fog. He brought them their lemonade and some sandwiches and then started in once more on the fog.

'But it isn't fog,' said the chronicler. 'No one knows what it is. They're doing tests in a lab.'

'And then there's that little matter of the jaguar,' said the waiter, who knew the chronicler. 'Didn't you read about it? In Colonia Cerrillos, which is in Entre Ríos. A jaguar that's put the fear of God into people. It's a terrible thing.'

'All felines are ferocious,' said Andrés. 'The jaguar is a feline.'

'Is the jaguar ferocious?' asked Clara.

'Yes,' said Stella. 'All felines are ferocious.'

The chronicler and Stella began to talk about the bone. The waiter would slip away to the counter and other tables and then come back to chat with them. The table was long and seated around it were

Clara next to Juan (but with a chair between them, occupied by the cauliflower and Clara's purse); then Andrés right next to Juan, occupying both the head of the table and one side,

so that at the other end in the first chair, opposite Juan and Clara, was Stella – chatting with the chronicler (and the waiter periodically pushing his nose between them).

And there was a loud, tense noise brought in from outside by the fog – amplified and at the same time dissolved. Just noise; not the noise of something or other; and inside the café the teaspoons always tinkling like little bells in the style of *Lakmé* and the shouts of the other waiters from Galicia with precise orders *SIX SAND-WICHES DELUXE, TWO WITH ANCHOVIES!*

Andrés wasn't sure he could speak with Juan without Clara's hearing. Clara was looking toward the Cabildo, the reddish streetlights, a soft mass in the fog, a balcony with shadows. A balcony filled with fog and shadows.

'I imagine you saw him, too,' said Andrés.

'Abelito? Of course I saw him,' said Juan. 'It was certainly Abel. That makes twice in one night.'

'At the House, you said you'd seen him. But running into him again here makes me wonder.'

'You know he's crazy,' said Juan. 'It could just be a coincidence.'

'I can't imagine Abel in the Plaza de Mayo,' said Andrés. 'If he came it was because he followed us.'

'Let him have his fun.'

'I don't like the idea of him having fun at Clara's expense,' Andrés was about to say.

Instead: 'If I were you, I'd forget about it.'

It's sad, he thought.

All fog, thought Clara. *We came fog, we talked fog, but it isn't really fog.*

'It isn't really fog, is it?'

'No,' said the chronicler, turning around. 'No one knows what it is. Down at the paper they're working on figuring it out.'

'It doesn't matter,' said Juan. 'He's crazy, what does it matter?'

'Listen to this,' said Andrés. 'Fiery souls are more open to rage. They aren't born equal; they're like the four elements of nature – fire, water, air, and earth.'

'What's all that?'

'Seneca. I read it this morning. It sounds like Abel, too.'

'Abel? Abel doesn't have a fiery soul. His ardor is like his clothes, which he wears on the outside. He can change his ardor the way he changes ties.'

'I'm not so sure,' said Andrés. 'Shadowing people, spying. Those are jobs that require dedication.'

'How about being bored?'

'Even worse. Everything around you grows then.'

'It may well be,' said Juan, looking Andrés in the eye, 'that what Abelito is doing is studying to be a boy scout. He's earning his merit badges.'

'Okay, okay,' said Andrés, shrugging his shoulders. 'If you don't want to talk about it, fine.'

But I do want to, thought Juan, turning around to smile at Clara. *I'd like to go on talking about Abel, protecting myself from Abel – together, with Andrés.*

'All those pumas and mountain cats are very counterproductive animals,' said the waiter as he walked away. The chronicler, looking meditative, nodded agreement, and Stella had goose bumps because of the jaguar story.

'I'm tired,' said Clara, stretching. 'I'm not sleepy, I couldn't sleep. But no one is talking with me. I'm all alone like a character in Virginia Woolf, surrounded by lights and voices, like a character in Virginia Woolf, and so tired.'

'Let's go home,' said Juan nervously. 'We'll grab a taxi and take Andrés and Stella. We can drop the chronicler off at the paper.'

'The thing is, I wouldn't be able to fall asleep. It's like being on death row – I'd dream of horrors, my special nightmares. You know my nightmares as well as I do, Juan. Models A and B. Model A for the night before. Model B for the *lendemain*.' She ran her fingertips over her face as if she were searching for cobwebs. 'No, Juanacito, let's not go home. Let's wait until the sun comes up in the city, let's walk and sing old songs.'

'She really is a character out of Virginia Woolf,' said the chronicler. 'Count me out. As we say in the foyer of the club, I must sleep.

> (*Il était trois petits enfants*
> *qui s'en allaient glaner aux champs*
> *s'en vinrent un soir chez un boucher:*
> *'Boucher voudrais-tu nous loger?'*
> *'Entrez, entrez, petits enfants,*
> *y'a de la place assurément.'*)

'Have some more lemonade,' said Andrés. 'That way you can gather more material and causticity for your articles. By the way, how pretty that tune you're humming is.'

> *How pretty she is with her eyes closed*, he thought.
> (*Ils n'étaient pas sitôt entrés,*
> *que le boucher les a tués, les a*
> *coupés en petits morceaux,*
> *mis au saloir comme pourceaux . . .*)

'Clara,' said Stella, poking her. 'And you say you're not sleepy. She's nuts.'

'I'm not sleeping,' said Clara. 'I was remembering . . . Yes, the song was also like a nightmare. How horrible childhood is, Stella. Weren't you afraid when you were a little girl? Didn't you feel an incessant fear? I did, and it comes back every night. Those nightmare images from childhood are the only ones that remain fixed and shining. Or, better put, have the sensation of being fixed and shining. Everything I see now is like the Cabildo over there, a whitish clot in the fog.'

'What you're saying, it's very good,' approved Juan, staring at her.

'That stuff probably isn't fog,' said Andrés with a sigh. 'Probably, just to continue Clara's line of thought, you're just getting old.'

'Things used to have volume – they came to an end, they glittered,' said Clara. 'Now all we do is know that they have all these attributes, and spread them on when we look at them like a coat of paint. I've gotten so dumb that I suppress my senses. I don't let them function. When I wait on a corner for Juan – and God knows the worm makes me wait – it happens that I *see him* two or three times. That's right, I see him – his face you see right here, his way of moving. It happened again tonight.'

'He's so common that anyone can stand in for him,' said Andrés.

'Don't laugh, it's really sad. It's the filthy projection of concepts, the logic machine. One day I was waiting for a letter from Mom. The mailman would always leave the mail on a chair in the living room. I went over and there were three letters. From the door, I saw the one on top (Mom always used long envelopes) – with large, beautiful letters. I saw my name, the "C" round and potbellied. When I had it in my hand, *I saw*: the envelope wasn't long, it wasn't Mom's handwriting, and the "C" was an "M."'

'Desire, a magic lamp,' said Juan. 'Poor Clara, you'd love to abolish everything that gets in the way.'

'I'd like to know who I am or who I was. And *be* that. Not this convention accepted by you, by me, by everyone else.'

'I feel the same way,' said Juan. 'Why do you think I write poems? There are states of being, moments . . . Look. Astonishing things happen when you're in between sleep and being awake: suddenly you feel like a wedge about to knock all obstacles out of the way. When you wake up (doesn't this happen to you, Andrés?), sometimes you have a knowledge, a memory. Then you look around – and standing there is the night table and on top of it is the alarm clock no less, and just beyond it, the mirror . . . That's why I'm usually sad in the morning, at least until I have lunch.'

'Paradise lost,' said Clara. 'But everything you said seems just like a filthy appropriation of Platonic ideas. Maybe in some dreams we actually reach those Ideas.'

'If only,' said the chronicler. 'But dreams are usually filled with telephones, ladders, idiotic flying around, and persecutions that are not in the least stimulating.'

'Wait a minute,' said Andrés, 'I've sometimes felt something similar to what Juan's talking about – but instead of it being left over from the dream world, it was much worse. Like this: one morning, I opened my eyes and saw the sun peeking in. At that instant, I felt a horror that was like a convulsion, a kind of rebellion of my entire body and soul (please excuse the terminology). I understood at that moment, *I lived*, purely, the horror of having lost a paradise – of being once again in banal Reality. The sun every single day. The sun again, whether you like it or not. It comes up at 6:21 whether Picasso paints *Guernica*, whether Paul Éluard writes *Capitale de la Douleur*, whether Flagstad sings Brünhilde. Little man, attend to your sun! And the sun attends to its little men, day after day.'

'Damn,' said the chronicler. 'You all just get more and more complex.'

'Quite complex,' said Stella. 'Why don't we get going?'

Clara, looking at the window facing onto Bolívar, made a gesture of surprise.

'Right, let's get going,' said Andrés. '*The night is young*, as someone probably says in "London Again."'

'There are no lyrics in "London Again,"' said the chronicler, offended. 'I think we should cut out. But there's the Chinese guy, and I would really like to ask *him* about it.'

'You know someone who's Chinese!' said Stella, *and she really put her hands together.*

'Well he's Chinese, mentally,' clarified the chronicler. 'A bit like

Andrés, except that Andrés actually uses Chinese dialectic. This Chinese only has a Chinese way of behaving.'

Andrés was watching Clara search for nothing in her purse, multiplying the signs of being busy. It seemed to him she'd grown pale.

> *'Gimme da dime you bastard,'* shouted the
> paperboy on the corner. *'You lousy mother
> fucker, son of a bitch.'*

'*Dixit*,' proclaimed the chronicler, delighted. 'What an animal. It's like a cursing marathon.'

'We Argentines are pros at that too,' said Juan. 'The increase in cursing must be in inverse proportion to the will of a given people.'

'It's not that simple,' said Andrés. 'It's more a matter of tensions. What you're saying is that our cursing is meaningless – just words we use to fill any void in life. We curse for no reason – we wind ourselves up, then we extend a little bridge over the thing that opens at our feet and threatens to swallow us up. Then we cross over the curses; the impulse lasts us a while, until the next time. But look at the symbol of Cambronne, which is formidable. Victor Hugo saw it clearly. The guy cursed at the *far end* of tension; the curses flew out like arrows, with all of Waterloo behind them.'

> *'All right, all right, take yer ten cents,'* said a
> shrill voice. *'What a lot of noise you make.'*
> *'I'm defendin' my rights,'* said the paperboy.

'Let me introduce you to the Chinese guy,' said the chronicler.

'On the other hand, tensions exist here more than in other countries,' Andrés went on. 'Too bad they have to be negative. Repressions.'

'All right, all right, you're going to trot out your favorite theme,' said the chronicler. 'If we'd only relax more, we wouldn't have such bitter stomachs and all that.'

'No, it isn't that, my dear café psychoanalyst. What I insinuated is that for us there are two levels of swearing: the *useless* level where there's a reason for it and we get riled up; and there's the *necessary* level that destroys us, born of *tragic* (excuse the expression) tensions. This necessary level goes on and on; if you look at it carefully, it's tragedy – and, as you see, my adjective turns itself into a noun very nicely. The tragedy is an immense, deafening curse against Zeus. And don't think the tortoise that fell on Aeschylus' head doesn't have its sequels. If Pascal had actually questioned Zeus instead of God the Father, I'm sure he would have been struck by lightning.'

'More and more fog!' said the waiter, bringing a coffee for Clara. 'There are going to be traffic accidents galore! That gentleman over there seems to know you.'

'Right, it's Salaver,' said the chronicler. 'Hey, man, come on over here. Allow me to introduce the Chinese gentleman, I mean Juan Salaver. Salaver, my friend, this young lady here is Miss Stella, shake hands. Sit down Salaver. Let's chat a bit before we leave. What are you up to?'

'Me? Nothing,' said Salaver. 'What about you?'

'Me?' said the chronicler. 'I'm writing a book called *Paludes*.'

'Oh,' said Salaver, who had walked around the table and was holding out a cereal-like, a rather dirty hand. 'How nice.'

'Are you a journalist?' asked Stella, who now had Salaver on her right.

'Yes, well, I write pieces. Tonight I'm gathering material for something about . . .'

And on the cross of my desires

(the guy singing must have had a problem with his adenoids, he'd been singing the whole length of Yrigoyen, and he raised his voice when he passed the café.)

> *Ah'l fill my soul wit mist*
> *The blue uv da sky will die*
> *Above my sleepless nights*
> *Seein' you leave*

'O Argentores, o Sadaic,' said Juan, trembling. 'But notice that it is symbolic. The fog has touched this guy's very soul. Of course, he calls it "mist," but not all of us are as cultured as he is.'

'. . . I'm writing about the religious spirit,' said Salaver.

The chronicler observed him fondly, focusing his gaze on Salaver's bald pate, on his triangular sideburns, and his long face. *The Chinese guy*, he thought. *A great man*.

'Well, well, let's talk about Eugenie Grandet,' he said, smiling at Salaver. 'When are you off to Spain?'

'If all goes well, within five squares,' said Salaver.

'He means five months,' translated the chronicler. 'Come on, explain it to the folks.'

Salaver took out his wallet, and extracted from it a card holder; and from the card holder he extracted a Celluloid calendar with a glamour girl wearing sunglasses that advertised Kirchner Optometrists, and also (it folded in two) an excellent picture of 1950 Liberator of the Year, General San Martín

> and on such-and-such a date, in Paris, Yehudi Menuhin would play Bach's sonatas for solo violin,
>
> and Edwin Fischer would be in Padua,
>
> and Arletty would be staging *A Streetcar Named Desire* – in Paris – and in Barracas Mrs Encarnación Robledo de Muñoz died.
>
> And someone, in a hotel, wept with his head in his hands thinking about Prokofiev's sonatas for violin; and a ranch owner in Chivilcoy stopped his car outside the Galarce and Trezza bakery, ordering one of his ranch hands: 'Okay, Bluebird, go on in and buy some macaroons!' While in Montreal a light rain fell.

'Five squares,' said Salaver, placing his calendar, dates upward, between two plates containing cold turnips.

'Oh,' said a distracted Clara. 'Of course.'

'Well, actually, it's rather clear,' Salaver said, happy to explain. 'You know that my Aunt Olga lives in Málaga. I want to see my Aunt Olga because I want to put into practice a plan I have about moving definitively to the peninsula.'

He talks like the late edition, thought Andrés, and then he remembered something said by Murena, an unknown comrade of solitude: antagonist in twenty different things, but – and this, this . . . – also connected in many other things,

Contributing, by means of perverting language, to man's becoming an anarchic spectator at a circus, the press . . . But the Chinese guy doesn't look anarchic, thought Andrés. *The poor man's just an idiot, nothing more.*

'To that end,' said Salaver, 'I've put order in the disorder, and I think that Málaga fits in the fifth square. Towards the right and down.'

'Around the 25th or 30th of August,' said the chronicler, studying the little squares filled with numbers written in red and black.

'But I'm not sure, you see, because counter-luck lends itself to the worst things.'

'Explain that counter-luck thing.'

'Everything is a matter of luck,' said Salaver. 'Everything. Philosophers have taught us that, and it's in lots of books. So you've got to go against it, and I've invented counter-luck, which is a way of life, you see. I can explain it this way: we all live in squares. The first thing we should do is construct a "super-luck" so that natural luck finds itself in difficulties immediately. My method consists in sticking a pin into a square, every morning, while I look up at the ceiling. Then you check where the pinprick is. If you've already been through it, it doesn't count, so you stick in the pin again. When you stick a place you haven't before, you observe the symbol conventionally designating the time when the sun is shining on that part of the earth and then you think. Water.'

'Take this,' said the chronicler, passing him his lemonade.

'Then you do the second part of "super-luck," which is most delicate. If you fall into what will be a (so-called) day, that is, say, two weeks off, you set about thinking how you're going to live that piece of the square, right? First the physical circumstance: if it will rain, if the wind will be strong or weak, if you'll have to write an article about how a quantity of combustible materials combusted in a place called Buenos Aires, or if the man holding the position of Editor will tell you to prepare a memo on the birth rate. Let's say all that will happen. You postulate those events.

That's super-luck. Then,' (at this point Salaver straightened up) 'then you prepare *counter-luck*. I was talking about wind and rain: when that day (so-called) comes, you walk out wearing a light-colored suit, whether it rains or not. I mentioned a fire; that day, you get to the paper and write about Beethoven even if Troy or Albion House burns down. So then, it doesn't matter that there is no fire, or that you aren't ordered to write about the birth rate. You've foreseen super-luck and sunk it with counter-luck.'

'No two ways about it,' said a delighted Juan.

'Didn't I tell you he was a great man?' said the chronicler, who'd never spoken of him before.

'It all sounds fine to me,' said Andrés. 'But will you be able to travel to Málaga?'

'It's entirely possible,' said Salaver. 'Fifth square, lower right, more or less easy.'

'Really?'

'The ships sail according to a fixed schedule,' said Salaver. 'That's an advantage: chance is already conquered in the most crudely practical aspect of setting sail, which is to have a ship to sail on. Against all the rest, super-luck arrays itself – and we attack with counter-luck.'

'You,' said Clara against her will, 'should be named Salaluck.'

'The "ver" in my last name does concern me,' said Salaver. 'I'm ahead of my time, so my very destiny orders me to look at what will happen.'

'Very interesting,' said Stella, obsessed with the calendar. 'Weren't we about to leave?'

'Yes, it's hot here.'

'Good-by,' said Salaver, quickly getting to his feet. 'It's been a real pleasure.'

'Bye-bye,' said the others.

AND ABEL WAS AT THE WINDOW

'The chronicler should pay, as punishment for the squares and Aunt Olga,' said Juan. 'I admit the guy has a certain Chinese quality to him, if we both mean the same thing by that.'

'Everybody pays his own way,' said Clara, putting two pesos on the table. 'Either I'm crazy or there goes Abelito again. Don't let Juan see him . . .'

'Out!' shouted the waiter kicking a bluish-black dog that was heading toward a fried turnip on the floor. Then he gave them their change, bade them a very cordial farewell, happy both for the kick and the mutt's howl.

The ladies exited first. The chronicler finished saying good-by to the waiter, and Andrés' hand lightly touched Juan's shoulder as they moved forward.

'Yes, I saw him too,' said Juan without turning around. 'What can you do, that's how he is. The amazing thing is how quickly he can fade away like smoke in the breeze.'

Andrés waited for the chronicler.

'*Like smoke in the breeze* is an expression to ponder,' he said. 'Smoke is the easiest thing to see! You'd become famous if you proposed in your column that thankful firemen erect a statue to smoke.'

'I'll do it,' said the chronicler. 'They could commission a statue from Troiani. But, man, the fog *is* getting thicker. What a night for walking around. It could only happen to us . . . Well, we must accompany the exam takers.'

Two columns of women were crossing toward Avenida de Mayo. They were very well drilled, escorted by young men carrying torches and flashlights. In the fog they looked something like a caterpillar turned loose, dragging itself along with the slowest movements. Someone with a high voice shouted, and Juan thought,

>*But Abel, that jerk. It's as if he's in the sirens of the ambulances going along Leandro N. Alem.* Switching the package to his left arm, he used his right to hold Clara close to him.

'How are you, old girl?'

'Okay. Wide awake. Very wise, a bit sad.'

'Clara,' said Juan in a low voice.

'Yes, I know. Why are you worried?'

'I'm not worried. It's just that it seems absurd. Andrés saw him too.'

'Poor Andrés.'

'Why "poor" Andrés?'

'Because he sees ghosts.'

'But don't we?'

'Yes,' said Clara. 'But Abelito is alive.' A violent desire to weep came over her. If she could at least get question number four.

The chronicler bought a newspaper, and they began walking along Bolívar to Alsina. A hot, wet drizzle was falling. 'Wonderful,' said the chronicler. 'Congress has approved a project for the protection of wildlife.'

As they were reaching Paseo Colón, slipping slightly as they walked down from Alsina, Andrés abandoned Stella's arm — she always made him serve as a tugboat — and fell behind, listening to the chronicler's shrill voice and Juan's angry humming, his way of holding on to Clara as if someone were going to take her away from him. He looked silly, with the package and Clara, shouting things to the chronicler, waiting for Stella to catch up to them, turning around to look at him, to get corroboration from him.

'How tired I am,' muttered Andrés. 'What a night.'

The light from the tall streetlights outlined Clara's ankles, her rapid walk. It would probably rain at dawn — one of those fine, hot rains that depresses you. 'I don't believe it!' shouted Juan, stopping on the corner. The light bathed Clara's hair, half her face; and Andrés paused, looking at them. He saw the chronicler, retracing his steps, waving for them to wait for him as he ran to the opposite sidewalk. Stella and Clara were talking with Juan; they had forgotten about Andrés in the shadow. *I too am a witness,* he thought. *You will give testimony . . . About what if not about myself? And even then . . .*

The woman stepped out of a doorway and whistled softly. She was very blond, tall, and thin, wearing a black dress that emphasized her breasts. She whistled again, standing in the shadow, staring at Andrés.

'Excuse me for not wagging my tail like a good little dog,' said Andrés, 'but I don't like being whistled at.'

'Come on,' said the woman. 'Come home with me, handsome.'

Andrés pointed out the group on the corner – Stella, who was looking back, and the chronicler with a package in his hand, catching up to them.

'Ah,' said the woman, her voice falling. 'You might have told me.'

'What can I say? Are you always around here?'

'Yes, sometimes. You can find me at one in the *Hafmoon*.'

'Okay,' said Andrés, waving good-by to her. He watched her go back into the doorway, her hair darkening. *Who knows?* he thought. *Who's to say that the best thing wouldn't be going off with that poor thing and getting drunk instead of* . . .

'A little wine of the first quality!' the chronicler was shouting. 'This is the time for *eutrapely*, my boy. 1:00 A.M! *Andiamo á fare una festicciola* in the Plaza Colón, and may the cops be deaf and blind, *questa sera*!'

'Andrés,' shouted Stella, watching him come along slowly, his hands lost in the deepest part of his pockets. 'Lonely little mouse, come along with your cat.'

'Kitty,' said Andrés. 'You're the angel who protects me from temptation.'

'Ah, so it was true,' said Stella. 'Clara said it looked like you were talking to . . .' She stopped, confused without knowing why. *It was a mistake to mention Clara by name*, she thought, but the thought didn't even enunciate itself, it yielded . . .

Andrés little cat

blond nice little . . . wine and the *festicciola* . . . a whore voice – Clara voice, as if she were angry, but senseless . . . Cat from Catamarca, so I . . . my RIGHTS!

                now oh those skinny arms

He never

           his heat his smell and inside

during love and oh what delight . . .

★

'Bah,' said Andrés, rigidly leaning forward (the way we always do when we have our hands in our pockets, the game of the dorsal hinge) and kissing her noisily on the hair. *To Clara it looked*, he thought, upset, happy. *She saw that I was talking with that woman*. Clara walked along listening to that velvet interior silence that throbs in the depths of our ears – the resistance of the body's night to the stridencies of the street and the lights. The others surrounded her, speaking to one another within her hair, through her ears, her skin. *Deep river*, she thought, *my soul is on the Jordan*. She was overcome with absurd desires to be alone, to be in Juan's arms, to listen to Marian Anderson, to read one of Poirot's adventures or an article by César Bruto, to drink water with lemon, to dream beautiful dreams, the early morning dreams when you squint your eyes and see that it's six, and delight in stretching your legs as far as they can go, cuddle against a warm, heavy back, let yourself go again into the depth

    and the diver

    but the ring and the cruel princess

    then the whirlpool; yes a ballad.

'You're sad,' said Andrés. They were walking along Paseo Colón, wrapped from time to time in shreds of fog, seeing cars and people pass by, alien and distracted things.

'No, it's just that the night is an appropriate time for thinking,' said Clara, in a slightly mocking tone.

'Excuse me,' said Andrés.

She touched his arm with the tip of her fingers.

'I didn't say that because of you. Talk to me. You should know that.'

'Yes. But it isn't the same.'

'Same as what?'

'The same thing as really wanting me to talk to you.'

'Don't be silly. How sensitive we are. Juan, Andrés is getting mad at me!'

'What a shame,' said Juan, moving ahead to join the others. 'Andrés' anger is noble because it's metaphysical above all else.

When it focuses on an object, it loses efficacy. *Aquila non capit*, et cetera.'

'Swine,' said Clara. 'You make me into a fly.'

'On the eve of your exam you should remember that if Homer says something like that it practically becomes praise. And how about Lucian, my dear? *I love flies, and it grieves me enormously when winter begins and they start dying on the windows and curtains. Flies are the chamber music of the fauna.* You, really, are the bitchy fly of invective. Bitchy fly, that's great!' And rocking his cauliflower he laughed like a madman

> (like a madman who laughed that way,
> but isn't true);

and a newsboy on the corner of Hipólito Yrigoyen stared at him and began to laugh slowly, fighting against it.

'Bitchy fly!' howled Juan doubling up with laughter. 'That's terrific!'

'What's he going to be like when he drinks this vintage Trapiche?' asked the scandalized chronicler. 'Come on, buddy, stop that. Stop acting like a baby.'

Andrés continued a few more steps and then stopped, letting them get ahead. He could just make them out in the fog. He remembered the little kid in Plaza de Mayo, the anxious and hanging faces of those watching the ritual. *Was that why the kid was there?* he thought. *Very likely, he's got the white face of those who really know horror.* He ran his fingers over his moist face.

'Let's cross the sweet plaza of *Cristóforo*,' ordered the chronicler. 'Watch out for the trolley. Stella, your arm if you please. Yes, it's vintage Trapiche; we've got to return to the simple rites, *eutrapely*, the art of pleasant conversation.'

The tall ghost on his back burst into view suddenly, his feet enmeshed by the agitated figures, the cross, the torsos at work. *Another one on his back,* thought Clara. *Another one staring at the water of nostalgia – useless path of escape.* A dog sniffed her skirt, looking at her with sweet surrender. She touched his hairy neck; he was wet, like Tomás when

her teddy bear, Tomás,
she left him forgotten outside and in the morning, at daybreak:

'Clara, Clara, that girl! Is that why we give you toys?'

And the horror, the remorse – Tomás frozen, Tomás soaked – my poor little Tomás soaking wet all night surrounded by fairies by cabbages by owls forgive me forgive me Tomás,

I'll never do it again.

'The War Ministry looks like it's made of cardboard,' said Stella.

'Nice image,' said the chronicler.

Anyway, it was odd to see Andrés so self-absorbed, such a friend of created silences (and how hard that is in Buenos Aires), and calling attention to himself two steps behind the others;

– the woman had blond hair, she walked brusquely out of the doorway, as if on stage – or moving on ahead and then waiting for them, with a monumental air.

As if he expected something from me, thought Clara. *As if I owed him something.*

'Then she came over and put an ant in his hand,' Stella explained to the chronicler. 'She's terrible. You never know what she's going to do. So naughty.'

'Kids,' said the chronicler. 'They're tragic.'

'They're wonderful!'

'They're death itself,' said the chronicler. 'Incredibly filthy and wild. You women love them with your skin, your noses, your tongues. But if you think about it a bit . . .'

'Men all say the same thing,' said Stella. 'Then they become fathers and start drooling.'

'I wouldn't drool, not even if I had my cheek pressed up against Gail Russell's pubis,' said the chronicler. 'Guys, we've got to sit down on a good bench and have a slug of this, while we contemplate Columbus and the progress of the stars.'

'You're more sensitive than you seem,' said Stella, interested. 'You play at being ironic, but you're really good.'

'I'm an angel,' said the chronicler. 'Which is why I don't live in fear of kids. What's eating you, kid?'

But Juan was looking into the distance, toward the hedges outlined in the fog. He took out a handkerchief, dusted the bench,

> (As did Darius to the sea,
> or was it Xerxes?)

and Clara sat down with a sigh of relief, making room for Juan, with Andrés on her right. Stella sat on the end with the chronicler between her and Juan. Then Andrés got up again, as did Juan, staring at the hedges.

'Come on, take a little rest,' the chronicler was saying. 'Here we are in the prettiest, most centrally located, most dilapidated plaza in Buenos Aires. No one comes here, except for lovers and people employed by the ministry. One night, I saw a black guy kissing a boy about fourteen years old. Kissing him as if he wanted to tattoo his palate. The kid put up a bit of a fight, ashamed to see that I was observing them from a distance.'

'And why did you have to butt in?' asked Juan. 'You shouldn't carry journalism over into love.'

'What things they say,' complained Stella. 'Kissing a boy, what a disgusting thing.'

'Not at all. It had its charm,' said the chronicler. 'They were like statues – which is always appropriate for a plaza. Come on now, Juan, your famous corkscrew.'

'I don't carry it anymore. We're screwed if you don't have one.'

But the chronicler did have one, although it shamed him to pull out his enormous yellow-bone jackknife – seven blades in one knife, Solingen steel, guaranteed.

'We've got to drink from the bottle. First the ladies, and a toast to Columbus dressed in fog. Stella, don't be so finicky. Follow Clara's example. You can see she's got a drinker's pedigree a mile long.'

'It'll take away the stickiness of the fog,' said Clara, passing her the bottle. 'Actually, you might have bought white wine.'

'It wouldn't have been proper,' said the chronicler. 'Completely incorrect. Like asking Charlie Parker to play a mazurka. Your turn now, Juancito. You look like a soldier on guard. Who goes there, Juan?'

'I'd like to know,' said Juan, grabbing the bottle. 'I think Andrés would, too. Did you see something, Andrés?'

'I don't know. It's so foggy. I think I did.'

Clara stood up looking toward the parking lot of the Automobile Club, following the confused form of the street, the lights of the A and C buses lined up at their stop.

'It looks like the first scene of *Hamlet*,' said the chronicler. 'Or was it *Macbeth*?'

'Let them rant,' said Stella. 'These three guys love to make up stories. What's that on your face? Let me get it off.'

'It's fuzz,' said the rather astonished chronicler. 'It's extremely rare that I have fuzz on my face.'

'The wind,' said Stella. 'And with the humidity, it stuck to your nose.'

Two ladies and a boy came through the plaza, stopping by a flower bed so the boy could urinate. In the silence of the plaza, the sound of the little stream hitting the gravel was clearly audible.

'And then they catch a cold,' said one of the ladies. 'All this time in your house, and he doesn't have to go, but soon as he walks out, he's got to.'

'At least that's all he had to do,' said the other lady.

'May you have children,' said the delighted chronicler.

'Well what do you want? He should sweat it out instead? Are you listening to this, Clara? Do you realize what he's saying?'

'No. My head was in the clouds,' said Clara. 'Andrés, why do you worry so much? You'd think he was going to eat us.'

'Who?' asked the chronicler.

'Nobody, Abel,' said Clara. 'A boy.'

Tired out, Andrés sat down again. 'Well, now that you've said his name we can talk about this. This makes three times that I've seen him tonight.'

'Twice for me,' said Juan and Clara at the same time.

'Or that we think we've seen him. This fog . . .'

'It isn't fog!' said the chronicler. 'I'm getting tired of telling you over and over. But you're all keeping secrets. What is this about Abel?'

'Nothing,' said Juan handing him the bottle. 'A guy who's not been right in the head lately.'

'Abelito is a little odd,' said Stella. 'But to see him three times . . . You'd think he was following us.'

'Brilliant,' said Andrés, patting her on the back.

'Don't be mean.'

'Okay. I won't. This bench is wet.'

'Let's go home.' Juan spoke into Clara's ear without lowering his voice.

'No, no. What are you so worried about?'

'I'm not saying we should go because of that. I'm afraid you're going to catch a cold. You've got to be in good shape tomorrow.'

'No one's ever in good shape tomorrow,' said the chronicler. 'I've got a million comebacks like that. You should see how much the Editor loves them. I'm what he calls aphoristic.'

'*Aphonic* would be better,' said Andrés. 'Who said tomorrow? It already is tomorrow, that's what this tapioca thing annoying us is.'

'What?'

ABEL. ELBA. BAEL. BELA. LEBA.
EBLA. ABLE. ELAB. BALE. EBAL.

'The air's really full of fuzz,' Stella said suddenly. 'I just swallowed some.'

'That fuzz is made up of the words people say, preserved and sent around by the fog,' said Juan. 'It is a night . . .

> "A night, one of those
> nights that bring joy to the soul,
> when the heart forgets
> its doubts and quarrels,
> when the stars shine
> like candles at an altar,

>when, inviting us to pray,
>the moon, like a holy Eucharist,
>slowly rises
>above the waves of the sea."
>Ten bucks says you can't name the author.'

'A Spanish Romantic,' said Andrés. 'Besides, tonight is the complete opposite of your poem.'

'Of course. I recited it so I could conjure up that perfect night. Stars: come out!
and you, Belazel, little sugar cube, come from above
and show us how to weave reeds and steeds!
I know lots of charms. I know many, many charms.'

>EBAL   ELAB   LEBA
>ABLE   BAEL

'Campoamor,' said Andrés.
'The Duke of Rivas,' said Clara.
'No.'
'Gabriel and Galán,' said the chronicler.
'No. Someone else? Núñez de Arce.'

>CERA   AREC   CREA
>ECRA   ACRE   RACE

'Well,' said Andrés. 'You sure found yourself a beautiful example.'

At the corner of Leandro Alem and Mitre, leaning against a doorway in the market, Abel lit a cigarette. For some reason, there was no fog in the market (a thermal difference or something like that). The people coming back from Plaza de Mayo emerged from a tunnel – the spotlights set up in twenty-five-foot intervals (after the attack against the Cardinal-Primate, in front of the bookstore with the sign 'Bookstore of Knowledge') sent light right through it, making it look like a tunnel of light.

When Abelito was lighting his cigarette (now the scene was prolix and minute) . . .

>EBAL   BAEL

Baskets and more baskets
the baskets of María Andrea, a paperboy was singing.

Abel dug around in the pocket of his vest, lower right. He needed a stamp. He delicately extracted a piece of paper and looked at it. A pink bus ticket. Maybe in the other pocket.

On my wedding night
I didn't sleep a wink . . .

ELAB

'More than two hours without mentioning literature. It's incredible,' said Juan, toying with the empty bottle. 'Shall we break a streetlight?'

'The perfect Buenos Aires gesture,' said Andrés. 'Go on, don't be left with only the desire.'

But Juan hid the bottle under the bench, slightly ashamed of himself.

'It's pleasant here,' said Stella. 'Less heat than in the Plaza.'

'Then let's take this opportunity to carry out a survey,' said the chronicler. 'What kind of education did you have, Andrés? Don't get annoyed. I can't stop being a newspaper man. *nihil humanum a me alienum puto*. Ever notice how the moment you quote something in Latin you look ridiculous?'

'In any language. Which is why the best thing is to quote from the Spanish and not say it's a quotation. Which is what I've just done by the way.'

'You're quite a guy,' said the chronicler. 'But really, I would like to get a hold of everyone and ask them: *What was your education? What did you read when you were ten years old? What movies did you see when you were fifteen?*'

'That's all?' asked Juan mockingly. 'Only fine arts and letters?'

'Let the chronicler talk,' said Clara. 'It's a great moment, a great plaza, a great fog to be speaking about these things.'

'I think we'd learn a lot about Argentina studying the cultural learning of people our age. Not that it would be of any real use, but you know that statistics . . . Man, statistics what a science! First they find out how many dogs were run over during the past five years and how many rivers overflowed their banks in the Sudan.'

'There are no rivers in the Sudan,' said Juan.

'I meant to say the Transvaal. Then they compare the results and derive a law about birth rates in families made up of Italian singers.'

'Careful now: statistics are democracy in its scientific state – essences isolated by means of individuals!'

'Listen to this guy!' said Andrés, laughing. Clara heard him laugh and was surprised at her own surprise. *So odd*, she thought. *It's good he laughs*. She touched his cheek softly, and he looked at her.

'The chronicler wanted to know how you came to culture. You're the first guinea pig,' said Clara.

'Second,' said the chronicler. 'I'm the first. The statistician should sacrifice himself on the altar of science, fill in the first note card of the story.'

'I had an idiotic childhood,' said Juan. 'But you tell, Andrés.'

'I don't like to talk about my childhood,' said Andrés, now surly, and Clara felt something like a violent taste of tenderness, of carob seeds, of summer saliva.

Childhood

how good it is not to speak   to leave it on its blurred corner on its hopscotch,

how good it is not to betray . . .

    Hiding place   watermelons, eaten all the way across; siesta,

    ladybug ladybug fly away.

    God the Father, God the Father. Smells,

    Carnival. Plays.

    I'm a 'Tarmangani' and you're a 'Gomangani.'

    Enough.

'. . . from then on,' said the chronicler. 'What I want to know is how you made the leap. When your adolescence ended, the onanistic period – self-abuse and the cultivation of lavatories.'

'Sweet chronicler, you most certainly did speak,' said Andrés. 'I can help you out in this business. Look, I was not precocious, but I began writing things with a great deal of rage, things I wouldn't have the nerve to say now. One funny thing: I wrote in a hypocritical language – without even the slightest obscenity. The characters always spoke familiarly to one another, and the action took place anywhere out of Buenos Aires. It's incredible how much you can aspire to universality. The idea of doing something local terrified me. I wanted my stories and my poems – yes, dear Juan, in those days I engendered some ferocious sonnets – to be as intelligible in Uppsala as they would be in Zárate. The language was stupid, but what I was trying to say had more power than what I'm writing now.'

'You're completely and utterly wrong,' said Juan. 'But go on, let's see which path you take.'

Andrés was smoking, having slid down on the bench, the nape of his neck against the backrest. 'Sometimes,' he said, 'determinism – well-beaten – bounces back off the ropes and splits your face open on the way back with a good punch. Look at me. Until I was twenty-five, I had a creative fever that was really notable. I won't tell you I actually wrote a lot; I carefully polished and reworked my things. But I filled more pages than I have in all the rest of my life, and when I re-read them I realized that I was on the right path. I screwed up, I wrote tons of garbage; but today I wouldn't be able to summon up the energy to write some of those things, or the style to produce a sonnet like the ones I wrote back then. Besides, I liked writing, I enjoyed myself as I did it. It was pleasurable suffering, like having a well-scratched rash – it bleeds but you like it anyway.'

'And why did the flow stop?' asked the chronicler.

'Influences, prejudices disguised as experience. The bad thing is that they were necessary, that they were good at the time. The good thing is that they turned out bad in the long run. Look, it isn't easy to explain, but I can give you an idea. I had a couple of friends who loved me a lot. I think that's why they almost never praised my stuff and tended to criticize it with self-sacrificing severity. I could never expect gaping astonishment from either one. They pointed out all my purple passages, everything useless; they saw something like an obligation to correct in me. That forced me, out of loyalty and gratitude, to close the larger valves of my creativity and leave only the small stream flowing. I would put my glass under it, and every few days – after nights and nights revising it, honing it down, taking things out, moving things around, cursing – something would begin to form that could stand.

'Also I was reading. It was the time that I first read Cocteau: I was nineteen and found *my* book in *Opium*. Now, I can recite it in French; but things like that didn't matter to me then. For very little money, I bought the Spanish edition. You can't imagine what that was like for me. The *Iliad* was my first jolt of the absolute; and bam, I sink into Cocteau. Cocteau was incredible! I spent weeks without combing my hair, being called an idiot by my sister and my mother, sitting in cafés for hours so I could be alone. Every one of Jean's sentences was a knife-edge of glass slicing through your neck. Everything else looked like liquid shit next to that. Imagine, not two years earlier I'd been reading Elinor Glyn. And Pierre Loti had made me cry, I shit on his Japanese soul! And suddenly I'm reading that book, which is a summary of an entire life – but a life over there, see, where at the age of nineteen you're no longer a Buenos Aires asshole. I dive in, and find myself with the drawings, they were there too. I discovered the plastic arts in those drawings – the last naiveté, "the most beautiful." Now I know they aren't anything that astounding; but I spent night after night staring at those geometric insects, those sailors, that opium madness – staring at them and suffering, smoking my pipe, and studying and staring at them right in front of me. A crustacean madness.'

'Holy shit,' said the chronicler.

'That's right. The formal severity of that book, how hard it was to understand – not only because of what it said, but because it alluded to things I hadn't a clue about at the time – Rilke, Victor

Hugo (in detail), Mallarmé, Proust, *Potemkin*, Charlie Chaplin, Blaise Cendrars – dimensions of seriousness were revealed to me without my realizing it! I began to fear writing gratuitously; I'd toss out the papers I'd scribbled on in Plaza San Martín or in La Perla del Once. The two friends I mentioned before, and that book, sent me straight to Mallarmé, I mean to Mallarmé's attitude. The thing is, I was drying up for lack of confidence and a desire to touch the absolute. I began writing poems so hermetic, I don't know more than four people who've been able to stand the first half-dozen. I began cultivating pure circumstance: to write only when I found an absolutely necessary reason. So I wrote an elegy when D'Annunzio died, I adored him wildly – but by contrast, see, because the same thing happened to him. Except that he wrote very little using a lot of words.'

'And then?' asked the chronicler.

But Andrés had closed his eyes and seemed to be sleeping.

'Then I began to write well,' said Juan, rubbing a finger over his forehead. 'I mean, well, he, like all of us, has the color of the moon. He's here, but the light comes to him from so far off. Cocteau . . . Sometimes the name of my light is Novalis, sometimes it's John Keats. My light is the forest of the Ardennes, a sonnet by Sir Philip Sidney, a suite by Purcell, a little painting by Braque.'

'And me,' said Clara shamelessly stretching.

'And you, my little mouse. Oh, chronicler, only provincials, very provincial at times, set up a poor little autonomous culture. Notice I don't say *autochthonous* because . . . But ultimately they place tremendous emphasis on the local. Are they right, chronicler, do you think they're right?'

'You contradict yourself,' opined the chronicler. 'It's possible to specialize in the local, but a culture is by definition ecumenical. Must I translate my terms? You can only appreciate your own culture when you're removed from it. I understand Roberto Payró because I've read my Mérimée and my Addison and Steele. To remain in the now and think you've got enough is fine for women and barnacles, begging the pardon of all ladies present.'

'It's so sad, chronicler,' said Juan sighing. 'It's so sad to feel you're a parasite. An English kid in a certain way, *he* is Sidney's sonnet or Portia's speeches. A cockney *is* your "London Again." But I, who love them so much, who know them so well, I'm just a handful of poems and novels, I'm nothing more than Echeverría's captive woman, the obstinate gaucho, the falcon's bell, Roberto Arlt's Erdosain . . .'

'It seems small-minded to complain like that,' said Clara, straightening up. 'It isn't proper for a man like you who fights to achieve the poetry that interests him.'

'All things considered,' said a bitter Juan, 'there's nothing brilliant about belonging to a pampa culture just because of some damned demographic accident.'

'But really, what does it matter which culture you belong to when you've created your own, as Andrés has and so many others? Does the ignorance and helplessness of those people in Plaza de Mayo really bother you?'

'They have their chimeras,' said the chronicler. 'And they're more from here than we are.'

'They don't matter to me,' said Juan. 'What matters is my contact with them. It matters that my boss at the office, because he's a jerk, can stick his fingers in his vest and say that someone ought to cut off Picasso's balls. It pisses me off that a government minister says surrealism is . . .

but why go on?

Why?

It pisses me off not to be able to cohabit with others, see. Not-to-be-able-to-coexist. And it isn't just a matter of intellectual culture – being able to appreciate Braque or Matisse or dodecaphonic music or genes or anything else. It's a matter of skin and blood. I'm going to tell you something horrible, chronicler. I'm going to say that every time I see limp black hair, long eyes, dark skin, a provincial accent,

it makes me sick.

And every time I see an example of the Buenos Aires dandy,

it makes me sick. And the chicks make me sick, too. And those unmistakably local white-collar workers whistling in the streets, products of our city with the wave in their hair and their shitty elegance, it makes me feel sick.'

'Okay, we get the point,' said Clara. 'He won't even stop when he gets to us.'

'No, I will,' said Juan. 'Because people like us make me feel sorry.'

Andrés listened with his eyes closed. *How miserable*, he thought. *Only in our passions, our elemental mud, are we equal to anyone. Couples marrying, values burning forth – the delicate fit of man into his world, his rigorous confrontation – that's where we get lost . . .*

The fuzz ball slipped between the moist leaves that held it prisoner; making a leap and falling onto the gravel. A policeman's boot came down next to it, just missing. A light breeze made it tremble and spin on its tiny tentacles of thread and dust, minuscule bits of fabric and fiber. When it entered a column of air it quickly rose to the height of the streetlights. It went from one to the other just grazing their opaline gloves. Then it lost its momentum, and it began to fall.

With his eyes closed, Andrés listened to the voices of his friends. The chronicler recalled some verses Juan had written a long time before. Clara knew them better and recited them in a slightly tired accent; but her fatigue seemed to be born out of the words rather than her voice. Perhaps the poem illustrated what Juan had just said in a very luxurious language. *You can puke into a tin bucket or a Sèvres bowl*, Andrés thought bitterly.

'Such elegance,' said Juan, breaking a silence that had gone on for quite a while. 'All that isn't bad – but those salt marshes, those conches . . .'

'Very pretty,' said Clara. 'With every new day, you have more fear of words.'

'It's good someone's afraid of them in these parts,' murmured Andrés. 'I'm with Juan.'

'But if we're always afraid of sounding pedantic, we run the risk of indigence. We shed more and more in terms of expression without gaining in the area of essentialism.'

'Perhaps if we could agree beforehand on the terms of this bitter argument,' suggested the chronicler. 'Words like expression, for instance.'

But Clara did not want to waste time. She liked Juan's poem and felt that salt marshes and conches were just fine. 'In every sense, we're losing ground,' she insisted. 'Our grandparents filled what they wrote with quotations; now it's considered vulgar. But, the quotations help us avoid saying what someone already said well badly; and besides, they point out a direction – the speaker's preference, which helps us understand the person who uses them.'

'Quoth the raven: nevermore,' said the chronicler. 'Even a parrot can say "Panta Rhei."'

'Just because he can say it doesn't mean he'll fool us,' said Clara. 'The fear of quoting, finding comparisons of a classic order, is a form of this rapid impoverishment. But I insist that the worst thing is fear of words – that tendency of ending up in a kind of Spanish for beginners.'

'Better Spanish for beginners than the Spanish of our Argentine classics, like *The Gaucho War*.'

'Don't waste our time,' said Andrés, as if talking in his sleep. 'Always the same confusion between form and content, ends and means. *The Gaucho War* is bedazzling because it's bedazzlingly

– keep an eye on that little adverb for me –

thought. All of which leads to this wise little saying: "Tell me how you write, and I'll tell you what you write." From bedazzlement to bedazzlization.'

'How much a person learns being with all of you,' the chronicler was saying as he stared at Stella, almost fast asleep at the end of the bench. Now all we need is an excursion through music, a touch of painting, two jiggers of psychoanalysis, and then everybody goes home – because tomorrow we go to work.'

'Tomorrow,' said Juan, 'there are exams to be taken.'

Andrés removed the fuzz that had flown into his mouth. 'If talking less and less meant speaking more and more, Juanillo, then the poet should be monophonic.'

'Yes,' said Juan, ironic now. 'And end up like Hermann Hesse's rag dolls, who masturbate facing the sun with their famous OM.'

'Funny, that Swiss gentleman annoys the hell out of me too,' said Andrés. 'But look, it's only proper we recognize the degree to which Clara is right. The language of the Argentines is only rich in exclamation – our false resentful aggressivity – and the remains of what's transmitted orally in the provinces. Listen, and the first thing that surprises you is how we've done away with all our adjectives. When you hear a Spanish cook describe a paella or a cake, you realize she's using a much richer repertoire of adjectives than what one of us would use to characterize a book or an important experience.'

'It's good that we depend on nouns instead of adjectives.'

'I agree, but do we really? I'm not sure. The modesty of the resentful leads to our epithets having opposite meanings. That's how there came to be this incredible catalogue of things like:

"What an animal, how he played Debussy!

He's a bestial artist.

What a *savage* the guy is, what talent that beast has . . ." or the appearance of magic adjectives that function as general expressions in small circles, comfortably replacing an entire series of words: "Fabulous" is one among us. And what people used to say, for one still with us: "phenomenal."'

'I don't think that's specific to Buenos Aires,' said Juan. 'But what you're saying is true in general. I remember that a long time ago I used to visit a house in Villa Urquiza, and a guy with a Catalonian name from Buenos Aires would also go there. It was from him that I heard these things you've discussed for the first time. He considered many things "horrible." They were the great things, the things that excited him. "A horrible novel, you've got to read it, right now today." I actually went to that house to be happy and to learn the technique of translation. Those were horrible years,' he added in a low voice, smiling to himself.

'If the condition of our language reflects the condition of those who speak it,' said the chronicler, 'then we're screwed. Our language is pasty, yellow, and dry – with a great need for Roget's lemonade.'

'Around here luckily, there are some people who don't hesitate to speak,' said Juan. 'I think I'm one of them: and I don't think Andrés is afraid of expressing himself in the most – well, I'll say honest – way. To express oneself honestly, without falling into comfortable patterns

– because when you get down to it, that's what they are, damn it –

of some sacerdotal language; a complex *trovar clus* that no longer has any meaning.'

'But it does have meaning,' said Andrés. 'It has *its own* meaning. Why would you deny an artist the right to express himself in good faith – whether it's with plastic material or words? It's good you speak about honesty and you see the two of us at least trying to write with honesty of expression. But accept the other planes as well – the possibility of a *trovar clus* as valid as your own immediate, essential language.'

'Andrés is right,' said Clara. 'The decisive factor is that language means what it says; and that happens very rarely around here. Our meanings are all still multiple – one thing is a poplar with nightingales, another is polenta and sparrows. The important thing is not to call grappa ambrosia and vice versa.'

'Shit,' said the chronicler. 'If you say that tomorrow, they'll ride you out of the University on a rail.'

'Very well put,' smiled Andrés, staring at Clara almost surprised. 'Of course! Roberto Arlt understood *Martín Fierro*'s moral better than anyone. He fought hard to unite language and its meaning. He was one of the first to see that what we call "the Argentine," as in any country, overflows the limits imposed by *refined* language – that language you call sacerdotal – but that only poetry and novels can contain it fully. He was a novelist and went to the street, which is where the novel runs. He let the taxis pass and got on the trolley. He was a tough guy and should never be forgotten.'

'It's actually more complicated than that,' said Juan, turning around on the bench. 'I accept that meaning should have its own language, should be its own language, and all that. I also concede anyone's right to practice *trovar clus*. Eduardo Lozano has as much right to his poetry as I do to mine, or Ulises Petit de Murat to his elegies with their open patios and atrocious wakes. The problem, when you get down to it, is never language but the meaning itself. I mean, is it really interesting to go out on the street? Is it really worthwhile? No sooner do you answer yes, than you realize only an idiot would attempt to write about the street in the banal style of *La Nación* or Dr Ricardo Rojas. Once he's made his decision, the intelligent novelist only has one path to follow, the one my wife has defined so beautifully: meaning which is at one with its language. But there *is* another question: What is the street? Does it represent, does it contain, more than Eduardo Wilde's salon or Eduardo Mallea's apartments with a view of the river?'

'Don't use metaphors,' said Clara. 'You know very well the street is the street because the person who walks along it is mankind, and that in fact, the street means the same as the salon, the apartment, or integral calculus. Up to here we are with you; but if you let yourself be fooled by your own metaphors, you won't even be able to understand yourself!'

'Ah, mankind,' said the chronicler. 'This girl always hits the nail on the head.'

'She sure does,' said Andrés. 'Arlt walked down mankind's street – his novel *The Seven Madmen* is about mankind on the street, I mean a *looser* being – less *homo sapiens*, less a character in a book. Notice the term "character" almost doesn't apply to these creatures. And notice that when we deal with Dr So-and-So, we quite properly call him a *character*. You've got to squeeze the juice out of these little things, my dear chronicler.'

'How about some coffee?' said Juan. 'But to go back to what I was saying. This man who is no longer a novelistic character, this Argentine walking along the street of the novels that interest us which, by the way, are very scarce;

does it seem to you that we can grasp him from top to bottom, that we know him and help him know himself, and that – for these reasons – we have to talk about him? speak about him?

in an absolute language, without brakes – a tongue that respects nothing but its own meaning, that has no other value than that of serving the novelist and his novelistic characters?'

'Yes, I do believe that,' said Andrés. 'I damn sure believe it.'

'Amen,' said the chronicler.

> *And the river was near, invisible,*
> *With a filth of buoys.*

By then, the plaza was almost empty. A few groups remained: one made up of people dressed in white who carried a white box; the police, also just up from the corner of Banco Nación; the laborers with yellow boots from a Department of Sanitation water truck, moving into the plaza to clean away the papers, the orange peels encrusted in the mud – washing the pavement and the surrounding sidewalks.

Two inspectors in a black Mercury kept watch. Day was beginning to break.

'The boss is an asshole,' said the short inspector.

'Let's not talk about that big son of a bitch in Parks and Walks,' said the inspector driving. 'You won't believe it, but he's got the papers for my transfer in a locked drawer and plays dumb. I know he's got them, but I don't have the nerve . . .'

'Of course.'

'to say anything to him'

'Sure.'

'Because you know how he is. When you least expect it, he'll pull a fast one and not promote you, *te la voglio dire*.'

'You can't make any kind of career in there.'

'What can you do?'

'All right, we've done what we need to do here. You think the water truck will be enough?'

'Yeah,' said the driver. 'Let'em give it the once over lightly and that's it. Anyway, they're going to start over again tomorrow anyway.'

From the orifice – black inside and tremulous on pink edges that vibrated, then contracted, acquiring for a second the perfect immobility of the circumference and then irrupted into the oval, the ellipse, the crude triangle of curved angles – flowed a material of a lighter rose color, agitated with its blind head and receding with the promptness of a whip, only to reappear: a decapitated salamander, crude, a formless phallus;

and Abelito licked the stamp twice, the first time to soften the glue, the second to feel;

> because all that did not change –
> Governments change,
> republics fade –
> but that foundation
> that affirmative compound adhesive;

the taste of the national glue, the sweet nausea caused by the layer that remains and sticks, the glue behind the face of Bernardino Rivadavia, one of the triumvirs – a man of the land, a founding father, and finally a refugee on the postage stamp

that remains as a homeland of heroes.

> A stamp is an important thing,
> it's what remains as a homeland of heroes –
> swept away and blown out,
> already in history;

but what does 'already in history' mean? –

When

history is a moment, a miserable word;
a miserable word that echoes, high-sounding and strong-souled?
(Despite all that, Abel stuck the stamp on the envelope according to the instructions handed down by Mail and Telecommunications. Perhaps because of that bit of rebellion present in every citizen of Buenos Aires, he put it a bit closer to the middle of the envelope than was proper

as if to incommode the cancellation machine, to force it to feel around, repeat its grand, iron foot-fall on the poor little blue flattened letter. So much flatness in that envelope:
the flat writing, the flat envelope
the stamp –
    (that remains as a homeland of heroes) also flat.

On the five-peso stamp, San Martín; on the ten-peso stamp, Rivadavia; and on the silence of the night, the enormous wing of the homeland.

(But the heroes are never there, they are never those ones, they don't fit, there are decrees that steal from them that glory beginning beyond the stamp: *To be born so some guy in the market can lick your nape before sunup. To be born so a cancellation machine smashes your face two million times a day.*)

    (Compare Mail Service statistics: the men on the stamps that cost more than one peso:
well-off,
less spittle required,
cancellations by hand, tolerable, and that is one of the ways of being-in-history.)

The worst thing, availability: Make yourself, construct yourself, commemorate yourself, baptize yourself, exhume yourself, repatriate yourself, transport yourself, mausoleumize yourself, stamp yourself, argue yourself.

That
that is what remains as a homeland for heroes: a handsome man unknown to others, his suave farewell,

and Bam Bam Bam

Bam Bam Bam

and the unfading glory and the labarum – the pure devotion of millions of tongues licking your neck and millions of cancellations breaking your face.

Mailbox, Abel, inside! Tomorrow:

in the power of the recipient;

and the envelope: into the garbage with his face, his unfading glory; San Martín. In with the beans and pieces of semolina pudding!

2

Suddenly he remembered. He was probably three or four years old and had to sleep in a bare room in an immense bed. At his feet grew a large window. It was summertime, and the window was open. He remembered even the smallest details. Waking up and seeing a livid sky seemingly stuck to the frame – a rubbery, filthy sky instead of the glass – the dawn. And *then a rooster crowed*, splitting the silence, a horrible tearing of the air. And it was terror – the abominable machine. Fear. Someone came, consoled him, held him in their arms, . . .

'My God.'

The taxi went slowly down Leandro Alem. The Post Office looked like a stage set, an illustration for Malet's history. *Wounded in an act of sedition, Lycurgus* . . .

'Please, driver, go as slowly as you can,' asked Clara. 'We want to see the sun rise.'

'Sure, miss. It's going to be a beautiful day.'

'Who knows,' said Clara. 'The air is so odd. We should have been able to see clearly by now, it's 6:30.'

She yawned, her head lolling against the cold leather of the backrest. Juan's eyes were closed. 'A rooster,' he murmured. 'What a son of a bitch.'

'What's all that about?'

'Nothing, a memory. In the beginning was the crowing of the rooster.

O *vive lui, chaque fois*
que chante le coq gaulois.'

'Did you notice the chronicler was hinting that you should make him a gift of the cauliflower?'

'That's not a joking matter.'

'But why would he want it?' asked Clara. 'He wouldn't eat it.'

'True. It's mine, anyway, and that's that.'

Clara caressed his hair, and her head took refuge on his shoulder. 'I think I'm a bit tired now,' she said.

'Me, too. What a night.'

'Bah,' said Clara, opening her eyes.

'Don't move,' asked Juan. 'I like to feel the scent of your hair. Listen to that train howl. Like my rooster.'

'Ah, your rooster. That train really is blowing. There must be a cow on the tracks,' Clara observed brilliantly. 'Cows do wander onto tracks you know – it's a tradition.'

'There are no loose cows in the port.'

'It might have escaped. But the train won't run it over. First, because the port trains are very slow. Second, the train is howling because of the fog and not because of some cow.'

'Fog, schmog. The chronicler . . . Driver, go up Corrientes. But slowly, very slowly.'

'Did you notice,' said Clara, 'that the chronicler saw those two cabs at the same time? What eyes!'

'He was the most wide-awake of all of us,' said Juan. 'I don't know how we could have walked like that all night. All that time in Plaza de Mayo . . . Stupendous – then the Chinese guy.'

'The Chinese guy, and then Abelito, and then that woman who started in with Andrés.'

'Right, the woman and Abelito.'

He ran his fingers over her mouth, tickling her nose. Clara bit him, moistening his fingers with her tongue. 'You taste like raw cauliflower,' she said. 'Look at those cops over there.'

At the intersection of Corrientes and Maipú, there were two patrolmen and some passersby staring at the pavement as if they were reading an inscription. The cabby stopped the car, and they saw that the pavement had collapsed – an area between six and nine feet long, just before the turn-off to Modart. Not a big deal, but enough to break a car's axle.

'It's the city's fault,' said the driver, speeding up a little. 'In my neighborhood, a light post fell over. It suddenly sank about a foot and a half, and then it tipped over. Bad foundations, I tell you! The city doesn't check up on those things.'

'I don't see how a truck could make the asphalt sink that way,' said Clara, half-asleep. 'The chronicler would explain it so well, so well.'

'She is good,' chanted Juan, letting sleep overcome him. 'She is very good . . .'

*And his face was white
under his blue hat.*

'She comes from Formosa, from Covunco . . .'

'Enough,' begged Clara. 'Please. When you think about it, all that stuff was horrible.'

'Yes, like my rooster.'

Clara cuddled against him. 'Tell him to speed up. I'm so, so tired.'

'I,' said the chronicler, 'have been thinking.'

'It's possible,' said Stella, who cultivated humor from time to time. 'These things happen.'

'I don't think,' the chronicler continued, 'that everything said about our literature tonight was accurate.'

'Ask the cabby to go up Córdoba,' murmured Andrés, who seemed to be asleep. 'And leave literature in peace.'

'No, man, it's important. At first I accepted your theory that we don't create because we're too soft. Now I'm not so sure that's the reason. Tell me one thing: why do you write?'

'To entertain myself, like everyone else,' said Andrés.

'Perfect, that's just what I needed. You didn't even use the term "amuse," which would have required a detour.'

'I will say,' said Andrés, 'that most of the time I yield to a necessity – a tension that can only be released onto the page. It's what those who write out of abnegation call "the mission," based on the reasonable idea that every flexed bow contains an arrow, and that the arrow's mission is to fly off and hit someplace.'

'But that necessity,' said the agitated chronicler. 'Does it really exist externally to you, let's say

as a moral imperative

a propaedeutic, a maieutic – something that obliges you ethically?'

'No sir,' said Andrés, opening his eyes. 'That we add later, like a hunter who talks about the damage to farms caused by foxes and how good an idea it is to exterminate them. In fact, writing is like laughing or fornicating – like releasing doves.'

'Agreed. But we've got to distinguish between what we call "pure" literature and – God forgive me – the essay used for didactic purposes. There's more to writing essays than entertainment; usually the person who teaches isn't just entertaining himself.'

'Essentially he is,' said Andrés. 'If you teach because of vocation, then in principle you're doing something to fulfill yourself, and I call that entertainment. To realize yourself is to amuse yourself. You don't think so?'

'Well, it's subtle,' said the chronicler, who was plagiarizing sentences from the Spanish version of *The Three Musketeers*. 'Poets, for instance, are extremely happy with their poems, despite the fact that it's considered elegant to assume the opposite. Poets know very well that their poems are their highest realization; and they most certainly savor the fact. Never believe any story about a poem written through tears; if there are any tears, they're dredged up – like those of actors. True tears, composed of sodium chloride, are wept for the sake of oneself – not to supply lyrical ink. Remember Saint Augustine when one of his friends died: *I wasn't weeping for him but for myself, for what I'd lost*. That's why elegies are always written much later, recreating the pain and being happy, the way we're happy when we listen to Isolde die or witness the fall of Hamlet.'

'Prince of Denmark,' said Stella.

'Of course the thing is subtle, as you said,' said Andrés. 'But I imagine that César Vallejo could weep while he wrote his last pages. Or Antonio Machado, if you prefer. For those poets, their pain was their humanity – you might say they were "given to" pain or "taken over by" pain. Believe me, chronicler, their last pages must have been their best moments; they transformed personal suffering into histrionics of the highest sort, by which, I mean, they transformed it into poetry. But if they were suffering in that moment, they were suffering the way a star or a storm suffers. The worst thing was what happened after, when they closed their notebooks, when they re-entered personal suffering. Then they *really* suffered, like dogs, like men broken by their fate. And poetry – like a broken toy – could no longer do anything for them until they found a new illumination and a new happiness.'

'That's the way it should be,' said the chronicler. 'Also, you might explain to me why card-carrying writers – they always give me a pain in the neck! – have to proclaim themselves martyrs to their labor. Why martyrs? In the worst case – if they really suffer while they're creating – they should be satisfied, like saints; because their suffering turns out to be the proof of the pudding, the corroboration!'

'Whenever I hear a writer say he suffers like a mother when he writes, I'm inclined to tell him to go to hell,' said Andrés. 'The poet's motto can only be: In my pain is my joy. And this brings us back to national territory again, old boy. Around here we don't suffer to the extent that our creative joy breaks windows and runs along the roofs. When I say suffering, I mean suffering on a grand scale, the kind that produces a poem like Dante's. As things stand, Argentina is in a bit of a limbo, a time-out – a soft, little happening between two nothings, as Juan said very well somewhere or other.'

'So you think that suffering should precede joy?' asked the astonished chronicler.

'No. Causality only has validity when you're talking about the *epidermic* dimension of destiny. To say that someone who doesn't cry won't laugh is absurd. Deep down, in the central laboratory, there is neither laughter nor tears, neither pain nor joy.'

'No?' said the chronicler. 'Explain yourself.'

'I'm speaking, always, about poets,' said Andrés. 'In the end, I suspect, the poet is that man for whom pain isn't a reality. The

English say that poets learn through suffering what they will teach by singing. But the poet will never accept that suffering as real, and the proof is that he metamorphoses it, gives it another purpose. And that is precisely what I mean about that kind of pain: you suffer and know it isn't real. It has no power over you because it's filtered through a prism and transformed into a poem. The poet enjoys himself as he does it, like playing with a cat that scratches his hands. Pain is only real for the person who suffers it as a fatality – or contingency – by giving it citizenship, allowing it into his soul. Essentially, the poet never admits pain. He suffers – but he is some other person standing at the foot of the bed watching himself suffer. All the time he's thinking that outside, the sun is shining.'

'You can drop me on the corner,' said the chronicler. 'I really didn't get where I wanted to. I mean with this theme, not about getting home. Aside from that, I agree with you. Stop right there at that oh so elegant door, driver. Well, it was a stupendous evening. The part with the Chinese guy . . .'

'That poor Chinese guy,' said Stella.

The cab continued along Córdoba where the street is divided by islands with trees on them and progress is as slow as if it were raining. Soon you're on Angel Gallardo: the entrance to Centenary Park – the vague perfume of the first hours of the morning. For Stella, who was staring at the street with blurry attention, the only things that had consistency were the recognizable cut of the corners, that pharmacy sign – *now the plesiosaur in the Museum, the baby whale* – the block shape of the apartment houses, the curved streets of the park – *where timid people were learning to drive in extremely old, rusted-out cabriolets*.

'It's going to be a beautiful day.'

Andrés seemed asleep, his legs pulled up, the back of his neck against the edge of the seat. He barely smiled, agreed with a slight movement of his head without knowing what Stella had said.

The miracle of nearness, he thought. *Meeting, contact. We were going along like this, and sometimes I held her arm and sometimes we argued –*

and sometimes she was bad and forgetful,
and a bit of a pain;
but so what
if we were, if it was, a corroboration – that unpronounceable moment when you leave your ego and say: you. You say it – you, you are it,
there it is, you are it. Oh clarity!

Pieces of image – to refuse to allow the voice to invent phrases that isolate. I simply remember, or better yet –

continue, am there still, praising the edge without words, the edge . . .

the gift of that night now gone.

'One day, it's over,' he said to himself. One day, it's over. To know from now on that a day would not even fit sideways in the street – barely to speak or coexist in a single image. We've broken bread, tonight;

and she poured me a glass of wine and said: 'Juan, Andrés is angry with me,' and she played at being Clara, at thinking herself this Clara who can still look at me and accept my nearness. But a time will come . . .

sparrows, little heaps of dust leaping, bathing themselves
simple happiness of pure material,
vacation of stone turned into birds.

One day it's over. She alone, or I. Suddenly: a telephone, and it's death. Yes, it was sudden. Oh my love, my love –

Revenge of language, flood of tropes, but yes, horrible, not to see her ever again, and to know that irreversibly –

so much on the side of morning
and then suddenly below so below
so sweet so cold so bare

'Stop on the corner. Sweetheart, let's go. Lord how asleep you are.'

Nothing can pay for this certitude, thought Andrés fishing out his wallet. *Only oblivion brings happiness. All foresight is horror. Fly allegro! stroll along the keyboard, untie breezes and oranges. I know, I know that the other tempo to come*———

is the lento, the terrible andante
it is what it was before this fleeting lie   present indicative

He was thinking about Clara when they went to bed. (Stella had made café con leche, and he took a long bath, staring at the plane trees on the street out the partly-opened window.)

And it was peace. Sleep taking over his hands.

He saw her again, hard and bitter (for him, only for him, and perhaps for Juan), her serene question a lie: 'Andrés, why worry so much? You'd think he was going to eat us.' And the chronicler asked: 'Who?' Then Clara said, 'No one, Abel, a boy.' One day – and by then he was sleeping, but it pained him to think it – one day, perhaps she'd say: 'No one, Andrés: a boy.'

'No one' being the subject of the sentence.

Stella, asleep, whined and turned toward him, putting her hand on his waist. Andrés let himself fall asleep; softness. Perhaps get a haircut at noon – Now he was near Stella, he didn't feel it when his hand, replicating hers, stopped on his thigh.

With the third try, the key was stuck completely. Juan cursed under his breath. José, the watchman on the corner, was having fun observing them from a distance.

'José!' Clara shouted, waving the package. 'At least we can't be robbed! *We* can't even get in!' José's entire fatigued face was filled with a laugh – with its Chinese factions.

'And to think,' Clara said to Juan, 'that we're carrying this beautiful cauliflower.'

'You just take care of the cauliflower,' muttered Juan in a rage. 'You'll probably shred it when we're thirty feet from a vase.'

'You're going to put it in a vase?'

'Of course. That is, if we get in.'

'It's good you look on the bright side, ma'am,' said José, in a high state of amusement.

'It isn't the lock,' complained Juan. 'The bolt is stuck. It's as if the door were out of line.'

But the door suddenly yielded, and from the hall there came

a soapy, nocturnal breath. Juan pushed open the door, leaning against it with all his weight; and it was then they saw that the floor was in fact no longer level. One whole side of the tiling had slightly sunk, bringing the whole door frame out of line. Clara sighed, astonished. They said good night to José and walked to the elevator, suddenly feeling a chill. It didn't take them long to realize that the elevator was stuck between floors.

'As long as there isn't a dead body with us,' said Clara. 'I've heard that a body can stop an elevator between floors.'

'Hold the cauliflower,' said Juan, who'd taken it away from her when they entered. 'I'll go up and see.'

'It might be between the fifth and sixth, but it's only eight flights,' said Clara to cheer him on.

'Right,' said Juan striding up two steps at a time. 'Stupid stairs.'

Later they slept, but Clara was still waiting for the elevator with Juan. The enormous apartment house. The little entry hall from the street (with José outside, but so inept, so much a watchman) had gotten dark and seemed longer – it isn't easy to prove that light doesn't affect the dimensions of things. The elevator shaft disappeared into the darkness

– yes, it wasn't daytime, it wasn't daytime –

where, doubtless, Juan was tinkering with the elevator.

(Why is that all you have to say is *doubtless* for the most extreme doubt to arise? End of chapter: 'And he separated tenderly from his wife, whom he would doubtless find safe and sound on his return from the expedition . . .' And the good reader thinks: 'Okay, here we go.')

But Juan was long in coming.

and the cauliflower, that heavy fruit, that whitish object wrapped in green veils, heavier and heavier – fatigue, everything is relative –

or perhaps a trifle larger since she'd begun waiting for the elevator

that wasn't coming wasn't coming.

        Breathing   what darkness the bars of the Otis cage.
        BECAUSE THERE ARE STAIRS, THE OWNER
        ACCEPTS NO RESPONSIBILITY
        FOR PROBLEMS WITH THE ELEVATOR
Oh Juan between the fifth and sixth floors –
          Sister Helen
          Between Hell and Heaven
  but a light   little light   and the light guided the shepherds to the   calendar   *shepherd's calendar*
  coming down   little light little light
          little lantern of the suburb   no, the elevator, finally the elevator and Juan;
  the elevator wrapped in light – slippery – finally coming down and Abel, laughing;
    but don't look at the floor, don't look at
    Abel's feet,
    because
    there on the floor . . .

Juan woke up with the scream. Clara was trembling, her hands covering her face. He shook her a bit (Clara now was sobbing in her sleep), but then she began to stretch out, calm now, and he supposed it was better to leave her as she was. He caressed her hair, barely a movement, before losing himself in that movement of the caress. Almost instantly he began to dream. The smoke came in under the door, and it was natural that the door was sagging because of the sunken floor, and there was a rather wide gap open on the hinge side. Smoke also came in where the window was partially open. *Here comes a candle to light you to bed, here comes a chopper to chop off your head.* –

The kid came out from under her skirt but it was the cauliflower. (How absurd, thought Juan, wrapping his bathrobe around himself.) Probably the smoke would hurt Clara,

would hurt the cauliflower, wilted by any smoke. But the thing wasn't serious because he still held the final trump card (He knotted up the belt on his robe, tightening it like an old-fashioned boxer.), which was to declare

THE DREAM IS FALSIFIED

'You, sir, can do nothing against me,' he said pointing two fingers at the smoke that eddied around the bed. 'Arise now, my pint-sized Brunhilde.' But Clara touched her heart with an exhausted air; it was necessary to try something else. 'The best thing would be for me to wake up,' Juan said brilliantly, and he did wake up. He was sitting on the bed, both hands squeezing the fat rolls of his stomach. And the fog was entering the room through the partially open window.

Without knowing it completely, she enjoyed the tranquility brought by Juan's caress. It was finished, nothing more than a nightmare. For an instant, Abel's face, his teeth, menaced her, then faded away, then nothing. The gallery was of noble beauty. It had brocades, and tables like those in the Pitti Palace – dazzling, tiny pieces of marble arranged in a minute geometry. She walked along, seeing portraits of her sister Teresa, all of them bearing the painter's name in large but illegible letters. At the same time, she felt she was being led by the hand (she could see no one). It was necessary to reach the basement. Under an arcade with a breakable air, she saw the charlotte russe. But it was a man in pink and white – he was also the arcade – and it was important to pass by him without speaking. Then came stairway after stairway; everything so Italian; open spiral staircases in which the descent was a highly pleasing slide – except for the fact of being led, knowing herself led. On the walls of the spiral stairway there were more pictures and on one of them the painter's signature was the painting itself, covering the canvas from lower left to upper right, barely leaving space for a greenish hand holding up eyeglasses on the tips of its fingers.

It sounded like a leak, changing tone slightly, higher, higher, lower, higher. Andrés was sure it was Madame Roland's heart:

but then he woke up convinced, happy. *What a stupid dream*, he thought, sitting up on the bed. Once again, he was annoyed at having yielded to illusion, to believing, accepting, that a noise might be something other than what it was. A moment before, the joy of certainty of the man of faith; that joy shamed him, as did his enjoyment of affirming it was just a leak. He remained seated in the dark room, leaning back against the headboard, listening to Stella's breathing. He felt around for the glass and drank with pleasure. But is it a glass of water? Who can guarantee that this substance, loose in the shadows, persists after you can't see it? Later he asked himself why his dreams were so silly, why he didn't dream the marvelous things other people told him about. A friend's wife had dreamed herself dead, buried, in the style of 'The Strange Adventure of David Grey.' From her crystalline depth, she could see the faces weeping for her, bent over the grave. Everything took place in great serenity, but even so, she wanted to shout, to say she was there, not alive, not the same person as before,

only that she was there

that she was seeing,

but, the mechanics of the grave wouldn't let her. Then she saw her mother, still weeping for her, planting a rose bush over her grave. From the glassy depth, she observed everything. And her mother left, but not the bush: it grew, and its root came down, growing like a white sword. She felt it reach her and pierce her chest.

Fingers holding up a pair of eyeglasses. The frames were ancient, as if made of worm-eaten plaster with green and pink veins. Softly, tiptoeing onto a step, Clara breathed again. Again she was being summoned, she had to get to the basement. She walked into the dining room in her house, laughing. 'Something really funny happened to me.' And her mother raised her eyes from her embroidery.

'I was going to work, and Andrés was waiting to sell me the paper. He was wearing a newsboy's cap and had a cruel air to him.'

'That is strange, because in general, military men are different,' said her mother. Clara didn't like the tone of her voice and went over to look into her eyes. She always did that with her mother when she was a little girl. 'I want to listen to your eyes,' she would say. (From her eyes, she learned when her mother was going to die, long before the hemiplegia.) *Ah, this table*, she thought, with discomfort, trying to get around it, but the table – as if covered with gulfs – got between her and her mother, who was again immersed in her stitching. *Why does she think that Andrés can't sell me the paper? And that way of not looking at me, that foxiness* . . . She pushed the table with her stomach and her hands. She moved forward as if leaving a river in sand made of air. The river was a softish water made of mahogany with a macramé doily at its center.

This time he liked feeling the belt of his bathrobe between his fingers. Being careful not to wake up Clara – she had slept badly and was once again tossing and whimpering – he walked to the window and closed it. The fog smelled of roasted chestnuts, chlorine. *Incredible that it can be so dense*, thought Juan. He sniffed it greedily, a bit surprised. *It may well be that the chronicler's right and that it's a new phenomenon*, he thought. Leaning his nose against the window, he moved until a crack in the outside shutter allowed him to see the house opposite them, the street, and a vague streetlight enveloped in an enormous halo. He was almost asleep standing there, pressing his forehead against the warm glass, and was looking at the light on the corner with half-closed eyes. His childhood in Paraná, a humid summer – Urquiza Park, with the gullies and the soccer pitch lower down. He'd played soccer and drank ginger beer, then swam at the island, dazzled by the sun and the terrible mass of the river, dying of hunger after his swim, eating sandwiches until he was full. But it was the light he was remembering now, the streetlights at night, the universe of the streetlight: thousands of insects in a madness of fulminating orbits around the light, vibrating in unison with a throbbing palpitation, buzzing with the movement of wings and the incessant rebounding of little bodies off the hot glass. The dung beetles dragged themselves along the ground, and at times a *mamboretá* unleashed its green nightmare. The rest were little parrots, *cascarudos*; little bulls, wasps; and sometimes a small, lost, yellow planet, a disconcerted bee, extremely dumb, that allowed itself to be killed by a slap.

The mosquitoes of Uspallata, he thought, returning to bed almost completely asleep, dropping his robe with a gesture of surrender. He saw the light at its zenith, a mountain stream, watercress and reeds; he heard a distant bleat, a shepherd's loud shout. In the air, a vibrant spindle-shaped mass of mosquitoes whirled in millions of luminous dots of light. Aerial screen – a space threatening to become concrete, the geometry of a living crystal, the mosquitoes! They occupied their spindle, made it alive and whirling; they spun within it, limit and content of their transparent world, without moving from the place they occupied in the air. Sitting a short distance away, he saw the spindle suspended in space, as if only *that* space were theirs and next to them or above it wasn't proper to reach. He never knew when the dance was over, where the mosquitoes went, and at what time the translucent phantom dissipated into the liquid air.

'But yes, yes, he sold me newspapers. Why can't I get closer, Mama?'

'Because your father would get mad.'

'Oh how ridiculous,' said Clara, stuck in the swamp a short distance from the table. And when she looked back, astonished at feeling herself hemmed in, she saw that she was now in the center of the table, that she had managed to move to its midpoint – she was a ballerina wearing a rigid tutu that paralyzed her. *Andrés, Andrés*, she thought – and her voice resounded as if in an empty chamber; but her mother went on embroidering without raising her eyes. 'Andrés, let's listen to fanfares.' It was urgent they listen to fanfares together, because that would be the sign of their pact, their meeting. It didn't matter that her mother had pronounced

that horrible sentence. 'A fanfare and a counterpoint.' Then it
would be perfect. 'Or just a fanfare.' She could distantly hear
  an echo of fanfare but it wasn't: fan fan la fanfarlo
  fanfan la tulipe
  the fan-tan the fan gogh *c'est l'Ophan* . . .

You've really got to be an imbecile, thought Andrés, slipping down
until he was flat on his back. *Madame Roland! Hipnos, how many
follies are committed in your name!* He was wide awake, feeling the
fatigue flatten his head into the pillow, unable to fall asleep. He
hypothesized plans of action, needful of something that would
distance him from the idea to which he always returned like a fly.
Clean up your life: stop going to the House, stay away from the
usual haunts, cultivate idiotic relationships that will, as a result,
keep you connected. Never go back to the House. Why go? Let
Stella arrange her own affairs. She should be with the Doctor, not
with me; and acquire learning on her own. Meanwhile . . . *That's
the rub*, he thought. *Meanwhile. Life is already an enormous meanwhile. Oh solitude, thanatogenic!* It wasn't a matter of being alone,
but of isolating oneself within a community, achieving total self-
awareness. After that it didn't matter whether you were in Florida
or Atacama. *But never to know oneself: to keep going to the House in
order to be close to Clara, hear Clara's voice. Living with Stella; always
self-doubting. dilatoriness that lasts a lifetime. putting off until the end the
only obligation that matters*: 'to thine own self be true.' How, without
knowing it beforehand, without doing anything to know? *In my
inaction is my action*, he thought, smiling bitterly. *Every day I choose
not to choose*. He began to fall asleep, still smiling. He managed
to think that there were no problems, that a problem is always a
solution facing the opposite direction. To decide, to choose . . .
Epiphenomenon – the other thing, the root of the wind, hidden
in the flesh of guilt. *It's a shame that this should be the problem; because
that isn't the problem*. Who would have said that? He fell asleep
laughing.

*

Before, and because the honey vision of the mosquitoes had filled him with tenderness and melancholy, Juan amused himself thinking about the likely development of the exam. I shall begin by summarizing, in general terms, the basic principles of Whitehead's metaphysics. It must be said that the structure of being, for Whitehead, manifests itself with the compact solidity of Parmenides' universe; the proof is that no sooner does he establish the analytic vision of the cosmos, the almost monstrous interdependence of each being with all beings, then he turns it into a game of . . .

'Young man, might it be possible to know what this "monstrous" business is?'

'Why yes, professor, of course. Whitehead
    White
        head   White Horse
o sleep sweet embalmer of the night.

In his little room, very near the stars, the chronicler was sleeping.

3

'But the government has categorically denied it,' said Mr Funes.

'Don't believe in their categories, Dad,' said Clara.

'And you, don't start in with your too-wise-by-half expressions!'

Juan whistled violently, astounding Clara's brother, Bebe, who with genius (if genius means having a lot of patience) was cleaning his cigarette holder with its anti-nicotine mouthpiece.

'*Che gelida manina*,' sang Juan, tugging at Clara, who was looking sulkily at her father. '*Andiamo in cucina, cara, Ho fame, savee*?'

'Just wait a minute here. We all saw that last night. Government denials, my foot.'

'Your foot,' said Bebe, blowing through the mouthpiece and then peering through it. 'Look on the bright side: at least you've got a foot. You have to take things as they come, girl.'

'You win, Bebe,' said Juan, patting him affectionately on the back.' You just unconsciously stepped on her little foot, but it doesn't matter because what you said had some singular moments. But, Clara's right, my dear father-in-law. We saw it last night, and no one can deny that the opening of the season is full of strange omens and even stranger observances.'

Clara smiled.

'The diabolic children have probably arrived,' she said. 'Gilles et Dominique, Dominique et Gilles.'

'Just hints,' muttered Juan, looking at Bebe's mouthpiece against the light bouncing off all the glasses in the cabinet. 'Nothing at all, really.'

'Some people go around playing the fool,' said Mr Funes, trying to make the strong impression that what he was saying had nothing to do with them. 'It's mass psychology, an irrational panic. Like when comets appear. The government's right to try to calm the people down. It's ridiculous to get carried away by all that nonsense. Like when they started in with polio whatyacallit.'

'Poliomyelitis,' said a very serious Bebe.

'That's it. Anyway,' said Mr Funes, totally convinced, 'there's nothing to be gained by spreading confusion, especially when no one knows what's going on.'

'Which is the best time to do it,' said Juan. 'Let's eat, Clara. Tell the cook to get a move on.'

'But the concert's at two,' said Mr Funes.

'Why so early?'

'It's a matinee.'

'Oh. But I think we can eat. Dad. Shall I tell Irma?'

But Irma was already coming in with the fish salad, and the four of them sat down in some haste and energetically spread their napkins. Bebe had nicotine on his fingers, sniffed them with disgust, and went to the bathroom. Juan saw his chance, mumbled an excuse, and went after him. Bebe was washing slowly, snorting. Not satisfied with soaping up his hands, he washed his face, snorting twice as much.

'Hey man, tell me something: what's all this with the concert?'

'I don't have a clue,' said Bebe. 'Just give me Pichuco or Brunelli and some chick to dance with. No classical music for me. No. Once and only once I was taken to Teatro Colón and saw an opera where there was a cave and God knows what else. Who needs it?'

'But what concert is it?'

'What do I know?' said Bebe. 'Besides, you two are the ones who are going.'

Juan went back to the dining room. *Incredible he would have us go to a concert today of all days*, he thought, eating fish salad with enormous appetite. *Of course, yesterday I told him we'd go, but what we should do is sleep some more to be fresh for this evening*. Clara had circles under her eyes. Her mouth was a little wrinkle of fatigue, and she spoke in a low voice.

As long as I don't panic, thought Juan, *like that time in first year or was it let me see no, it was in third year, third-year philosophy. They asked me who Hegel was, and I said a friend of Copernicus* . . . Then he choked on the wine, and Bebe, who was just coming back, started pounding him on the back. Juan hit him back hard, amused in the extreme.

'Juan laughs all by himself the way crazy people do,' said Clara, caressing his cheek to remove a tear that was sliding down.

'Even if it means plagiarizing Chesterton,' whispered Juan as he cleared his throat, 'it's important you know that no madman laughs by himself. What you really call laughing, you know: the right to skip having to talk to someone and nevertheless laugh: that is divine laughter, granted only for the most elevated beings. It's divine because it creates itself and is also gratifying. A kind of epiglottic masturbation.'

'He was just like this last night lying in bed,' complained Clara in coddling tones. 'You called me a bitchy fly, and then you tossed and turned for five minutes. Hey, Bebe, how's the lady from Apartment 8?'

'Better, I think. Dad asked after her last night.'

'She almost died,' said Mr Funes. 'Complications from old age. She's very fond of you and always asks after you. All the neighbors always ask about you.'

The shadow of a pigeon passed over the tablecloth. Irma served the stew and brought in the telephone: for Miss Clara.

'Titina? How did you know I was at Dad's house? Oh, of course!'

'Titina is an incommensurable item,' Bebe informed Juan. 'A friend of Clara's from high school. Incredible. She rows and likes to drink.'

'I know all about her,' said Juan. 'I cozied up to your sister so I could get closer to Titina. Isn't that right, Clara?'

'It's a lie,' said Clara, covering the mouthpiece. 'But of course, Titina, whenever you like. I'd love it. Oh that . . . Yes, last night was weird.'

'See? Here we go again,' said Mr Funes. 'I bet one half of Buenos Aires is calling the other half to scare them with this nonsense. They're even saying a ship sank in the port.'

'It might well be true,' said Bebe. 'In movies with fog, there are at least foghorns. Hey, give Titina a big kiss from me.'

But Clara had already hung up and was eating stew.

'Turn the radio on. Not too loud, Bebe,' said Mr Funes. 'Let's see if there are any more news bulletins. It looks as if the sun's setting!'

'Actually there hasn't been much of what you'd call sun,' affirmed Juan, staring ironically at Bebe manipulating the radio. 'But it's really odd. In this fog, there's such a brilliant dose of solar light. Did you see that pigeon pass over the tablecloth? A shadow, barely for a second.'

'If it was a shadow, then there must have been sun,' said Mr Funes. 'Find the State Radio Channel, Bebe.'

He's afraid, thought Juan. *He's scared out of his wits, this father-in-law of mine*. And in a flash he understood the business of the concert, the need to do something, to avoid being chased
by
by what

Girls are not
Love toys

'Get rid of that tango,' said Mr Funes. 'Would you like some cheese and sweets, dear?'

'Yes, Dad,' said a somnolent Clara. 'Girls aren't love toys. So what are they then?'

'They're the love of toys,' said Juan. 'Now, dearest, who was the first to suspect the greatness of Delacroix?'

'A Category 3 question,' said Clara. 'No one knows, but probably it was Delacroix himself. And then Baudelaire.'

'Very good. And what is the title of Tristan Corbière's famous book?'

'*Les Amours jaunes*. And who speaks ill of Emile Faguet in an essay on Baudelaire?'

'Menalcas,' said Juan, winking. 'And what do you think of Symbolism?'

'For the purposes of the exam, I think exactly the same as Dr Lefumatto.'

'You'll pass, but you're going to wear yourself out,' said Juan. 'Don Carlos, I think your daughter's going to pass the exam, if she gets to the end safe and sound.'

'And what's that supposed to mean?'

'Nothing, nothing at all,' said Juan, half surprised. 'No one can know if he'll pass happily over the River Styx of Category 7. Actually, and excuse me for saying so, this idea of going to a concert before the exam . . .'

'Who knows,' muttered Clara. 'Maybe it'll be good for us. It's useless to go on studying.' The telephone right next to Clara's plate rang. She made a sudden gesture and knocked over a glass of water. 'Hi. Yes. Oh, Mrs Vasto. I'm fine, ma'am.' She waved to Bebe to lower the volume of the radio, which was blaring a full orchestra's *allegro*. 'We're all fine. Oh, what a shame. But is he better? Of course, in this season . . . No, why?'

'Here we go again,' said Mr Funes. 'Another one telling tales.'

Scared out of his wits, thought Juan, almost envying his father-in-law. *An opera box: the great refuge, the snail in his shell. I've got to hand it to you, buddy.*

> At lunch, at dinner you
> will be happy if —
> gave Splend —
> and they swam and they swam all over the dam —
> proved by Hugo del Carr —
> — curity counsel of the United Nations convened
> in . . .

'What a shame,' said Mr Funes. 'They already gave the Argentine news. We'll have to wait until the next report.'

'And I hope they all get better,' finished Clara, who was talking with her eyes closed — which in reality is how one should speak over the telephone. She hung up and looked at the palm of her hand. 'What humidity. You stick to everything.'

> Rácing opened the golden gates for him so he'd fly
> high! And Huracán gave him an opening as wide

as the sky so he'd reach the height of a condor! And Uzal – epitome of the professional player – gave his all to the new division; which is where we see him today – magnificent, tricky, with his acrobatic strikes, intelligent, vigorous; ready to put a stop to River Plate's aspirations!

'Turn off the radio, Bebe,' said Mr Funes, 'and come eat your fish salad. Irma, at six, go down and buy the papers even if I haven't come home yet.'

'Yes sir,' said Irma. 'All three, sir?'

'All three. Pass your plate, Clara.'

'Just a little, Dad. Dad . . . is the box for four?'

'Yes. Pass your plate, Juan. Do you want to invite someone?'

'The chronicler!' said Juan. 'That's it: let's invite the chronicler. Hey look!'

But the shadow had passed so lightly and rapidly over the tablecloth that they only saw Juan's finger grotesquely pointing at nothing.

'Hmmm,' said Clara cautiously. 'Okay, invite the chronicler.'

'Did you have another candidate?'

'No, I wasn't thinking of anyone.' She passed him the telephone. Irma removed the fish salad and left a letter next to Juan's free hand. He was laughing at the chronicler's sleepy voice. Clara glanced at the envelope, glanced at Bebe, and then back at the envelope. The writing was large, irregular. She brusquely opened the letter.

'But my dear boy, come on,' Juan was saying. 'It's fine that the paper squeezes the cephalic liquids out of you, but they have to let up once in a while. When do you get a day off?'

'What do you call last night's infinite wanderings?' the chronicler was saying in the tiny voice of a man with a cold.

'Come with us. It's a box. You'll see a lot.'

'I can't. And stop harping on the box. Besides, I can't imagine you in a place like that. Why are you going?'

'I have no idea,' said Juan. 'Since we're prepping for the test, it's a good idea to amuse ourselves with something. So you won't come?'

'No. They're going nuts down at the paper. They almost suspended me because I didn't call them every hour on the hour as it seems I was ordered to do.'

'What's that all about?'

'Nothing, the mushrooms,' said the chronicler. 'The nutty things going on. They still don't have their analysis of the fog, but there have already been two bulletins from the police; and an old lady caused a horrible brawl at the intersection of Diagonal and Suipacha. Just half an hour ago. Hysteria by the bucket, my friend.'

'At least you're having fun,' murmured Juan. 'Anyway, I understand why you can't come.'

'I'm glad you understand,' said the chronicler. 'Hey, last night I recited one of your poems so I could get to sleep. Ciao.'

Juan hung up, laughing. He felt Clara's hand in his jacket pocket, the rustle of paper. 'Don't read it now,' said Clara, looking down at her plate. 'No, Dad, I don't want any more stew. Give some to Bebe, he looks thin.'

Juan locked the door, put down the lid on the toilet, and after lighting a cigarette and making himself comfortable, began to read the letter. Through the beveled glass in the bathroom window came a yellow, violent glow from the banks of fog. From a radio on another floor came the voice of Toti Dal Monte, cackling actively like a hen. But Mr Funes, still in the dining room, turned on the radio again in search of news, and with Bebe's help, moved the dial from one end to the other. He would have liked to call *La Prensa* – a last, sibylline resort, an *in extremis* consultation with the oracle – but he was too ashamed.

Clara excused herself for a moment and carried the telephone to the room that had been her mother's, where Bebe's collection of pin-ups was now displayed. She thought about Juan reading Abel's letter, because it was certain he was reading it in the bathroom – the space allotted to secrets, our first cigarette, to the first ghost we embrace with a whine. She dialed Andrés' number.

'Shadow of the gods,' said Andrés' voice. 'Hello.'

'That's pretty,' Clara congratulated him. 'Very nice. Do you have a varied stock, or do you always repeat the same thing?'

'Actually what happened was that I pinched my finger when I closed the door,' said Andrés, slightly confused. 'And to what do I owe this exalted honor?'

'If you could only hear,' said Clara. 'A magpie's screeching in the palm tree at our house. Delightful.'

'The telephone is for loud noises, insignificant things.'

'Yes, and now you're talking to me,' said Clara. *Then why is it I always say everything truly important over the telephone?* she thought. On the other end of the line there was a long silence.

'I didn't mean it that way,' said Andrés after a long pause.

'I didn't take it that way. But what you said is true. Actually, the two of us hardly ever talk.'

'Probably because we see each other everywhere.'

'That's also true.'

'But it's great that you called,' said Andrés; and Clara noted the clever effort he made to be abstract, avoiding the 'me' that would have been an interjection of vanity. *I must speak to him about that*, she thought, with a strange pain in her temples and in the roots of her hair. *The halos of the saints must burn in the same way*. She heard Andrés cough, turning his mouth away from the telephone.

'It's hot,' she heard him say. 'Could you sleep?'

'Badly, a lot of tossing and turning,' said Clara, and she felt a strange desire to weep – as if he had asked her something extraordinary, ineffable. 'What about you two?'

'More or less.'

'It's the heat.'

'I guess so.'

'Listen,' said Clara, imagining Juan with the letter in his hand, his face, 'Dad has a box for a concert by Jaime something-or-other.

Would you like to go with the three of us? We're leaving in ten minutes.'

The silence communicated Andrés' obvious vacillation.

'Shadows of the gods,' said Clara, not intending to mock him, simply giving him support. *I can't tell him over the telephone*, she thought. *But at the Colón, perhaps for a moment, just outside the box. But why, when* . . .

'Look, Clara, thanks a lot,' said Andrés.

'It's all right. You don't have to go if you don't want to.'

'Thanks. I don't think I have to beat around the bush. It's just that I'm not in the mood for music.'

So now I'll have to tell him about Abel, thought Clara. She heard Mr Funes in the living room banging with his cane to get them back to the table.

'I don't know, I would have liked to talk to you,' she said. 'Oh well.'

'I was thinking about going to the University tonight.'

'And why do you have to go to the University!?' she shouted hysterically. 'Do you like to see people being hung? Sorry.'

'Yes, I know. The heat,' said Andrés in a strange clown-like voice, distancing himself.

'Bye-bye. Sorry.'

'Bye-bye.'

When Juan came in, she said, 'I called Andrés to see if he wanted to go to the concert.'

'Hard to imagine he'd come.'

'Right, he didn't want to. A shame.'

'Yes, a shame,' said Juan, staring at her. 'I suppose you wanted to talk to him about this.'

'I did. It would be good if he knew. You know how fond he is of us.'

'Your father's fond of us, too, but we won't say a word to him.'

'It's different,' said Clara without looking at him. 'After all, it's not such a big deal. We should simply pay no attention. We aren't going to call the police or anything like that.'

Juan sat down on the edge of Bebe's bed. Mr Funes' cane was coming down the hall, and he entered the bedroom in a fury. Two blows with the cane. Another. Like in Molière, or just about.

'What the hell are you doing here?'

'Making a call,' said Clara, pointing at the telephone as if it were an insect.

'Come back to the dining room,' said Mr Funes. 'Don't you want dessert?'

'But there's no hurry, Dad.'

'It's 1:30,' he said. 'The sooner we leave, the better.'

Fine. They'd go to the concert. It was worse to wait and smoke or pace the floor. Passing in front of the mirror, Juan saw his face was dripping with perspiration. At the window in the apartment opposite theirs, a boy was repeating, 'You'll see, you'll see, you'll see, you will.'

Clara was finishing her dessert, and Bebe was cutting another pin-up out of *Life*. On Juan's plate, the cheese was oozing like yellow rubber.

'Extra creamy,' he said to Bebe. 'Very good for those taking exams.'

'Just think, it comes from the refrigerator,' said Mr Funes.

'Are you happy with your refrigerator?' asked Clara, eating distractedly.

'It's perfect. Nine cubic feet, marvelous.'

'It's huge,' said Bebe. 'It makes you want to get inside.'

'Like a mummy in a case,' said Clara.

Juan listened, as if at a distance. More dessert appeared, and he ate a little; but the memory of something the chronicler said about mushrooms worried him. Poor chronicler.

'The six cubic-feet refrigerators are worthless,' the father was saying to his son.

'Very small,' said Bebe. 'You put a head of lettuce and a carrot in, and there's no room for anything else.'

'And besides, this one has a *dry* cold.'

Clara went on finishing her dessert, then rolled her eyes back, resting her forehead on her free hand.

'The people in Apartment 4 have one that runs on kerosene. Disgusting, huh?'

'That's garbage, Bebe. You can't tell me that kerosene makes cold.'

Sighing, Juan got up so he could sit farther away on the sofa, the one that had been his mother-in-law's favorite. He began to write, sadly, having forgotten about Abelito and the exam. He passed the paper to Clara who had come over to keep him company. She could see that the verses were written on Abel's envelope, which was now coming apart, spread-eagle like a cross. On one end, Juan had made an awkward drawing of a refrigerator.

'Enthronement,' Clara read aloud.

Here it is, they've brought it in, contemplate it – o sugared snow, o tabernacle!
The day was propitious and mama went to buy flowers; and the sisters sighed, deceased.
Air of expectancy, access to jubilation, here it is!
Hallelujah!
Heart without teeth, cube of the most crystal of crystals, ivory inlay!
(But the father disposes pure pause, and perfumes.
The silence with joined hands: let there be contemplation.
   We were there. We dared,
barely –)
Here it is; they've already brought it, snow tabernacle.
As long as it accompanies us we shall live
as long as it wishes we shall live.

Hosanna, Westinghouse, hosanna hosanna!

'You're nuts,' said Bebe.

'And after all that, you can't understand a thing, as usual,' said Mr Funes. 'Aren't you having your dessert?' He called Irma to bring in dry plates, please, and Irma apologized, saying it was the humidity of the day – she took his observations to heart. Bebe defended her with wit and she thanked him, vigorously drying a flat plate so Mr Funes could have cheese.

'It's cruel,' Clara murmured, leaning on Juan. 'Everything you write these days seems so cruel to me.'

'It's to the point: Reasons for anger.'

'Poor us,' said Clara, as if she were asleep. 'The distance we've yet to travel today, and how tired we are.'

'Traveling doesn't make you tired. If we could only learn to disassociate those two things.'

In a very low voice (and Mr Funes was fuming now), he added: 'I need a poetry of denunciation, see? Not social-consciousness idiocy, not a correspondence course. What do the facts matter to me? What I denounce is *antecedent* to the fact – the thing that you and I and the rest are. Do you think poetry is possible, Clara – in this material, which is so corroded and angry?'

> 'Listen to the news, Bebe, and during an itermission I'll call you from the concert hall.'
> 'Yes, Dad.'

'I don't know,' said Clara. 'It's so strange that poetry not be the daughter of light.'

'But it is possible, dear,' murmured Juan. 'Poetry ascends to its true homeland. It knows the regions where song is not possible and joins the battle to free itself.'

> 'Above all else, pay attention to any detail.
> There's nothing worse than panic.'
> 'But of course, Dad.'

'I don't know,' whispered Juan, lost. 'I wish I could cry a whole night through and wake up afterwards to my truth. I feel as if I'm constantly walking around houses, sleeping on the streets.'

'*I'm* a little piece of truth,' said Clara. 'How dumb that sounds, right? God, soap operas have eliminated tenderness.'

> 'My keys!'

'Irma, Mr Funes' keys.'

'Forward march,' whispered Juan, getting up. 'Come on, old girl. How do you feel?'

'Horrid. But I'll do fine on the exam, I think I'm going to have phosphorescence.'

'Hegel, friend of Copernicus, right?'

'Go ahead, laugh at me. Laugh.'

But Juan didn't laugh. *But now is the thing*, he thought. *The street, the hours left. How stupid of Abel to threaten her that way. The idiot. Anonymous letter, written in that dumb handwriting we've known all our lives.* He almost felt sorry for Abelito; but no matter what, he would have to do something, to put a halt to that advance of Abel's toward them. First the face:

SO WHITE

under blue hat

and then his handwriting, the first direct action. Ignoring him was no longer enough. *We'll take the test*, thought Juan, shaking himself as if he were a wet dog, *and then I'll go find him*. Like all planning, this made him happy, ordered his thoughts. *How to Stop Worrying and Start Living*, twenty pesos. Write or call.

4

As César Bruto puts it so well: what with all this demolition, Buenos Aires ain't what she used to be. *Non sum qualis eram bonae sub regno Cynarae.*

And thus it was that Mr Funes (noting that the taxi was bringing them along 9 de Julio Avenue, over the strip that was Cerrito) froze as he contemplated the rear façade of Teatro Colón, where the authorities had just set up a canopy *pour faire pendant.*

'But just in front here was a café,' he said.

'There was,' agreed Clara.

'A café where musicians would get together.'

'Yeah.'

'Extraordinary,' said Mr Funes. 'How everything's changed in such a short time.'

He looked all the way down the avenue, the confused traffic, the vague perspective between banks of fog. The taxi skidded as it turned up Tucumán, and Clara was overcome with something like nausea at that instant.

'Dying must be like that,' she said to Juan. 'Like a change of movement. In reality, the movement of the car is the same, but in the skid it's different: something soft, unreal, as if it weren't touching the

'It touches it, but the wheels aren't moving,' said Juan.

'Exactly. The person who dies is like the wheel:

still, but entering into the new movement of its quietude. Daddy, it's 5.70.'

'Don't be silly,' said Juan getting out the money. 'It's all taken care of, Don Carlos.'

'I'm sad they knocked down the café,' said Mr Funes. 'And how strange Teatro Colón looks with that part exposed, and . . .'

Obscene, thought Juan. *That's right. certain naked façades, and suddenly it's pornography.* He wondered if that guy on the stairs might not be

but of course it was . . .

'In fact, I'm here because of a professional obligation,' said the chronicler, slightly embarrassed.

'Great!'

'No, really. We've got so much work that . . . ,' and he said hello to Mr Funes, whom he'd never met, while he winked at Clara. 'Man, it's exciting to have a box. Now I know Colón the way I know my way around beef – every part but the sirloin. Good joke, huh?'

'Rancher-style,' said Clara, looking around at the people in the foyer, the white faces, the gray faces, the devilish facets, façades, falsies; she saw decolletés, handbags (quickly evaluated because she adored pretty handbags), lights, and a lame gentleman who went up the stairs oh so slowly – with a soft unreality thanks to the silence of the carpeting; she listened to the chattering of already-organized groups, boxes prefabricated, going up to slip into their containers; then, for the first time, with violence, with terror, the exam.

She seized Juan's arm, foolishly squeezing close to him. She could hear the chronicler explaining to her father that the paper had already published two special editions and that another would be out at 4:00 P.M.

'The paper wants to get a sense of the mood of different sectors of society,'

(it was extremely amusing to hear the chronicler plagiarizing newspaper jargon)

'and because of my cultural background, it has assigned me the task of looking in at this concert.'

'In that case you should be sitting in the paradise of the last row in the balcony, where the commonfolk sit.'

'You know very well that news flash about paradise here on earth is made up. Good one, huh?'

'Your paper and your opinion polls seem pretty stupid to me,' said Juan.

'Well, what do you want? It isn't enough for people that things actually happen – they're only true if they read about them in the late editions.'

'Do you think there's a big panic?' asked Mr Funes, who did think so.

'Well now, Mr Funes, panic is a pretty big word. What there is is apprehension, and no one believes anything except lies, with the result that the government's communiques are a huge and prodigious success.'

'The yellow press meets the yellow nineties,' said Juan, mocking himself. 'Uh oh, time to sit down.'

The box was at balcony height, on the right. In the packed orchestra seats, there was anxious chatter, as if all news had to be shared before the lights went out. Sitting next to Juan, in front, Clara heard her father impatiently interrogate the chronicler, who seemed in no way disposed to discuss either his work or any information to which he might be privy.

'We've got to be discreet,' he was saying. 'We won't get anywhere tossing out theories that scientific analysis will disprove.'

'Scientific analysis?' asked Mr Funes.

'Yes, of course. The paper is conducting an analysis of the fog. We still don't have the results.'

'An analysis of the fog!'

'An analysis of the fog, exactly.'

Juan caressed Clara's hair, noticing how pretty she was.

'Want me to let you see the jewel of great nights?'

'Yes,' she said, as if suddenly remembering. 'Yes, hurry up, before the lights go out.'

Juan took off his glasses and carefully held them up close to his chest. Leaning over, Clara looked at the reflection in the lenses: the chandelier was reduced to a double gold coin, glowing like yellow eyes inlaid with ivory – tiny points of light.

'Balzac's eyes,' said Juan. 'Remember? Gold dust? I forget who said it.'

'And the eyes of that character in Felisberto Hernández,' said Clara, 'I think he's an usher in a movie theater and light comes from his eyes.'

'A dreadful trade, dear. Look, look, the lights are going out.'

The eyes faded without closing, and instead of light, there arose the vaulted shape of the concert hall, a pink disk where the pupils, opaque now but still present, seemed to see their own contemplation, like the eyes of enraptured bodhisattvas. Juan enjoyed the parallel fading of the lights and the whispers. *It's the voices that are going out*, he thought, *and it's valid to say the lights fall silent. But there's fear in this hall*. People in the higher seats were coughing – dry, crackling, annoying coughs. *Soon they'll be suffocating from the heat, even now it's disagreeable. As long as the fog doesn't get in . . .*

'What are they playing?' asked the chronicler. 'I hope it's something by Borodin.'

'Well that's progress, considering we caught you with Eric Coates last night,' said Juan. 'Look, there he is – wise and old, like Homer; and like Homer in need of a cane and a boy to lead him.'

'A unique case of artistic devotion,' said Mr Funes.

The blind man was ushered in between two employees in livery and wigs. The virtuoso grasped his violin and moved forward taking small steps, which on the stage looked like tiny dance steps. The corpulent accompanist followed and went straight to the piano where he began to arrange the music, while the soloist remained in the perfect place to greet the audience with a grave bow (perhaps there was a chalk mark on the floor so the ushers wouldn't miss it). Then he shook his head as if making sure the ushers had left him alone.

'Man, how disappointing,' said the chronicler between two rounds of applause. 'I thought he was a pianist.'

'You too?' said an angry Juan.

'The violin is a noble instrument,' said Mr Funes.

He talks like Andrés' girlfriend, thought the chronicler. *Now he's going to say it's the instrument that most resembles the human voice.* From the box next to theirs came a whisper: '. . . censorship. But censorship isn't going to fix anything.' Someone went on applauding stubbornly. People in the orchestra hushed him up. There was a great silence, and the violin rose to the virtuoso's chin. There were rubbing noises, like those of some insect, as he tuned the violin, leaning a bit toward the pianist. *The great cricket of wood*, thought Juan. *The hard, implacable bug, the key of songs.* He felt for Clara's hand, and their moist palms touched. A small, localized anguish that didn't pass beyond their wrists.

The pianist had stood up – imperturbable, immobility – and was now demanding absolute silence. 'The master,' he said in a strong Balkan accent, 'must rest between movements of the *Kreutzer Sonata*

because of the delicate state of his health . . .'

The audience applauded loudly, making it impossible to hear the end.

'But why the hell did they applaud?' asked the chronicler, whispering into Juan's ear.

'They were born for that,' said Juan. 'Some people do things and others applaud. That's what's called musical culture.'

'Stop being a light-weight Zoilus,' said Clara. 'Enough raging against everyone else.'

'Silence,' ordered Mr Funes, whose emotional state was visible. He vigorously blew his nose, drowning out the beginning of the sonata for those around him. Clara had her eyes closed; Juan wanted to tell her he was a light-weight Giorgione, but the music stopped him. He wanted to think, to entrench himself in his rapid rage at this hysterical applause which recalled the reaction of audiences to Primo Camera; but instead, he abandoned himself to the rhythms, to the slightly dry and, as it were, schoolboyish sound of the blind man. Squinting, the thin figure of the artist shrank to a silhouette drawn in ink – a puppet that moved in abrupt starts, whose white hair is shaken by a sudden wind. He had something of the sacrificial victim to him, of the stations of the cross. Out of his hands came all the sins of the world; the melody was malignant, uselessly beautiful. And this was born, like all voices that matter, from a world of darkness, falling into a falsely dark hall, full of murmurs and furtive reflections – exit lights, sunflowers of jewels. The cricket chirped, and the entire theater depended falsely (its attention loaded with idleness, affection, escapism) on the almost ridiculous language – its angry dialogue with the yawning mouth of the piano, the back-and-forth shift of voices; its encounters, its flights; the material – irritated, incongruous, but forged together by force by the blacksmith from Bonn. *A blind man playing a deaf man*, thought Juan. *I can't wait for someone to lecture me about allegories after this*. The applause fell like a rain of sand, and the lights came on suddenly, almost with the last stroke of the bow.

'But this is absurd,' said Clara. 'I understand he's very old, but taking a break between every movement destroys all the unity.'

'They probably sit him down in his corner and fan his face with a towel,' said the chronicler, watching the employees with wigs lead the virtuoso away. The accompanist stayed on stage, and since people went on applauding, he began waving, sometimes from the piano, sometimes standing and moving to the proscenium.

'Grabbing all that applause, it's as if he were taking the Lord's name,' said Juan, watching a redhead in the orchestra put on lipstick.

'You're bored,' said Clara.

'Yes.'

'Well, you'd be just as bored at home.'

'Maybe more so. The most humiliating form of tedium is the kind that grabs you when you're in your pajamas. Then there's no salvation. Chronicler, how about a cigarette?'

They all took a stroll, observing the women in that comfortable mode of intermissions. The groups in the foyer and in the mirrored salon had a more deliberate air to them. People were not talking about the concert.

'Practice your observations,' suggested Juan. 'I can help you. How about, I tell that lady over there that the Torre de los Ingleses just collapsed? You go up to the last balcony and time how long it takes the news to get there.'

'Yeah, yeah, but listen to this dilemma,' the chronicler was saying as he looked over at some teenage girls. 'When I leave here, I have to go to a poor neighborhood; I don't know if I should choose La Boca or Mataderos, which are both excellent ears of Dionysus. The bad thing is I'm still tired from last night, and the list of chores waiting for me . . .'

'Why do you keep on working at the paper?'

'Because I can't find a better job.'

'Anything's better than the paper.'

'Don't you believe it,' said the chronicler staring at the floor. 'Sometimes you get to go to concerts, or you're one of the few who get to see a widow's cadaver. Are people panicking here?'

'No,' said Juan, looking at the various groups, discovering himself, thin and unkempt, in a mirror. 'These people are Romans watching the barbarians enter, but the difference is no one's entering here. Science has cured us of many real fears by showing us that the worst deaths are the kind you can't prevent. You can imagine a man of our times trembling because of a metaphysical fear in the presence of a bouquet: beauty, first level of the terrible;

and no sooner is he concerned when a flying fortress drops a bomb on his head.'

'How retro,' said the chronicler. 'Bombs, flying fortresses. Bah.'

'At least you give me the bouquet,' said Juan.

By the time they got back to the box, the virtuoso had appeared, just before the lights when down suddenly, and alone; the lento began. Juan had bought mints for Clara, who was docilely tending to her father but she was beginning to concentrate more and more on the hands of her wrist watch.

'When will we go?'

'We'll leave straight from here,' said Juan. 'We'll have café con leche in the bar on Viamonte.'

'It will begin late, as usual.'

'Sure, but it doesn't matter.'

'We can chat with Andrés,' said Clara. 'He told me he was going to come.'

The beam from a flashlight ran along the floor of the box. Juan felt someone hand him a paper. The usher left, and they heard him trip as he entered the box next door. Someone hissed. Clara put her mouth against the felt covering the ledge and sniffed it; the music was cutting, but at the same time there was something silly to it, something tired, something of the conservatory text book. *The fertile plain of the Nile supplied the Egyptians with huge crops of wheat, and the periods of flooding and low water of the wide river . . .*

and the program they had was for the following Thursday: 3 concerts for piano and orchestra, seats at eighteen pesos

'. . . straight home,' someone said in the box next door. The movement was ending, and when the first applause began to sizzle up like meat in a skillet, the blind man raised his bow menacingly and launched into the *allegro*. The pianist seemed rather put out; but now the two were playing very well.

In the hall was created that fluid which later disappears to be replaced by the word 'success.' Almost no one coughed. When the sonata came to an end, many people in the orchestra were on their feet, and from the upper balconies there came a strident roar, as if from a moth or a grater. Mr Funes applauded for the four of them, even Clara was moved. And the virtuoso's blindness suddenly seemed to her like an immediate quality, as if it were *her* blindness, a hint of the sonorous world where the blind man moved around in small jumps, with his cricket, his tiny, varnished coffin, his pretty, singing mummy, telling the future. Now the artist had finished waving to the audience, and the two employees wearing wigs were at his side; he was leaving, but stopping every few feet, turning his chest toward the hall, toward the piano, making vague gestures of happiness, suddenly rejecting the employees' helping hands. A gentleman wearing evening clothes appeared at the left, gave some instructions to the employees, and they firmly took hold of the artist and carried him along. The gentleman brought up the rear along with the pianist, who had put away the music in a glistening briefcase and was walking along without looking at anyone.

'Let's have a smoke,' Juan said to Clara, who still had her nose stuck in the felt.

'Take a whiff,' she said, forcing him to sniff. 'Take a whiff.'

'It smells vaguely of rot and salicylate.'

'It must be what they call the smell of time,' said Clara with a shiver. 'Oh, it's fascinating. How well Beethoven went with this felt.'

'And with us,' said Juan, lowering his voice. 'With us in the box.'

Outside, they ran into Pincho López Morales, an expert in hot jazz and the poetry of Xavier Villaurrutia. Pincho informed them that the virtuoso had just fainted and that perhaps the rest of the concert would have to be canceled. The chronicler was mixing in with the people in the foyer, in the area right around the cloak room; Mr Funes set out in his quest for comments on the news. Pincho was concerned with the problem of how he was going to fill up the two empty hours before he could take his first evening drink.

'The idea of going outdoors with this sunshine, you understand . . .'

'But the sun isn't shining,' said Clara. 'You made it up just so you could get mad. You haven't changed a bit, Pincho. You are egoism plus.'

'Look, my dear ex-classmate, I don't wish the artist ill. By the same token, it isn't right to ruin the program this way. Planning is everything, as you well know. These two hours are like a hole in the wall. If I look through, what will I see? Libertad, Corrientes, the broad and alien world. At least with the walls, you can put up pictures between this and that.'

'So true, Pincho, so true.'

'All that aside,' said Pincho, 'the street is – how can I put it? – pretty strange. Mom wants me and Wally to go out to Los Olivos. I'm almost convinced she's right.'

'The technique of the ostrich,' said Juan. 'Of course I can say that because I don't have a ranch like Los Olivos. By the way, Wally, I must tell you I *do* think Schumann didn't compose music exactly, that *Die Davidsbündler* and *Carnaval* are at the gates of a different kind of art.'

'Really?' said Wally López Morales. 'But the elements are the same.'

'Both prose and poetry use words, but they don't resemble each other in the slightest. Schumann *intentionalized*

excuse me for saying it this way

his music; he brought it closer to an enunciative form that was no longer esthetic

or, better put, was not only esthetic

and, of course, it wasn't literary, either. That is, he didn't try to pull a fast one. To me his music sounds a bit like a rite of initiation. That never happens to me with Ravel, for instance – or Chopin.'

'Yes, Schumann is strange,' said Wally, who was a great woman to talk to. 'Perhaps madness . . .'

'Who knows? Listen, Wally. Schumann knew he was in possession of a mystery – by which I am not saying that it was a transcendent mystery. His work reveals that he had a dark awareness of this mystery – but it was as unknown to him as it is for others. The anti-Socrates: All I know is that I *do* know something. I just don't know what. He seems to have waited for his music to tell him, the way Artaud expected it from his poems. Look how alike they are.'

'Poor Artaud,' said Wally. 'The perfect kaleidoscope. His work goes from one person to another, and at that instant the inside glass shifts (the person changes), and then it's something else.'

'Perhaps,' said Clara, who was standing between them, 'the works that matter aren't those that mean something but those that reflect. I mean, that allow our reflection to appear in them. Quite a bit like what Valéry said.'

'From which we may deduce a rather conceited conclusion,' said Wally. 'Which is that the important part is us. Your idea is something a readers group would come up with. As far as I'm concerned, I'd rather forget myself and let the book take over me.'

'You must be one of those people who reads two books a day,' said Clara, in a slightly mocking tone.

'Sometimes I do. With the number of books around these days, it's good there are some voracious readers.'

'Too bad,' said Clara, 'that the writer is always counting on a different kind of reader, one that'll always be carrying him around in his pocket.'

'In that case, why do they print five thousand copies? Why write five or ten different books? It's like bowling — each new book knocks the others out of the way.' These last words Wally spoke smiling, waving good-by with her cigarette holder. Pincho took her by the arm, and the two of them ascended the lateral staircase, Wally leaning over the balustrade and gesturing toward the woman selling candy, something that did not meet with Pincho's approval.

'They're colossal,' said Clara. 'So clever.'

'So clever,' murmured Juan, 'that before tomorrow they'll be on their ranch. Look at those people over on the left, no, further on. The woman with the bluish hair.'

'She seems to be hiding something,' said Clara. 'A little like us, like me.' She squeezed Juan's arm, while he looked at her and smiled. 'Juan, why hasn't this day gone by? It's 3:15, only 3:15.'

'It's always an hour before . . .' said Juan. 'And you can skip the rest of the sentence. Is it the exam that's put you in this state?'

She didn't answer. They returned to the box, where the chronicler was explaining to Mr Funes about the takeover of the National Lottery and the effects of a farm-worker strike up north. They'd barely taken their seats when the lights went out (suddenly), and a gentleman with a double-breasted, pearl-gray suit walked briskly onto the stage.

'The theater views it as an obligation to put to rest the *malicious* rumors that have been circulating about the physical condition of the artist, who is honoring us with his recital,' he said in a burst. Some dry applause was heard. 'The artist is perfectly fine.'

Someone – just one person – clapped two, three times.

'We beg the audience to pay no attention to unfounded rumors. In a few moments, the second part of the concert will begin. Thank you very much.'

'I've never understood why people say thank you in situations like this,' said the chronicler. 'Besides, the guy really did collapse.'

'We believe you,' said Juan. 'You're obliged to know. What else is going on?'

'Aah, things. I'm leaving for the paper in a minute. If you want, call me tonight, and I'll give you the latest gossip. In the foyer, I saw Manolo Sáenz from *La Razón*, and he told me tons of things about the mushrooms and the nervousness of the people on the street. He wasn't really worried about that. A lady had just told him about the virtuoso's private life, along with the fact that he isn't blind and that his great-grandmother was black. Can you imagine the sources that lady must have? Manolo thinks she's a total mythomaniac, but he took careful notes of all the gossip. He's got a reporter's blood, much more than I do – I was really born for contemplation and music. Anyway, I've got to satisfy the needs of a thirsty Editor; though I don't really have much.'

Juan was going to ask him another question when there was a burst of applause. The two bewigged employees placed the artist on his spot, and the artist said something into the ear of one of them that seemed to disconcert him, as if he didn't understand. Then the artist turned toward the other, with the same result. Exchanging a glance, the employees released him and left, more quickly than necessary. The blind artist hesitated, moving around a bit, first leaning back, as if the piano offered refuge; then he walked toward the orchestra pit, while a murmur of warnings, of shock grew in the orchestra. Mr Funes was on his feet, waving his arms and breathing heavily. In the box next door, a lady shrieked, with the dry and extremely high-pitched screech of a trapped rat. Clara felt a dizziness and held on to the ledge of the box with both hands. People stood up everywhere, and a bank of lights came on and then went off. The artist raised his bow, as if feeling the air in front of him, and went back to his place with an air of secret mischievousness. Before the audience could quiet down, he was already playing Bach's *Partita in D Minor*.

'Well, well,' said the chronicler. 'He was a foot away from becoming news.'

'Don't be nasty,' said Juan. 'Do you think he did it on purpose?'

'Of course. This guy knows what he's doing. The great thing is how closely they're watching him. Just look on the left there.'

The man in the pearl-gray suit was clearly visible behind one of the bewigged employees. Posted just outside the half-closed door painted old-rose, which led backstage, they feigned indifference.

Allemande
    Courante
        Sarabande
            Gigue
                Chaconne.

'A bit long,' was Mr Funes' epitaph, 'and the violin got a little lost when the piano wasn't there.'

'Yes, of course,' said the chronicler, whose voice was trembling with rage. 'It's much better when forty violins play the prelude to *La Traviata* together.'

Clara glanced at her father and saw he was delighted to have the chronicler's support. She was returning from Bach with a feeling of displacement – of having traveled vertiginously. She found nothing to say, would have wanted to stay right there for hours (and for the applause to stop, so that the virtuoso not return to the stage and leave escorted again by the two bewigged employees). She was pleased to be left alone during the intermission. Ensconced in the secretive forward part of the box, she covered her face with her hands and closed her eyes. Sleep, Bach, the beautiful sarabande, sleep, bach, sleep – She saw stars, red dots; she pressed harder on her eyes, shaken. Snapping out of it, the fear. Get the right number on the exam. As if that mattered now.

She heard a distant shout (an extremely long time had passed for her, perhaps she'd nodded off). Running feet. It was nothing, of no importance. Someone shouted again '... *Listen to unfounded rumors. Thank-you very much.*' Sleep. *Get the right number question on the exam. Sleep.*

With Mr Funes between them, Juan and the chronicler wandered the corridors. There had been some vague talk about raiding a *Gentlemen* (which in the Teatro Colón was called: *Men*), and Pincho and Wally were devouring mints.

'Hey, the guy got better!' shouted Pincho, delighted to see Juan. 'Now we're off our heels and on our wheels!'

'The guy's obsessed with motion,' said Juan to the chronicler. 'Beautiful world, where the horror of the unforeseen is covered over with the ink of a road map. I don't think anyone's better than the good citizens of Buenos Aires in this masquerade of elaborating plans.'

'You're too critical,' said the chronicler. 'In fact, a life isn't made up of anything else. Planning is a way of going against chance a little, remember the Chinese guy.'

'There is no chance. Chance is the bounce caused by our weaknesses, mistakes in our plan for life.'

'Is that so? Then an earthquake that catches you in bed and . . .'

'But that isn't chance,' said Juan a little defensive. 'That's poetry, which is something greater.'

They stood aside for Mr Funes and entered the lavatory behind him. There were many men relieving themselves, smoking, and laughing with one another; but others were washing their hands with intense concentration, waiting their turn to use the little nylon comb connected to the shelf over the sink by a chrome-plated chain, under the mirror.

'Formulas delight you,' said a slightly resentful chronicler. 'If chance turns out to be poetic, it's hard to tell what's chance and what's poetry.'

But Juan had already spotted Luisito Steimberg standing at the urinal next to his. He was paying close attention to Luisito's opinion of the concert. Pincho also came in and stood nearby, delighted at how well everything was going. The chronicler opted for a urinal on the opposite wall, where he could watch Mr Funes waiting to take his turn with the comb. It was getting hotter and hotter, but when the doors moved – further away, in the cubicle modestly dividing the lavatories from the hall – a breeze entered, saturated with perfume and hot talcum powder, perceptible even amid the overpowering ammonia smell that, as Mr Funes said to a crinkly-haired gentleman standing behind him in line, was shameful,

as if the Colón couldn't use good deodorizers, the powerful ones mentioned in *Reader's Digest*. The crinkly-haired gentleman answered in a German accent that it was always the same, which didn't satisfy Mr Funes. He was still one turn away from the sink. Then the chronicler heard Juan calling him over to meet Pincho and Steimberg, who became quite interested when they found out he was a journalist. They wanted to ask him some questions; the chronicler was a bit uncomfortable – not because of the questions but because it bored him to foresee them and foresee at the same time the lie or distortion in his answers. Now another group of men came in, and from the toilets emerged gentlemen (men) with the false naturalness of those who leave those places (which lengthened the line, now crossing the room from end to end and doubling back on itself). And there came a moment when the crowd was huge and someone was heard to remark to someone else that those who'd already urinated should leave, because otherwise they were just taking up space for the pleasure of it.

'Always the same,' said Mr Funes, surprisingly. 'The young rooster wants to kick out the old one. No sooner do they enter than they want to take over.'

'Ah,' said the crinkly-haired gentleman. 'That's youth for you.'

'It's bad manners, that's what it is,' said Mr Funes, who now stood before the sink, where his predecessor had just carefully rinsed the comb and deposited it on the shelf. Mr Funes stepped to the left to put himself opposite the mirror, stretching out his hand toward the comb. The chronicler was staring at precisely that space (hearing in the distance the clapping of the ushers signaling it was time to return to the box);

and Pincho was saying to Juan that the police had the mentality of hens, that they were acting with an inefficacy that was mon-stru-ous,

which seemed to please Steimberg;

and the pull on the little chrome-plated chain was so sharp and unexpected that the chronicler saw the comb fly through the air like a shiny projectile,

eluding the hand of Mr Funes, who stood there as if suffering a terrible abuse – a brief path was traced to the fingers of the man behind who had grabbed the chain

until the comb was in his hand. The guy took a step to the right, visibly dislodging Mr Funes, pushing him away from the mirror,

and bending over slightly in order to use the comb more easily

the little chain was not very long.

'Well, that beats everything,' said the chronicler, taking Juan by the arm so he'd look.

'Wait a second,' said Juan rapidly – he'd asked Steimberg something (people who work in government ministries always know things) and didn't want to miss the answer. With the chronicler's second tug, he turned his head and saw in that instant Mr Funes, red and reckless, take a step forward, causing the man with the comb to lose his balance, drop the comb, and grab hold of a blond man smoking a cigar.

'What the hell's going on?' said Juan. 'Let's go. Don Carlos! . . .' Juan couldn't see him clearly, partly because of the line (which was shaking and coming apart) and partly because Pincho and Steimberg were between him and the sink. He tried to get through, but the chronicler was there first, just in time to see the man with the comb, livid with rage, shove Mr Funes, putting his open hand against the old man's shirtfront and flexing his arm like a spring.

The chronicler grabbed hold of the back of his jacket and pulled him away — not knowing exactly to what end — but the man violently freed himself (grabbing the young blond man smoking the cigar a second time). He half turned to face the chronicler, unintentionally elbowing a very short fat man right in the face. The injured party stumbled, dazed, emitting a strange shriek. Cursing him out at the top of his lungs, the chronicler went toward the man with the comb, who had an air of knowingness mixed with astonishment; and just then Juan interposed himself (he'd suddenly understood what was happening or he simply leapt in). Luisito Steimberg broke the line, which oscillated, already shaken in its herd-like consequences, and the whirling extended. The small gentleman stood there, his face covered in blood, amid a confused entanglement of arms and torsos;

the general objective was to reach the exit doors, but in order to accomplish that, it was necessary to pass through the most narrow space, which led to the cubicle, all of which went against the efforts of Mr Funes, determined still to reach the comb (which was hanging by its chain below the sink) and take control of it like some sort (it might be supposed) of affirmation against the man who was now a short distance from the chronicler, but now Juan and Steimberg were between them. He was staring at the chronicler, as if inviting him to take the first swing, saying something to him that the high-pitched imprecations of the short, bloody man drowned out, aside from the general racket and the pounding of the double doors being pushed by numerous new men entering the washroom. Mr Funes was seen, finally, to raise the comb up and almost immediately lose it because Pincho, presumably intending to calm his excitement, pulled on the chain, yanking it out of his hand; and at the same time, other hands (the chronicler, definitively separated from the aggressor, saw those new men entering in great numbers, faces known or never before seen piled up at the entrance, forcing their way in)

at the same time that other hands grasped from all directions at the chain, pulling it with all their strength until Pincho shouted with pain and let go of the comb, which, when it slipped, cut open two of his fingers, making him swear at the top of his lungs and land (with his bloody hand) a ferocious right on the blond man with the cigar – the cigar fell into a corner and burned slowly like an eye watching the insane rotation and movement of dozens of pairs of shoes.

At that moment, Juan shouted to his father-in-law to get out of the fight, but Mr Funes was by then holding on to the chain, very close to the comb, and the first usher, white with fear, was just arriving, raising his arms;

the shouting was a single roar carried by the acoustics of the washroom to all the floors of the theater, where the alarm was spreading . . .

> *and the masseur signaled to the blind man not to move from the daybed. He tossed a blanket over his naked torso and ran to the door to listen. (In the box, Clara heard a shout.)*

although no one could locate the site of the disturbance, because the first usher was still trapped with the men who'd come in after him – the doors could no longer be opened from the outside and in the access cubicle there was a horrifying agglomeration;

through a rare acoustical phenomenon,

you could hear the terrible, anguished blows: the men locked in the stalls striking against the doors, vainly trying to open them against the sea of shoulders and backs that rippled in all directions, pinning Luisito Steimberg like a mummy in a urinal,

encased back-first in a way no one had ever before seen. Steimberg was cursing in Yiddish, which suddenly came to his mouth like hot nails, but was unable to get out – even though the chronicler (who asked himself, what the hell, but no, it was a mistake) tried to reach his hand to him over the head of the very short, bleeding gentleman in order to get him out of the hole;

he was wondering at the same time if he'd seen clearly among those men who came in at the end, wondering – although in fact there would be nothing odd to it, it's a small world and if the guy liked violin music –

no doubt he was wrong.

There went Mr Funes pushed by others. In the air a piece of chain – Pincho with a hand in his mouth was extremely pale –

shoulders blocking, Juan like a top delivering blows to get to his father-in-law; the comb was in the hands of a heavy man with dark hair who held it aloft shouting 'Drop it! Drop it!' as if someone else were actually holding it; a stall door opened inch by inch, on the side where Luisito Steimberg had just freed himself from the urinal and was stupidly smoothing his jacket over his hips,

opening little by little and a shaved head, some eyeglasses, really a turtle that comes out to see what's going on –

the opposite of what good turtles do –

with huge blows on the other stall doors by trapped men, and one final, ferocious general shake that sent the comb flying through the air until it fell into the sink, into the water

and no one put his hand in there, where there were a few hairs but calm was being restored, starting with the aggressive guy who was near the exit to the cubicle, his arms fallen, and staring at the cop who was entering like a projectile, breaking the shell of bodies – terrible, respectable, the end of the affair.

The chronicler (now he was sure he'd seen correctly, seeing a few even escaping in the back, into the cubicle),

he sighed as if coming out of anesthesia. *It's crazy*, he thought. And then, *Which is why it happens*.

'You'll see,' Pincho was saying to Juan, who was straightening out Mr Funes' clothes. 'Now the virtuoso's going to get mad because of this mess. I'll bet you money he doesn't play the third part and he screws up the matinee.'

Juan was laughing, smoothing out Don Carlos' jacket, putting the shoulder pads where they should be. He took a comb out of his pocket and lent it to him, it was still difficult to move his arms.

The chronicler heard the policeman's order and showed him his press card. For a second he thought the cop was going to take him in with the others.

'Don't you remember me?' he asked. 'The other day. That case with the kid on Peña street.'

'Oh yes, sir. Okay.'

'I'll tell Clara,' the chronicler shouted to Juan. 'Where are you going to take them, officer?'

'To the press room. Then we'll see.'

'Aah, it was nothing. No need to cause a panic. Bye-bye, then.'

How he disappears, thought Juan, amused beyond belief but breathless from a punch in the ribs. *Well, so much for the exam.* He carefully put away the comb Don Carlos had returned to him; they began to walk between a double file of spectators who crowded the corridor. The lights in the hall were going out. Wally stared at them making the kind of serious expression where the mouth seemed on the point of whistling.

'It was incredible,' said the chronicler. 'You can't imagine, Clarita. It was the apotheosis, the end of the carnival, the apocalyptic, the universal mess!'

'But are they all right?' asked Clara, astonished at how calm he was.

'Juan got in several good shots, and your Dad fought like a lion,' the chronicler said with a bow. 'Everything's okay except that they're under arrest.'

'Well, that certainly finishes everything,' said Clara, without unduly upsetting herself.

'Think so? There's too much going on outside for them to worry about this. They'll just say it was because of general nervousness and in half an hour –

But I wonder why they're turning off the lights when there's no concert? –

Oh,' said the chronicler, remembering. 'Something very odd did happen. I saw someone you all know. That guy who was following you last night.'

★

There was a hasty meeting in the Manager's office. The man in the pearl-gray, double-breasted suit delivered the final statement: 'He refuses to play. First, he insulted me in the grossest possible fashion, and then he started in about art and respect and all that bullshit.'

'We can't make him play,' said the Manager.

'Right, but it's going to be my job to go out and be a jerk in front of the audience.'

'You do it better than anyone else,' said the Manager. 'I mean, you know how to talk to those sons of bitches.'

'Abel?'

'That's the name you all use.'

'But you don't know him,' said Clara, staring at him in surprise.

'Madam, I'm a reporter, ergo, I use my eyes; ergo, it wasn't hard to spot the lad who's got you all upset. In the bushes at Plaza Colón?'

'And he was in the fight just now?'

'Not exactly. He peeked in at the end. I think the cop didn't give him enough time to dip his toes in. Okay, here we go . . .'

The man in gray indicated to the people in the orchestra that they should sit down. People were shouting everywhere. The air was unbreathable.

'Ladies and gentlemen. We regret to inform you that the final part of this concert will not take place. A minor indisposition afflicts our great artist

who was crying, face down on the day bed

and will deprive us of the charm of his art. I also want to calm the ladies who have been upset by an insignificant incident that took place a few moments ago. Nothing serious has occurred, I assure you . . .

he was wailing with his face in his hands and the masseur was contemplating him.

The exits have been opened.'

★

'Abelito?' repeated Clara. 'Then it's true.'

'What?'

'That he's crazy.' She glanced involuntarily toward the shadows of the forward part of the box. 'It's unbelievable. Please, where is Juan?'

'In the press room, with the others.'

'Let's go.'

'Certainly, but let's not hurry. Let everyone leave, look how furious they all are.'

The man in gray was sent on his way with three claps and a terrible whistle from the last balcony, and in the orchestra the people were moving around listlessly, dying from the heat, shouting to each other from row to row. So Abel – but the absurd has degrees too, who can accept the idea of voodoo while standing in the heart of Buenos Aires? The box, that tower they would have to leave (and the chronicler, full of good will, was waiting with his back turned to the front, like Lancelot, or Galahad, or Geraint.)

AND THE FULFILLMENT OF THE OBSCURE PREDICTIONS

I just can't believe it, thought Clara, imagining herself disdainfully (one eye; nose; half a mouth; the other eye little mirrors those replicas of the soul, that continuous parcelling out

never tell your left hand what . . .

Yes, but my right will never know. What does my tongue know about how my foot lives? *What a horror* – and now there wasn't even pure

thought, no words – like that disgust at the avoidance of thought when you're listening to the radio; an evasion of oneself that she should somehow impede, reorder, distribute. Now that Juan was another region of her skin:

find him and –

but where might they be holding him? *I asked Andrés to come*. Feeling the need for Andrés (because where might they be holding Juan?) . . .

Poor chronicler, poor Kurwenal . . .

I asked him to come, and he didn't want to. He'll come to . . .

with a final glance at the stage (but not seeing it), where one of the bewigged employees was lowering the top of the piano.

There was a detective in plain clothes, the uniformed cop who arrested them, and two more policemen. Outside, there was the murmuring of those leaving the theater without having found out much.

'Form a line facing me,' said the detective. He was standing solid and safe behind his table.

'Please don't all of you speak at once,' he said. 'Who started the fight?'

Mr Funes stepped forward, but a cop put a hand on his shoulder. 'Please,' stammered Mr Funes, staggering a bit. 'I did it, sir; in defense of my rights.'

'Did you now?' said the detective, as if distracted.

'The gentleman is my father-in-law,' said Juan stepping forward, 'and as you can plainly see, he is not psychologically capable of explaining anything.'

'Get back in line,' said the detective.

'Certainly, but let me explain what happened.'

'Okay, start talking.'

Juan realized he knew nothing about what happened. He vaguely identified the comb as some kind of spoil of war, and then – strange slip of the tongue – as a war flag. He smiled involuntarily, and the detective stared at him with narrowed eyes.

'I know what happened,' said Luisito Steimberg. 'This gentleman with the big wave in his hair took the comb away from this gentleman's father-in-law.'

'You saw it?'

'Not exactly, because at that moment . . .'

'That's what happened,' said Mr Funes. 'It was my turn to comb my hair.'

'Whatever,' said the man with the wave, who seemed bitter. 'I saw the comb on the shelf and picked it up.'

'That's a lie,' said Mr Funes, trying to step out of line. 'You weren't on line, and you didn't grab the comb, you grabbed the chain.'

'What's the difference?' said the man with the wave. 'If you're closer to the chain, you pull on it and get the comb.'

'But it was my turn to use it. And besides, I had it in my hand. I'd just picked it up when you yanked on the chain and snatched it away from me.'

'Seriously endangering the gentleman's hands,' said Pincho López Morales. 'Look at my fingers. The comb cut them when some bastard or other snapped it away from me.'

'Watch your language,' said the detective. 'And don't speak until spoken to – the same goes for you and you.'

'They're making a big deal out of nothing,' said the man with the wave, not very calm.

'Shut up. So it was pulled away from you?'

'Exactly,' said Mr Funes, calmer now. 'And then I was shoved, yes sir, a BIG shove, that almost knocked me flat on my back against the other gentlemen.'

'Bull,' said the man with the wave. 'You should have seen the shove he gave me.'

'So what was I supposed to do – say thank you?'

'Shut up!' shouted the detective. 'And then what happened?'

'Well, sir, after that things got confused,' said Pincho. 'I'd dare say it was as if twenty people were trying to liquidate nineteen and take control of the comb. Sociologically . . . ,' and he began to laugh, looking at Juan, who was just as tempted. *What an incredible nut*, thought Juan. *At least he's all set now for the rest of the afternoon.*

'Things won't go well for you,' said the detective extending a telescopic finger, 'if you keep on being a smart aleck. Okay, you over there' – he pointed to a young man with a frightened face who hadn't said a word – 'what happened next?'

'Pandemonium,' he said. 'I was shoved all over the place.'

'And you of course, like a saint, never lifted a finger.'

'At first I did nothing,' was his surprising response. 'Then I did what I could to get the comb.'

'You too, eh?'

'Well, the comb was going from hand to hand.'

'Like counterfeit money,' murmured Pincho.

'And when did the fighting stop?'

'When I came in, sir,' said the fierce patrolman. 'Straightaway, I brought them here.'

The detective looked the man with the wave up and down. He wiped his face with a filthy handkerchief. Outside, there was a warning whistle, and the door opened a few inches. It remained that way, as if waiting for someone to walk in.

'Get out your identification,' said the detective, looking down at his handkerchief, wiping his face again. Without saying a word, he listened to the mutterings, the but-I-didn't-bring anythings, who'd-ever-think-he'd-have-to-go-to-a-concert-with-his-identification-papers, *you can call my house! this is an abuse of my rights, I have nothing to do with all this!*

and my wife is waiting for me outside . . .

'Shut up, all of you,' said the detective, slapping his hand down on the table. 'Start giving me your names.' He sat down with a blue notebook in his hand. The telephone began to ring sharply; one of the policemen looked over at the detective as if waiting to be told to answer it. Through the partially open door came the conversations of those outside, the high-pitched shout of a newsboy, another whistle.

'Campos, answer that,' said the inspector to the cop who'd made the arrest. 'Why is that door open?'

'Someone's come down from headquarters,' said the cop standing next to the door. 'He was just coming in, but he stopped when . . .'

'All right now, you,' said the detective to Mr Funes. 'Your I.D.'

'I didn't bring anything,' said Mr Funes, panting a little. His shirt collar was soaked. 'If my social-security card will do . . .'

'*Ma sí, ma sí,*' said the patrolman on the telephone. 'Call later, there's no one here now.'

The detective looked at the card, at Mr Funes, at the card.

'I will cooperate in any way I can,' said Mr Funes. 'I behaved as it was my obligation to behave in the face of an indescribable abuse. I put myself in the hands of justice.'

'That much I do believe,' said the detective. 'Now shut up.'

Juan slipped around the patrolman. Only the table separated him from the detective.

'You shut up,' he said. 'You have no right to treat this gentleman that way.'

'Get over here,' Pincho was saying behind him. 'Don't start anything.'

The detective stood up. The patrolman at the telephone was instantly next to Juan, his hand on his holster. Through the partly open door came an enormously fat, mulatto officer. After him came the noise: 'Knock it off!' shouted by a high-pitched voice, but the door shut, cutting off the words.

'You wait a minute,' said the detective in a low voice, fixing his eyes on Juan, who felt a chill in the pit of his stomach. He left the table to speak with the officer waiting for him near the door.

'I know what's going on,' said the officer. 'Get back to Moreno immediately. It's serious.'

'But these people . . .'

'Send them home right now. Nothing happened here. Get rid of them.'

'But look . . .'

'These are orders from higher up, man.'

Pincho walked out first, saluting courteously. Juan picked up Don Carlos' card, which had been left on the table. He walked out with Mr Funes and Luisito Steimberg. The detective turned his back on them, and one of the policemen held the door open as if he had a branding iron in his hand.

'Finally,' said Clara, trying to smile. 'Did they torture you?'

'Yeah, they gave us a real third degree. Come on, let's get the hell out of here.'

'What heat,' said Pincho, sighing. 'And all those people packed in there, you'd think we were in the Nuremberg trials. Excuse me, madam, excuse me.'

The light on the street made him blink in confusion.

'I forgot it was so early,' he complained. 'Wally, mirror of fidelity, let's go somewhere cold and dark.'

Steimberg, tacit and somewhat fearful, followed without saying good-by. Juan and the chronicler escorted Mr Funes and Clara. By chance there was a cab on the corner of Tucumán and Libertad. Juan looked at his watch.

'You go home, Don Carlos, and rest for a while. Clara and I will go downtown,' he said.

'You've got time. Come home and have hot chocolate.'

'No, no,' said Clara. 'Go home, Dad. Take a nap and a bromide. Tomorrow . . .'

A fire truck passed by, drowning out her voice. Juan sniffed the air in surprise. He saw Luisito Steimberg standing in the shelter on Libertad waiting for a streetcar. None to be seen, just a few cars.

'All right then,' said Mr Funes. 'Good luck to both of you.'

'Thanks, Dad.'

'Thanks, Don Carlos.'

'Can I drop you off?' Mr Funes asked the chronicler.

'No thanks, I'll walk a bit with these youngsters.'

A police car, its siren wailing, turned onto Tucumán. They thought it was going to stop at Teatro Colón, but instead it went up Libertad. They saw Mr Funes leave in his taxi, waving his hand.

'Poor old guy,' said Juan. 'What he went through. Let's go have a beer, I'm dying of thirst. It's a good thing that you're coming with us, chronicler. I'll tell you all about the interrogation. It was really something.'

'I'm sure it isn't newsworthy,' said the chronicler spitting out some dust. 'But the beer part is.'

There was no beer in the Edelweiss, where a white-haired *garçon* tried to convince them to drink cider. They made no fuss, it was well known that there had been a lack of beer in Buenos Aires for three days. They went to the Nobel instead, and Juan washed the fresh blood off his left hand – not his, but someone else's.

'I'd like to listen to the *Kinderszenen*,' Clara was saying to the chronicler. 'When I was a little girl, a friend of the family would play them at night in our dark sitting room.'

'In the sitting room, of course.'

'Of course. I grew up in a house with a sitting room, and everything possible was done so my intelligence would furnish its own sitting room in my head. Don't laugh. My uncle Roque has a perfect little cultural sitting room. With anecdotes about General Mansilla, admiration for almanacs, and vague, perfumed soaps. I adore sitting in it and breathing its fine dust.'

'Sometimes you stay too long,' said Juan, throwing himself into his chair. 'Don't think our apartment today doesn't have a sitting room. It's invisible, but the threat of it is still there – in the radiotelephone, home remedies and everything colored old rose.'

'The good old days,' said the chronicler, as if he'd said 'The goddamn days.' 'In any case, I think your invisible sitting room is rather impoverished in terms of consoles, macramé, and shrouded harps.'

'No need to be excessively cruel with sitting rooms,' said Clara. 'They were the least physiological part of life for females – the only place where trays of sweets, the filthy siesta (procreation I'm talking about, whether you wanted it or not) didn't enter.'

'It's hot,' said Juan drinking his beer. 'It keeps getting muggier and muggier. I feel something here that's . . .' Through the open windows came the cries of a black paperboy selling the latest edition. The voice came up by itself from an almost empty street where some people were rushing along. Far off (and Clara remembered Leandro Alem the previous night), an ambulance siren echoed.

'*Crítica*'s second special edition,' said the chronicler. '4:30. They're punctual as Scotsmen. Meanwhile, I should be in the office of my own paper.'

'Take the subway with us, you'll be there in ten minutes.'

'Right. Well, that was quite a concert.'

'Poor Dad,' said Clara. 'The one time it occurs to him to listen to music.'

'Are you kidding? I hope you don't think he didn't have a good time,' said Juan. 'After he rests, he's going to feel very proud of himself. You should have seen him dishing out the kicks and shoves. This was his great day – a day worthy of a souvenir anchor with fifteen real rubies.'

'Don't be mean.'

'But he's right,' said the chronicler defending Juan. 'It's going to be a beautiful memory. His battle of Hernani. These days we have even more need of memories. Notice how people forget?'

'You've got some soot on your nose,' said Clara. 'And I don't think we forget more now than before. The thing is that before, people lived with that wonderful escapist idea that "all past time is better," et cetera. Or the other way around – the religion of the future and all that. Now . . . well, that's it: now. There's no place for memories.'

'But you know that the now doesn't really exist,' said the chronicler.

'It doesn't?'

'What the chronicler means,' said Juan, 'is that the person giving meaning to the now, I mean, the before or the afterward – that's the most important thing.'

'I didn't mean that in the slightest,' protested the chronicler, 'but it fits nicely with the general idea. People remember less now because, in a certain sense, all their memories are accusations.'

'How right you are,' said Juan. 'This thing that's floating in the air nowadays, this awareness that we're guilty of something, that we've been accused . . .

At times it even becomes incarnate: like William Wilson, *je suis hanté, hanté, hanté, hanté, hanté!* And poor Josef K . . . Even us, without going further . . .'

'But what right does the past have to accuse us of anything?' asked Clara, carefully closing a small gap in her lipstick.

'None whatsoever,' said Juan. 'It isn't the past that accuses us but we who accuse ourselves. Our evidence comes from the past: what we did, and what we didn't do, which is even worse. It's a break that can't be crossed over.'

'Look, this subject is talked about too much and understood too little,' said the chronicler. 'People say we're failing for lack of style, because we've stepped out of the frieze, the golden mean. Do you think that's the source of our neurosis?'

'It's something much worse,' said Juan, drying his hands on a paper napkin that turned into a filthy little wad on the edge of his plate. 'If at least we'd lost what you call style. But no, we're like the awakened dead in the Last Judgment in Bourges cathedral.

Remember the photo, Clarucha? The figures have one foot out of the coffin and the other still in. They're trying to get out, but they're still trapped by the habit of death. Between two waters, like Mr Valdemar; "and we shall suffer opprobrium as long as this transitory life lasts."'

'You're on the right track,' said Clara, sighing, 'but you're so confused.'

'What I'm trying to say is confused. Give in, chronicler. Rimbaud saw the horror of existence better than anyone: "*Moi, esclave de mon baptême*," he said. You grow up within the Christian structure, reduced, it's true, to a turtle shell, where you stretch out and fit yourself in until you fill it. But if you happen to be a rabbit and not a turtle, you're obviously going to be uncomfortable. Turtles – like the Great God Pan – have died; and society is a blind nursemaid who insists on putting rabbits in the turtles' corset.'

'Nice image,' said Clara, her mouth filled with charlotte russe.

'You grow up wrapped in the great fixed ideas, but one day you make your first personal discovery. It's that those ideas aren't applied in practice. And since you're no jerk and you like to live, it happens you want to choose freedom of action. Bang, you smack into the ideas – into your baptism. I'm not talking about external decrees.

Listen, because this is important. Not practical compulsions, which drive half-assed rebels to despair –

in that form, believe me, you can always get around them more or less.

The thing is you realize these ideas are *within yourself*: your baptism, man.'

'Orestes' furies, right?' said Clara.

'You're a Christian!' said Juan. 'From the way you cut your nails to the shape of your war flags – you're the Christian West.

Trapped, the panting begins. Imagine an eagle brought up among sheep, and one day it feels the presence of, no, the need for, its eagle strength –

or the other way around, because no one should be smug.

Just imagine it – and there you have it.'

'Fine,' said the chronicler. 'Unfortunately, there's no way to resolve the thing.'

'That doesn't matter,' said Clara. 'What does matter is that it be that way, *indubitably* that way, *cleanly* that way. And that's not always certain.'

'I think it is,' said Juan. 'At least, I can't help but believe it. I know that every authentic gesture is reined in, repressed by a conformism in my nature. With each minute, when I decide: *Tomorrow* – then my rebellion arises. What is *tomorrow*? And why *tomorrow*? Then, you see, the Swiss watch starts going – well-oiled and perfect – and the cuckoo I keep here in my head sings to me: "Tomorrow is a new day, at sunrise it will be cloudy, and temperatures will rise steadily, the sun will appear at 6:22, Saint Cecilia's Day. You will get up at 8:00, you will wash –"

look at just that: you will get up,

you will wash –

that alone is your baptism, your handcuffs, your Western structure.'

'And you feel bad because of that?' asked the chronicler. 'The answer is to get up at eleven and rub your face down with alcohol.'

'That's stupid and doesn't fool anyone. Look, if you're born a sheep you've got to live a sheep, and the eagle needs room to take flight also. I can accept the form of the sardine can. I've been stuck in it since Jesus was forced on me as my third eye. The can is one thing, but the sardine is something else. I think I can own up to the fact that the can is mine; it's enough that I've been able to distinguish myself from it.'

'From distinguishing yourself to escaping . . .'

'I don't know if it's possible for me to escape,' said Juan. 'But I know it's my obligation, with regard to myself, to try. The results count less than the actions.'

'Your obligation with regard to yourself,' murmured Clara. 'You're going to realize yourself on your own?'

'I count only on myself, and even that to a slight degree,' said Juan. 'I have to discount that part of me that is the enemy, that's cultivated to kill my free part. The part that should be a good boy, love his daddy a lot, not stand on chairs or step on the guests' feet. I count on so little of myself; but that little bit of myself stands guard, pays attention. Baudelaire was right, chronicler. It's Cain – the rebel, the free man – who should care for the extremely soft, the viscous and well-mannered Abel . . .'

He stared fixedly at Clara.

'Apropos,' said Clara. 'But go on, I'm not interrupting you.'

It isn't viscous, she thought with an absurd tenderness.

'I've said all I have to say. I'm happy not having a God. No one's going to forgive me; there's nothing I can do to gain forgiveness. I go about my business without any advantage, without the great recourse to repentance. (It wouldn't be worthwhile for me to repent of anything. Within myself *there is no forgiveness*. And it's possible there's no such thing as repentance either.) My fate is absolutely my own: I know, that when I break one of my own commandments, *I* am doing it. And I know and can guess pretty well why. And what I've done is *unforgivable*. If I were to repent, it would still be useless. I'd be falling into self-compassion or high mindedness, and I'd rather die a hundred times.'

'That's what people call pride,' said the chronicler, adding up the three checks.

'No, that's what's called being your own self – going at it alone, and having faith in yourself. I think that only someone who isn't going to screw up can foresee his risk with such clarity. And vice versa.'

'A little Sartrean Orestes,' mocked the chronicler, tenderly.

'Thank you,' said Juan. '*Muito obrigado.*'

At the corner of Talcahuano, they had to make a detour and follow the confused orders of a municipal foreman, who was rerouting traffic. Some barrels, lanterns, and red flags gave the street the air of a barricade – all complicated by a distracted Chevrolet that had just crossed the forbidden line and was there with one of its front wheels in the hole where the pavement collapsed. It had that grotesque air all machines have when they're yanked out of their norm. The dialogue between the driver and the foreman was of such violence that – according to the chronicler – it was highly unlikely they'd start throwing punches. Curious, there were very few people surrounding the antagonists; and the show was lost in the foul-smelling mist hovering close to the ground in that sector of town.

'Well, we can go up Talcahuano until Lavalle and then turn to get the subway,' said the chronicler. He walked ahead, leaving Juan and Clara walking silently arm-in-arm, alone.

At the corner where the Court building was, there was a fire truck and its entire crew along with a lot of water – on the side where the court stairs led from the plaza. The chronicler was going to ask a fireman what was happening, when a huge 'Keep Moving!' put him in motion once again. Two cars with official license plates were parked with their doors open at the turn into Lavalle. Like a river of ants, employees with piles of forms and portfolios went up and down. One of the cars was already almost full. *Are they going, as the song says, with the music to another place?*

'I don't know if you did it on purpose,' Clara said brusquely. 'When you mentioned his name you were looking at me.

'As soon as it came out, I realized it,' said Juan. 'I noticed the coincidence, so it was natural I look at you, to see if you'd noticed as well.'

'Sure, how could I not notice,' said Clara. 'The chronicler told me he saw him at the fight.'

'No!' said Juan, stopping dead in his tracks.

'At the end, when the gawkers slipped in. Which is why he could get away before they arrested all of you.'

'He must be mistaken,' said Juan reluctantly. 'Of course, it's all the same.'

'Sure, but this is getting to be a bit much,' said Clara. 'It's disagreeable always having to check to see who's behind you. In the box, I was afraid. Now I'm with you – but I might get afraid again, and I won't like it.'

'Look at this,' shouted the chronicler from the corner of Uruguay. He was pointing to an enormous truck that had fallen over. Dozens of boxes of eggs were scattered in the direction of the fall.

'Just when they've gotten so expensive,' said Clara. 'Pardon my reaction.'

Juan was silent, staring at the eggs and the street, breathing in the fog that suddenly made them spit out something like dust balls. Standing outside the Martona milk bar, there was an enormous black man, standing guard at the door on the Uruguay side. Clara froze in her tracks because he was whistling the themes from *Petrouchka*, one after another. He wrapped them up in his clear whistling and then released them into the mist.

Like bubbles with smoke, thought Clara, deeply touched. She was going to say it to Juan, but he was still walking with his eyes lowered

as if skating along with his eyes, thought Clara, extremely happy with her use of Juan's verb. A bitter happiness, really, from the neck up. It was better to get to Juan through his arm, hold on to him and draw him closer, close to your own tranquil respiration. *There's so little time left*, she involuntarily glanced at her watch. *After*

4:00. She thought about Andrés, who would probably be there, quiet and amiable, with a book under his arm (always the least expected one: De Quincey, Sidney Keyes, Roberto Arlt, or Carr Dickson,

or *Adán Buenosayres*, which he liked so much, or Tristan l'Hermite, or Colette – and so on the other side sometimes, so passed onto the shore of his authors. Andrés far-off, cinerary image – greeting of a storm, suddenly, a brutal flash, the bursting of a rage into fire, denunciation;

and how could anyone walk happily along the streets with him walking just ahead, or standing in a courtyard studying a door knocker or listening to the echo of his own footsteps –

Like Juan, who . . .

Yes, like a Juan without poetry, a green plant without fruit, almost without flowers. *Andrés*, she thought, pressing her lips closed against the fog. *How I dumped you*.

'Now there's a notice I don't like one bit,' said the chronicler as he began to cross Uruguay. 'Imagine we're left without subways.'

The notice was written in green ink and stuck to a board attached with wire to the bars of the Corrientes subway entrance:

The company assumes no responsibility for the regularity of trains.

'What company?' asked Juan in a fury. 'Doesn't all this shit belong to the State?'

'Some flunky or other wrote it.'

'And in a big hurry,' said the chronicler. 'Green ink, how disgusting.'

'Let's just go,' said Clara. 'Somehow we'll get downtown, even if they don't assume responsibility.'

Sliding along on the slippery stairway, they reached the long tunnel that led to the first level underground. A huge number of people had congregated there in a bar; and in the dense, filthy air a smell of hot sausages was winning the day. The fog didn't reach that far down; but the humidity was condensing on the walls, and the floor was dotted with puddles and enormous mounds of garbage.

'They haven't cleaned up here for days,' said the chronicler. 'I'd pinch my nostrils shut, the way you always see people do,

if it weren't for the fact it would force me to open my mouth, which is much worse. I've always thought that smells are just deficient tastes. And if you smell something through your mouth, you can eventually taste the smell; and you can understand that in this jelly . . .'

'You're too delicate,' said Juan. 'It's obvious you were never drafted.'

'I never was, but I do go to soccer matches a lot. Look, the other kiosks down here are closed. That is news. When they close the kiosks it means that people are passing them by, or simply not passing.'

'Think so? Look at this mob stuffing their faces.'

'It's inevitable. I've proved that people from Galicia breathe through language,

and if they don't speak they die – asphyxiated by the silence. On the other hand, people from Buenos Aires breathe through their stomachs. And how they eat, My God! Just think of those huge steaks they call "Baby Beef" on menus – nowhere else do they have beef like that.'

'We're machines for manufacturing poop,' said Juan. 'Who said that about us?'

'Someone who passed by this bar. Wait a minute. I take back everything I said! Those people aren't eating.'

From a distance, they watched as two girls helped a woman back to her feet who'd slipped. The chronicler was right. The people at the bar were wrapping packages. They were carrying on some obscure business with the fat owner, who was wearing a mangy smock.

'They're selling all their stock,' said Clara, who felt a wave of fear,

and felt Juan's hand squeeze her arm.

'What sons of bitches,' said the chronicler. 'Where's a telephone? This is the beginning of the black market!'

'Bah, I'll bet they already know it down at your paper,' said Clara bitterly. 'Your Editor probably has his garage filled with bags of sugar and potatoes.'

'I hope they rot,' said the chronicler. 'Juan, my dear, got any change?'

'Here.'

At the bottom of the stairs, crumpled newspapers were piled high, along with a broomstick, and the cover of the magazine *Cuéntame*. They heard a bark that came up out of the tracks. Clara took hold of the handrail but instantly pulled her hand away in disgust: it was oozing, as if alive.

'Here, wipe yourself off,' Juan handed her his handkerchief and supported her by holding her arm. 'You made me remember that night when I went into my room in the dark and picked a record up off the table – the Seventh Symphony (which I've subtitled "the apotheosis of the Dance"). I grabbed it in the darkness, and I felt something move in my hand. You can imagine my reaction: the Seventh flew to the other end of the room! – and I was feeling all over for the light switch. When I could see, my hand had moving centipede legs on it. The disgusting arthropod was on its spine, and it was enormous.'

'I hope,' said Clara, 'that the Seventh was smashed to pieces.'

'Not at all. Those records can take it.'

'Do you hear barking?' asked the chronicler.

To think I got excited over César Franck, thought Juan. *That I liked that praliné* . . . Clara thought: barking, *Beethoven, Castelar's house, 'Turk', Mozart, the Turkish march, the horns in the Fifth:*

all that had a meaning   THERE WAS BARKING
that was incomprehensible
deep
(a well in moonlight, frogs)
'a carbuncle' – there are beautiful words like carbuncle and gem,
a reach, and it was, yes,
a vision – of what who could say   THERE WAS BARKING
for what purpose;

a vision, a reach in the night, of . . .
pulse without words   the fountain.
Naked living   *That's how destiny barks at the door.*
Living, like an
immobile fall through the music in the vertiginous circle;
with *names*: fervor, pretty, stay, tomorrow, die, sacrifice, gem. Sandokan.

'Be careful,' said a guard. They ran into him at the bottom of the stairs. He seemed to be standing watch at the bend where the platform started. 'I wouldn't be surprised if it had rabies.'

'Damn,' said the chronicler. 'You mean the dog that's barking?'

'Yes, sir. They come out of the tunnel. This is the fifth one I've seen today.'

'But if it barks, it doesn't have rabies,' said Juan, who'd read all the novelized lives of Pasteur. 'Now, a dying dog with hydrophobia and blood-shot eyes bites because it doesn't cry.'

'Go ahead and joke, but if it bites you . . .'

'The fifth today?' said Clara. 'Where do they come from?'

'I don't know. This has been going on for a few days. Look at him, there he goes.'

They instinctively stepped back. The dog came along the platform, skinny and hairy, with his head drooping down, his tongue hanging out like a rag. The few passengers were on the other side of the exit to the stairs, and some shouted for the guard, who waved a broom with rapid horizontal movements. The dog stopped about six feet from the broom, whined, and started panting. It might well have been rabid. From back in the tunnel, came another bark, muted.

'How do they get in?' asked Clara, clinging to Juan.

'They get in everywhere,' said the guard, carefully watching the dog. 'I've called ten times to the central office to have a cop sent down to shoot them, but they're all asleep. And then the mess with the traffic, there was a train wreck at Aguero. I'm going nuts!'

'They must be trying to escape from the heat,' murmured Juan.

'Maybe the fog. They go down into the darkness. But why do they bark, why do they seem so miserable?'

'Poor doggy,' said Clara, seeing the dog stretched out at the edge of the platform, still panting, looking around and trembling slightly.

'That dog doesn't have rabies,' said the chronicler. 'He's thirsty and frightened. Hey, look down the tunnel, way down.'

In the tunnel, there were two eyes almost at ground level, staring at them. The eyes were there for a second, and then the white shape of a dog could be seen going back inside. The hum of the train could be heard coming from the west.

'It's going to smash him to pieces,' said Clara. 'How can he get away from it?'

'There are walkways on both sides. Let's go, this is our train.'

They walked out of the stairway, passing next to the guard, who was still watching the dog, his broom ready. The train emitted a dry snort as it came into the station and moved quickly forward. Clara and Juan looked at the dog, expecting to see it get up in fright, but the animal seemed still unconscious, bobbing its head a bit. The guard gathered his strength and hit him with the broom right in the center of his body. He calculated correctly because the dog fell onto the tracks a second before the train passed, and its howl stopped exactly when Clara's scream did, both swallowed up by the noise of brakes and metal.

5

'Just take a look at that!'

López, the news dealer, like an entomologist, was showing him a box on page two of *La Nación*:

THE MINISTRY OF PUBLIC HEALTH WARNS THE POPULACE THAT UNTIL SUCH TIME AS THE RESULTS OF THE ANALYSES BEING CARRIED OUT AT THIS MOMENT ARE RECEIVED...

> (He read clicking his tongue, making mental disapprovals, clearing his throat.)

NO ONE SHOULD EAT THE MUSHROOMS THAT APPEARED IN THIS CAPITAL – EVEN IN VERY SMALL QUANTITIES.

'Tell me, sir, if that isn't just the worst.'

'The mushrooms or not being able to eat them?' asked Andrés with a sigh.

'I mean the tone of the announcement. Hypocritical, Mr Fava, that's what I'd call it! Hypocritical. They're out to hoodwink folks. As if anyone would think of eating such disgusting things.'

Mysterious now, he lowered his voice. Giving him a signal (the old vendor to an old customer), he brought Andrés behind an enormous pile of books published by Santiago Rueda, Acmé, Losada, and Emecé. Bending over, he examined a low and empty shelf. Then he stood up, snorting triumphantly; and while looking around with an air of innocence, he gestured for Andrés to bend over and take a look. In the back of the shelf, two silvery little mushrooms were glowing weakly. Andrés stared at them with interest – they were the first he'd ever seen.

★

'It's this filthy humidity,' said the salesman, another López. 'They can say anything, but I know what's going on. There's never been heat or humidity this horrible.'

'That's true,' said Andrés. 'The air's stickier than Rachmaninoff. But I don't think these mushrooms...'

'Believe it, Mr Fava. It's the humidity, you've got to realize it's the humidity. I've been telling Mr Gómara something's got to be done here, inside. Look at this book, its physical condition. It's all curled up!'

Andrés took the book, entitled *The Rainbow*. It was soft and smelled of suet.

'I never thought a book could rot, just like a man,' he said.

'Well, now...' (Slightly scandalized.

Rot.

When there are such pretty words that mean the same thing;
    but that tendency of young people
      to, and only to apatay luh burshwa.)

Andrés walked through the vast ground floor of *El Ateneo*. *My years as a student*, he thought, drying the palms of his hands. *My two little pesos, my little five-peso notes... And it's all so much the same. What did I buy first? I don't remember —*

but not remembering is like killing yourself — a betrayal.

I was here one day, I walked through that door, I looked for a salesman, I asked for a book.

And now I don't remember.

Leaning against a reddish column of Casares' ideological dictionaries, he closed his eyes. He wanted to remember. A dizziness came over him and he opened his eyes again. He whistled softly:

    It's easy to remember
    but so hard to forget.

Damn, the young Bing Crosby. But now he did remember one of his visits: he'd bought Aeschylus, Sophocles, and Theocritus in the little one-peso volumes published by Prometeo in Valencia —

didn't Blasco Ibáñez edit the series?

And also (again) *The Picture of Dorian Gray* in the Biblioteca Nueva series.

Now he remembered the second-hand bookstores where they sold books by the pound. That's how he'd bought O'Neill, Neruda's *Twenty Love Poems*, *Sons and Lovers*. Then to a café – 'Waiter, a coffee and a knife, please' – cutting the pages, you could almost taste the books. Being happy, so happy. The days were lofty. Misfortune helped happiness a great deal.

The taste, the aroma of cigarettes, he thought. *And the shadows of the trees in the plazas*. He picked a book off a pile, put it back. He was constantly having to dry his hands. Raising his eyes, he saw the employees on the second floor winding their way around the balustrade. They looked like insects. One of them was whistling 'Solveig's Song.' *What an animal*, Andrés thought tenderly. He'd entered *El Ateneo* to buy Ricardo Molinari's most recent book and stood a while in the doorway watching the Eighty Women parade by. The first of them carried a strange poster of which a few newspapers had taken note: the reference to the prophecies of the sibyls, the invitation to join.

> DON'T WASTE A SINGLE DAY
> A SINGLE DAY CAN WASTE YOU
> OH WOMAN
> SISTER OF THE EIGHTY
> WHO PRAY WHO PRAY

And also their music, those plastic rattlesnakes they frenetically shook;

> OH WOMAN

while an announcer hidden in a van from which pamphlets were tossed – with loudspeakers – held forth in a strange, proselytizing monody.

Purification, thought Andrés looking at the women. *What are they afraid of? of what portents are they aware?* . . . The procession paused in front of the Gath and Chaves Clothing store and then disappeared down Florida. Andrés had entered *El Ateneo* at 4:00 P.M., and another van had passed by rapidly, repeating an official announcement that contained the paragraph about the mushrooms.

'Mr Fava, what heat,' said Arturo Planes from the other side of the Colección Austral books. 'And how's it going, old man?'

'Surviving. Listening to people talk.'

'You can hear more than that,' said Arturo, holding out a big red hand dripping with sweat. 'I'm fed up with these loudspeakers. You don't live downtown, I think – but those of us who do . . .'

'I can imagine. Selling here on Calle Florida –
what a pain.'

'And having to sell books, which is so boring,' complained Arturo. 'At least there's more diversion in this place these days. You won't believe this, but upstairs on the second floor
(he was suddenly choking with laughter, furtively looking up),
 – man, this is something –
upstairs, they've pulled out all the stops. They think this is the end or something like that. Beginning the day before yesterday – when the north wind started blowing.'

'What do they do?' asked Andrés, distracted, caressing a volume of tales by Luis Cernuda. He remembered:

> *Of what use was summer to us,*
> *oh nightingale in the snow,*
> *when only an orb so small*
> *vainly wraps the dreamer?*

'They wash themselves,' said Arturo, convulsed with laughter.

López passed by, his arms filled with volumes published by Kapelusz. He was followed by two timid teenage girls, who seemed afraid they might lose their books. Andrés looked at them remotely. *Everything passes*, he thought, *and they'll still be studying the rivers of Asia, isobars*

and the sad isotherms. One of the girls looked at him, and Andrés smiled faintly at her, seeing how she lowered her eyes. She looked at him again – forgetting him. He felt himself fall into the girl's oblivion, his image disintegrating in an instantaneous nothingness. Kapelusz; isotherms; *the average*; Tyrone Power; *I'll be seeing you*; Vicki Baum. They went too.

'Hey man, listen to what I'm telling you,' whined Arturo. 'Are you in a daze too?'

'Of course,' said Andrés. 'So they wash?'

'Yes, right in the office. I swear on a stack of Bibles. Look, go right up. Don't be afraid. I can't leave the store area. Go up and then tell me. You want one of these bricks here in my section?'

'What's your section?'

'Urbanism. Traffic,' said Arturo with some chagrin. 'Things on functional cities and reinforced concrete.'

'That isn't really my line,' said Andrés, replacing the Cernuda volume. *The indolent man*, he thought, remembering Cernuda. *To elaborate a life so that its most beautiful moment culminates in a stone house at the beach: sand and water until the end* . . . He smiled at the bark of a loudspeaker in the street. A nun in charge of a frightened little Chinese girl was staring at the piles of *My First English Book*. The sweat was hanging from the fine, black fuzz on her upper lip, while from time to time, she'd shoo away a fly with an impatient wave. López and Mr Gómara were closing the double doors to keep out the fog – which made it impossible to see the sidewalk outside.

The stairway was empty. He threaded his way through tables and book cases, unenthusiastically searching out what amused Arturo so much. Leaning over the balustrade (*now I too will look like an insect*, he thought), he waved a sign of confusion to the salesman. Arturo energetically pointed to the side where the offices were located. Andrés saw the paltry little windows. He remembered the credit he'd requested in order to buy Freud, Giraudoux, García Lorca – all read, paid for, almost all forgotten. The employees were emerging, not very gracefully, by a little door on the right, which opened almost into the balustrade. Andrés had the impression . . .

SISTER OF THE EIGHTY
WHO PRAY
WHO PRAY

— the voice reached him from the street drowned out, but accompanied by a mixture of horns and crackling noises —

he had the impression the employees were restraining themselves prodigiously — one was so pale, others were red-face, and moving around the store continuously —

as if obeying an imperious password. *They're not going to let me in there*, thought Andrés. *It's a shame I'm not with Juan or the chronicler.* A telephone was ringing on his left, and the pale employee

— now there were seven or eight employees, either walking up the stairs or leaving the offices —

ran to answer it. 'Wrong number,' Andrés heard him say. He'd barely hung up when it rang again.

'No, no. Wrong number,' repeated the pale boy, looking at Andrés with a supplicating air, as if he could do something.

'Now they'll call again,' said Andrés at the same instant the phone began to ring.

'Hello. No, no! Wrong number. Dial correctly. Well, that isn't the number. No. Call the operator. I don't know.'

'Tell them to dial nine-six,' said Andrés.

'Dial nine-six. Bah, they hung up.' He stood there staring at Andrés as if still expecting something. Someone called: 'Filipelli, Filipelli!' from the center of the stairway. The pale salesman left Andrés standing in front of the telephone, which rang again. Andrés laughed, answering.

'Menéndez?' said a fine but slightly urgent-sounding voice.

'No, this is *El Ateneo*.'

'But if I dial the Menéndez number . . .'

'It would be better to speak to a supervisor.'

'How do you do that?'

A SINGLE DAY CAN WASTE YOU

'Dial 96, miss.'

'Oh. Nine-six. And then?'

OH WOMAN

'Then you ask for the supervisor. And you tell him what's happening with the – whose number was it?'

'Menéndez. Thank you, sir.'

'Good luck, miss.'

'I need it,' the voice said incredibly, hanging up. For a short time, Andrés kept the telephone in his hand, without thinking, living the telephone;

that thing through which for a second something of yours and something of another's are united, without being united.

OH WOMAN

Listening to himself still on the phone, but why?

and who might it be?   united without being united

Contact for a second –

and then nothing; like Clara, *like Clara again*.

DON'T WASTE A SINGLE DAY
SISTER OF THE EIGHTY

He hung up. To sit down awhile on the leather benches, to watch from above, with the consolation of looking down on others: López's bald spot, Arturo Planes' boiled-crab hands, the books.

WHO PRAY WHO PRAY

But since the employees didn't seem to concern themselves with him, he took advantage and made his way to the little door of the offices. The door swung back and forth lightly; and through the thin partition and the opaque windows, he heard a splashing noise, a collective murmur, a muffled cough. He entered, both hands in his jacket pockets, without looking at anyone in particular, barely stepping aside for a fat gentleman with white hair, who tripped over the doorjamb and swore (not at the door but at himself).

Andrés had ample space to lean on some shelves packed with folders and survey the scene. He was a bit blinded by the yellow glow in the large windows – where the fog had taken hold, erasing

the buildings across the street. But then he got used to the glow and could see clearly the tub in the center of the room. They'd rearranged the desks to form something like a small circus ring, like a neighborhood circus complete with sawdust-covered floors.
SHOULD NOT BE USED   AS FOOD.
He saw the woman who was the head of credit at the edge of the tub, with two younger women flanking her; and some men – eight or nine of them – a bit further back and at the narrowest end,

> (because it was a zinc-colored kiddy pool, shaped like a
> nautical coffin, with its charming edge and its gray color
> that the water filled with white stars and blue reflections).

And they stood as if it were the intermission of a ceremony. The back of the office where Andrés was standing was dimly lit – the yellow glow illuminated only the circus' center – but Andrés had already seen more employees crowded in beyond, where a long figure was stretched out on a sofa with split-leather cushions, as if sleeping or in a faint.

Almost no one spoke in that moment, and although the women glanced at Andrés, and he was certain everyone had noticed his presence, things went on. The head of credit signaled to one of the men, who left the group and

... UNTIL THE RESULTS OF THE ANALYSES ...
('What pains in the asses they are with their analyses,' said one of the men in back)

came to stand next to the tub. When the head of credit signaled him a second time he bent over slowly and put his hand in the water, picked it up in the palm of his hand, leaned his head over, and washed his mouth and chin.

One of the young women waited with a towel that was already quite wet, and the head of credit said something Andrés didn't hear because he was crossing over to the window side, approaching the employees in the back who were now looking after the man on the sofa. López entered through the other side, extremely nervous, carrying a bath sponge that was soaked in vinegar, or so Andrés thought. (It smelled of vinegar, but then it could have been ammonia, or a mixture of salts like what Stella carried in her purse on the days when . . .

although the smell of vinegar predominated.) Behind Andrés, the murmuring continued, the splashing. *They've lost their minds*, he thought. Then he thought they hadn't, that perhaps what they'd *saved* was their minds: purification technique –

because this was a . . .   OH WOMAN

a clever way of . . .

Yes, they were sponging the man's lips, and then Andrés saw the man who'd fainted more clearly; his extended, inert figure and his face – but of course, now he realized – seen in so many lectures. They'd taken off his glasses, and one of the employees was holding them. He saw the thick eyebrows, the clean-shaven cheeks, the thin neck over which fell, folded and ridiculous, the loosened blue tie. Without knowing who he was, Andrés had the shock of recognition: fraternity of groups, teams, gangs.

'Not fraternity,' he said to himself, 'rather security we feel, knowing we always run into the same faces in bookstores, writers' societies, the House, concerts. And this guy . . .' He'd seen him in art galleries, in theaters – where the two of them (now he realized the parallelism) had stayed to the bitter end of movies starring Marcel Carné or Laurence Olivier. *He was at the Isaac Stern concerts*, Andrés thought, suddenly becoming anguished, *at Batlle Planas' last show, a course given by Don Ezequiel, Borges' classes at the Cultural . . .*

'He fainted near the door,' said López, recognizing him. 'It seems he was picking out some books, and someone saw him collapse. This will bring him around; and you, Osvaldo, you'd better bring up some water. See if there's some cognac. With this heat . . .'

But López knew (and Andrés knew he knew – he knew that everyone knew)

that the sponge was a gesture; the vinegar (with ammonia) a gesture.

'Can't you get a doctor?' he asked, tired, holding on to the back of the sofa.

'But it's nothing, some dizziness that's all. It happens here all the time.'

Andrés was looking at the body, the short, dark, disordered hair, the scuffed shoes, the long legs. One hand (enormous, bony) was resting on a knee: the other was palm-up, as if begging. From between the eyelids came a greenish reflection. *Who can he be? And why suddenly . . . ?* He closed his eyes, staggering a bit. López glanced at him nervously. Andrés opened his eyes when he felt the burn of the ammonia in his nose. He took a deep breath, smiling.

'It's okay, it's nothing,' he said, pushing away the sponge. 'Who is that man?'

'I don't know,' said López. 'He always came in a lot, but he didn't have an account here. He looks very young. I helped him sometimes.'

The others were looking over the body. Andrés heard the splashing again behind him, the murmuring. Before he left – because he really had no business being there, standing at the foot of the sofa – he looked down at the dead man, taking him in completely. The hand that was palm-up closed imperceptibly, but it was a trick of the light.

Sitting on a stair and leaning against the wall, he watched the shoes running up and down. Osvaldo passed by with the glass of water. The pale young man who'd had the problems with the telephone passed by.

'I just don't know what to think,' murmured Andrés. 'Maybe he died at the right moment or he deserved to go on a bit more. What a disappearing act. What right did he have to die that way, right now?'

He felt irritated and kept on seeing that face which was so white, so bereft of relief – the protruding cheekbones, the weak chin, and sunken temples. *Escapist!* he thought, enraged. *Between the fog and the Eighty Women, escapist! Coward!* And he was suddenly overcome by tenderness. Now he visualized more clearly the thin figure he'd seen in the corridors of the Odeon, remembering an accidental collision and exchange of excuses outside the ticket booth at a movie. Always alone, or speaking with friends, but alone. Who was he? Andrés wondered if he'd left some book or piece of music behind. Smiling, suffering, he reproached himself for that need to qualify. Everything he could say, everything worthwhile, was contained in Marlow's statement about Lord Jim: *He was one of us*. And, really, even that didn't help much.

All right, he thought, *now he's going to rot. He'll go through all the phases of a proper cadaver* – and it was curious because he saw himself. He thought about the dead man, but it was himself he saw decompose. Why not? If there was one thing you could be sure of it was that final – saponification. Foreseeing it (even if your whole body jumped back like a horse that smells bones) was almost a moral victory. To ponder the notion of life, of having been a man, up to its final consequences. *I'm not finished when I die*, he thought, burning his mouth on his cigarette. *I've been my body, and I owe it the loyalty of accompanying it to the end. My imagination goes to the door and says: good-by there, loving hostess. But no, let's follow it out onto the street, let's keep going. If I'm really finished when I die, if my body – which I feel living right now, which is myself – goes on horribly night after night, swelling, growing, decomposing, shrinking, the least I can do is foresee its destruction, look at it from life. Ah, Orcagna, painter of putrefaction!*

People passing by on the stair watched him out of the corner of their eye. One of them going up was carrying a briefcase. *They must have found the doctor. What for?* thought Andrés. *They're just going to pinch his arms and chest, the doctor will give him a shot just to show how efficient he is – shake him, strip him, and vilify him.* He wanted to go back, to shout at them that the man was dead. All of them knew it very well, but they all hoped the faint was nothing.

'I'm getting old,' muttered Andrés. 'I sentimentalize everything I touch.'

From his stair, he watched people buying books, watched Arturo running around his section. They'd just reopened the doors, as if there were less fog. The loudspeakers on the street were no longer audible. Osvaldo passed by with the same glass of water, and Andrés saw that the glass was full. *How odd it didn't occur to him to empty it in the tub.* Then he had the horrible thought that they might throw the man into the tub to get him to respond. *But of course, if he's already got the necessary form. Ars moriendi.* But dying isn't an art. *That day I discovered that I've died other times – so clear, so without solemnity. It isn't a show, as with dreams, but a light passage instead, like a bird: repeated death,*

returning.

Rotting again, as many times as it returns. Obligatory ransom of a season in the sun.

> The Sunne who goes so many miles in
> a minut, the starres of the Firmament,
> which go so many more, goe not so fast,
> as my body to the earth.
>
> – Donne

Blackmail of the soul, sermons, thought Andrés. The trumpets will revive the bodies. Isn't that what it says? Death for them was all the sun, all space. Death denies the world: I am not my death, I am the world, I hold it up like an orange against the sun. My death I throw to the depths of myself – to that which is so distant it doesn't exist. It is my limit, just as my body's limit is not my body – even if I cut it out of the air and imagine it.

(He would have sworn that hat in the novel section . . . but he could no longer see it.)

Dying is like writing, thought Andrés. *Of course, my dear little Pascal, of course we die alone.* He remembered his first notebooks of essays, his awkward novels. Everything he discussed about them with his pals – the ideas, the locales, the arguments about how to set things up. And later, in his little room, the bitter *maté*, late nights; at times his black cat on his lap, distant but so warm. Alone, facing the notebook; without witnesses. Like dying – because the employees hadn't seen the unknown man die, only collapse. Perhaps in that moment he was with others – thinking about others; perhaps the last thing he saw was the spine of a book, the last thing he heard was the noise of hasty heels behind him. *If a book could at least attain the dignity of a death*, thought Andrés, *and, at times, vice versa*. What a temptation to make metaphors. How death invited you to embrace it with words, follow it out to the street, ascribe it attributes, negate its negative qualities.

But it most certainly is him, there he was again! Some coincidence. And Arturo was speaking with . . .

After all, dying won't be any business of mine, thought Andrés, mocking himself, his throat tight because of the memory of the man upstairs. *If I'm anything it's alive, right? I'm alive, I exist. Therefore, how can I stop living without ceasing to be?*
Oh reason, oh marvel!
   Then, clearly, it follows that
      if when I die I'm not myself,
         it's someone else who's died. So what should it matter to me? I can feel sorry for him beginning now, right this minute. It's now it grieves me that the guy I was is dead! Poor lad, so meritorious! He wrote and everything. With such a pluperfect future . . . He lit another cigarette, staring in surprise at his fingers shaking. Abel was standing in front of the economics books, his hands in his pockets

– indeed, indeed; with both hands in his pockets,

and he was softly negating something he must have been thinking: his blue hat continuously swinging back and forth. Andrés forgot him. The figure stretched out on the sofa got up, hard and useless. Cadaver. A horrible nuisance.

He should come sit down next to me, thought Andrés. *Leave the other guy on the sofa,*
      unless they've put him in the tub;
should come here and tell me: he died. And we'd smoke together. But I, who was his life, what do I care? If he didn't come, watch out, if he didn't come,

then it's serious. *If he doesn't come, then it's not enough just to think about this; something atrocious impedes the break. The living person goes off with the dead one . . . But it can't be, it isn't right, it isn't fitting. I've just felt so clearly that it isn't I who will die one day . . . It can't be that he, in some way – air, image, or sound – isn't here, that he isn't walking around free . . .*

Tired, he let his head sink. *You've done nothing but argue, nothing more than create a double for yourself – the way others create a soul. The ka, old boy. You're late to this, you repeat yourself* . . . And nevertheless he'd *known* that only life was his, was he; and the other . . .

'So it's dispossession,' he murmured, tossing down the butt and stepping on it. 'Enough fantasizing. Don't ask from discourse what is proper to poetry. Nice, eh? 5:10, the kids, the exam. Let's get up, vitalist.'

Arturo was waiting for him at the bottom of the stairs, giggling.

'Did you wash your face too?'

'No, and I really need to,' said Andrés, glancing at his wet, dirty handkerchief. 'It just didn't seem right for me, only being a regular customer who gets a 10% discount . . .'

'Bah, they're nuts,' said Arturo, shaking. 'That idiot Gómara wanted me to go up. They're loony.'

'You can always use a washing,' said Andrés. 'If I were you, I'd go. It's gotten very amusing. There's a dead man and a lot of first aid.'

'Are you kidding?' asked Arturo, looking at him out of the corner of his eye.

'Go on up and see for yourself if you don't believe me.'

'You're kidding me.' He looked at Andrés without looking at him, containing himself. Suddenly he burst into laughter (Andrés recognized the brittle quality of it – the other source of sobbing), and he ran upstairs. Slowly lifting his head, to give him time to arrive, Andrés followed his running steps. He was close to the balustrade and didn't step aside when López came from the other direction. López, stepping aside, saw him run in. Behind López came the doctor carrying the bag.

How bizarre, thought Andrés, amused. *How he slips away.* He looked for Abelito behind the book cases, in the entryway to the elevator, over at the cashier. Then he went out onto the street desiring to walk, to smell the yellow smell. On the corner of Corrientes, a first-aid station had been set up; through the fog he could see the nurses and the orderlies wearing blue smocks. The station took up the diagonal route of the sidewalk on the Mayorga side (it was there they gave injections and distributed flyers about the danger of the mushrooms); but it extended into the middle of the street

since – after the pavement had collapsed on the corner of Maipú, and there had been more mushrooms since morning, and now they were opening in a star-shaped pattern – the superintendant in person had ordered the detouring of traffic off the street, as well as off Maipú, Esmeralda, and Lavalle. Only ambulances could enter, running over the northern sidewalk of Corrientes. They were made to come from Suipacha, with the stretcher bearers waiting on the corner of Bignoli to bring down those who'd fainted or were overcome by fumes. A federal police truck was on the side of Trapiche, with a detachment ready to intervene, in case (because of that excess of imagination typical of the citizens of Buenos Aires, which tends to see beyond communiques) there might be some panic in the area around the first-aid station.

'They won't be able to get to the University,' said Andrés, who was beginning to practice his long-standing tendency to talk to himself out loud right there on the street. He distractedly heard a loudspeaker enumerating the exemplary fines that would be levied against businesses that closed before the legal hour. Bignoli was closed, and Ricordi as well. A ferocious fight involving loudly barking dogs amused a squad of policemen. It was broad daylight, but the area around the first-aid station was illuminated with spotlights set up on roofs and balconies. At regular intervals police whistles could be heard. Ambulances (there must have been a lot of them) announced their presence from a distance with short and continuous howls, but people no longer seemed to listen to them. It was curious that there would be such a crowd in the street and on the corners, and that the police would allow them to stand around, getting in the way of the workers in the aid station. A column of people (actually, compact groups all moving in the same direction) came up Florida, passing by the station and moving on;

but when they crossed Corrientes, the light leapt onto their filthy faces, their matted hair, and clothing wrinkled by the fog, the kids eating peanuts and drinking Coca-Cola; and the heat getting more intense in the agglomeration

they went up toward Lavalle and faded getting lost again in the yellow darkness of the fog.

Andrés slipped along staying close to the buildings, trying to see through the peepholes in the canvas of the first-aid station. No one said a word when he took advantage of an empty space, and entered, peering into the more or less protected space, where people were setting up cots for those overcome by fumes. The light came from above as it would onto the floor of a big-top circus; everything had a circus air, including the white smock with enormous bloodstains of a doctor who was bending over the body of a boy. Two nurses were pulling down the boy's trousers so the doctor could give him an injection in the buttock. The kid howled. His eyes were shut, as if he were afraid or ashamed. One of the nurses laughed and gave him a mocking pat on the cheek. Up above, against the spotlight, the summer insects were fluttering about, anticipating the night; a moth with ashen wings began to walk tremulously along Andrés' sleeve. Andrés patted it as if it too were the child's cheek. Two accident victims were brought in, and from the side of the Mayorga sidewalk appeared orderlies and a nurse. One of the nurses glanced at Andrés, who wasn't moving. On the cot to his right, an elderly lady was shaking. The moth flew from Andrés' sleeve and landed right on her hair.

'Go take a rest,' a recently-arrived doctor said to the one who'd given the injection to the boy. 'There's hot coffee.'

'Okay, but go see what's bothering that woman.'

He passed next to Andrés. They were not surprised to recognize each other.

'What are you doing here, man?' asked the doctor. 'You don't feel well?'

'I'm okay. I just thought I'd take a look.'

'Well, there isn't much to see. Come and have some coffee. It must be a century since we saw each other last.'

'Since the meeting of the cellar group,' said Andrés. 'Since that long.'

(And through some unfathomable mental association, he remembered an old record by Kulemkampf playing a *siciliana* by von Paradis; but they didn't play that record at the meeting of the cellar group. More likely Louis Armstrong and *Petrouchka* or *La Création du Monde*.)

'I can see you've got your hands full,' he said, to say something, hoping to get rid of this vain, useless
    like so many others
               catalyst of memories.

'They're driving us crazy,' said the doctor. 'This afternoon I must have seen almost four hundred asses, some really weren't that bad. Come over here.'

They went into another room, almost completely dark, where relatives waited for the sick to be returned to them. The doctor pushed his way through, but Andrés saw that he wasn't shoving out of ill will. He was just trying to pretend he wasn't fed up and worn out. They took refuge in a space barely nine square feet. A soldier was attending a camp kitchen, and frowned when the doctor asked for coffee.

'You're going to have to wait. That bastard Romero . . .'

'What's going on?'

'He took off. He was shitting in his pants from fright, so he ran. He left everything to me.'

'We're doing just fine,' said the doctor lighting a cigarette instead. 'So they've still got these jerks helping us who don't understand.' He lowered his voice, staring intently at Andrés. 'But if I were to tell you that a plane just left and that . . .' He stopped, glancing at the soldier. 'Bah, why get all steamed up?'

'How long have you been at it?'

'I haven't slept in two days. Things were bad in Liniers and in La Boca. But since last night . . .' He inhaled on his cigarette until he couldn't, and exhaled as if with a groan. 'What a life.'

He looked at Andrés indifferently, actually talking to himself, using Andrés as a comfortable mirror. Andrés smiled at him, happy the doctor didn't dive into that 'confidential puddle.' Flies settled on their hands and they let them stay there. *Svelte youth*, he thought, weakly. *The horror of these encounters. Alumni banquets, silver-wedding anniversaries, diplomas, remember those times, old man* . . . He trembled, averting his eyes. The doctor was speaking with the soldier, who showed him a stain on the back of his hand. Andrés silently backed up, and stepped out into the street through an opening in the canvas. It was drizzling.

'But your trousers are soaked,' said Stella. 'Is it water?'

'Worse, wine,' said Andrés, collapsing into a chair.

'Wine! How could you get so much wine on you? Your whole left leg!'

'It was at the intersection of San Martín and Tucumán, my dear. Waiter, bring me a dry *caña*. Actually, bring the bottle.'

'I thought you'd never get here,' said Stella. 'What happened?'

'First you tell me what miracle got you here.'

'No miracle,' said Stella. 'The 99 streetcar.'

'It's still running?'

'Yes, but a lady said it was the last, and the conductor had heard an inspector say so.'

'Any way,' said Andrés. 'The thing is you managed to get here.' He drank two shots of *caña* and a glass of water. He was stupidly happy. He reached over and lightly brushed Stella's hair. A dust ball stuck to his fingers. He had to use his other hand to get it off. Stella was still waiting for his story.

'Just to test your English, Stella, I'm going to recite this bit of William Blake,' said Andrés, extremely happy. '"Sund'ring, dark'ning, thund'ring! Rent away with a terrible crash . . ."'

'Translate it for me.'

'It isn't worthwhile,' Andrés smiled. '"No light from the fires, all was darkness in the flames of Eternal fury."' Which is the same as saying that the corner of the Railroad Savings Bank was a perfect pandemonium. It was a big mistake for me to leave Florida. Everything was going so well on Florida.'

'But the wine . . .'

'It was a wine delivery truck. It broke an axle in a pothole. Actually, there were whole stretches of pavement that sank, dearest.

> *And on the sofa, under the yellow light.*
> *The loudspeakers THAT PRAY THAT PRAY.*
> *also that skin so white, ready to sink to . . .*

'So it splashed on you.'

'So it splashed on me. Actually, the accident with the truck happened earlier. It seems they posted a cop to keep an eye on it. I say "seems" because he wasn't there when I passed by. What was there was a crowd enjoying the hell out of itself. They were putting all the empty bottles at the entrance to the Railroad Savings Bank and dancing on the solid part of the pavement. For dancing, they took a radio from some poor guy wandering around like a lost soul, begging them to give it back. Just when I arrived they'd managed to get a Uruguayan station and were dancing, I think, to one of Pedro Maffia's tangos. I don't know if you noticed that our stations are only broadcasting news.'

'I did. I was listening before I went out. But how did you get soaked?'

'I committed the indiscretion of getting in the way of some girl who was vomiting,' said Andrés. 'Maybe the poor thing didn't like Pedro Maffia's tango. Luckily, there was a faucet working at the Bank. I took off my pants and did a decent job of washing off the affected part. I wrung them out and put them back on. Incidentally, I can tell you that the perpetrator was carried out feet-first and that there was very little wine left.' He passed his hand over his forehead and studied the perspiration on it before drying it with a paper napkin.

The *Florida*, where they were sitting, was almost empty. A student café. Andrés liked it out of habit because he was unable to let go of that nighttime past: The groups of people with no other object than that of having no object, the verbal skirmishes, rapid love, coffee, paintings, Clara and Juan, nights. With each day that passed, he was further from all that;

but the higher the kite – and he smiled, cruel – the heavier the string weighs on it, its history and support.

Another dry *caña*, and potato chips (which were moist, aside from not being made from real potatoes).

'I had an easy trip. Nothing happened to me,' said Stella. 'Well, wait: on the corner of the University there were some trucks, I think they were shoring up the wall of the Institute.'

'It's 6:30,' said Andrés. 'Outside, you can barely see a thing.'

'People have gone home,' said Stella. 'Oh, the porter was at the door of the University. I said hello as I passed, and he didn't recognize me. You could hear people inside, but I don't think there were very many.'

'Let's go over there,' said Andrés. 'That way we won't miss the kids.'

But they stayed a little longer. A boy at a table next to the wall was reviewing some papers, taking notes. Occasionally he would pass his fingers through his hair, would fidget around nervously, then go back to his work. *This guy keeps at it*, thought Andrés. *When you see people like that, it makes you think that after all . . . But he's probably going over a dialogue for some soap opera*. He felt himself softening, spongy, like the potato chips. *We should learn the art of the sponge – full of water, but separate from it, conforming it, a different substance . . .* Stella was waiting for him, very attractive in her blue-silk blouse, her thin legs with the golden down. Passing next to the boy with the papers, Andrés resisted the temptation to stop and talk to him. 'Perhaps he's as lonely as I am,' he said to himself, articulating each word in his dry throat. 'The writer's moral: *noli me tangere*. That's how you get there, but that's also how you die. Like . . .' and then there were no more words,

only a vision: leather sofa   long rigid legs
                          hand   up

(and the glasses – he remembered – dancing on the fingers of one of the employees, the lenses through which things would no longer pass for sensitive cells to sort out;

he suspected that all that out there: WORLD.

The world, the world, the world . . .)

'It's incredible,' he murmured;

> by then he was next to Stella, at the door.
> 'I am also this thing
> that continues in the fog
> copying itself remaking itself saving itself.

Oh final unity! Access!' ('But I've already figured that it isn't that way,' he said to himself in admonition. 'I've brilliantly demonstrated that I have nothing to do with the guy who's going to die. I go on, I am. Is that just talk? *Here*, this thing I touch. Take a deep breath. *This*, right now. *I*, still, always. What can nothingness do to me?'

'Stella, my love,' said Andrés. 'We are safe from nothingness.'

'Nothingness?'

'Yes, Stella. Safe. And we didn't even know it. Before, I had an inkling – but now I'm beginning to live it. Safe, safe, Stella. Nothingness is for others. For that guy who's dead in a bookstore, he can no longer deny it. But it isn't just that he no longer is. Irrevocably, we are *not* the nothingness. We have nothing to do with it! It doesn't mix with us. When we yield to it – because it's inevitable – then it advances; but it is *not* us. It's useless to look for words. If we stop singing, it seems that silence takes over the music; but it's a lie, Stella. There's no silence. It's only that there's music or there's no music. Never accept the idea of silence. Watch out for the cab.'

They crossed to the pharmacy at San Martín and Viamonte, orienting themselves by means of some vague lights at the edge of the street – two red lights signaling a *depression* in the roadway. What they thought was a taxi was a black car with government license plates, filled with cops guarding someone they couldn't see.

'You have to be careful with ideas,' whispered Andrés, and Stella realized he wasn't talking to her.

★

'Papers?' asked the policeman at the door.

They were halfway up the stairs. Andrés and Stella stopped and stared at him.

'No one enters without papers.'

'Why not?' asked Andrés.

'I've got my orders, and that's that.'

Stella took out her identification card, and Andrés had to hunt around in his wallet until he found his. When he looked up, he saw Clara staring at him from the sidewalk. Juan and the chronicler were bringing up the rear, involved in an argument.

'Hi,' said Andrés, holding up his identification card with two fingers.

'Hi,' repeated Stella, marching up the stairs. She had showed her card to the policeman and went inside.

Clara stood next to Andrés. Silent, they went up the stairs together. The policeman looked over their documents and let them pass.

6

Juan and the chronicler had been chatting since leaving the subway at the last stop. (The Florida Avenue stop had been closed, and people were saying – Clara heard a young soldier say it – that the station was being used as an emergency hospital, taking people overcome by fumes after being attended to at the first-aid station on the corner.)

The two of them weren't much in agreement about the House and the University. It was true both institutions hated each other, that on one occasion, a Reader from the House had said about the University: 'It's distinguished only for its solid stairway,' and that a dean from the aggrieved side had invented the title *Only His Master's Voice* for the House.

To the chronicler it seemed that . . .

but when they saw Andrés at the door, they were so happy they stopped arguing. ('A trivial theme,' said the chronicler.) And in the vestibule inside from which ascended the

solid stairway,

the five came together to chat, waiting for a chance to take over the bench next to the cashier of the . . .

and they stared in some surprise where two proctors were sitting at a table occupying the center of the space, now reduced, with the result that the movement of students became slow and complicated.

'First time I ever saw the proctors looking so important,' said Juan, patting at the sleeves of his jacket as if they might lose the humidity that was wrinkling them that way. 'Look at them, they're Olympian.'

'They've always been very majestic,' said Clara, leaning against

Juan, worn out. 'But the table bit is pretty unnecessary. Let's sit down on the stairs, anywhere.'

'Can we get into the classrooms?' Juan asked the proctors.

'No.'

'Why?'

'They're locked up.'

'Couldn't you open one for us?'

'No.'

'Why?'

'We don't have the keys.'

'Who has them then?'

The proctor looked toward the other proctor, while Andrés took one step back and assumed control of the end of the bench. He tapped Clara's shoulder and waited for her to be seated. The chronicler placed himself next to them, and the students occupying the rest of the bench squeezed together to make room. 'It would only occur to me to go out wearing this suit,' one of the students said, as if speaking to himself. 'But it's great – it's light as a feather.' Clara listened as she collapsed in fatigue, having lost all will power in the arrival, then the immediate scene. 'But she likes me to get dolled up,' she heard the student say. Andrés was staring at her – against her – but folded into himself in a violent attempt to make contact with her not matter.

'You're a wreck,' he said to her. It sounded like a clinical evaluation.

'I am. I'm done in. What a day it was . . .'

'*It was?*' said Andrés. 'I don't know, somehow I get the impression it's barely begun. There's so much suspense in the city.'

'Don't talk like you're in a ghost story, Andrés,' said the chronicler. 'Man, if I could just take off my shoes. If I were in the office, I'd have taken them off already. I really should be at the office.'

Then he explained he'd come to the University to keep them company, but that he didn't intend to stay until the exam because there was no doubt his absence would be commented on at the paper.

'Think so?' asked Juan, who'd taken a seat on the floor and was facing them.

'To tell you the truth,' said the chronicler, 'I have the impression that at this hour they don't give a damn if anyone's at the paper or not. What a pretty blouse, Stella.'

'It is attractive, isn't it?' said Stella. 'I see you have good taste. The best thing about it is that it's light.'

'That woman who was strangled on Rincón Street was wearing a blouse just like it,' said the chronicler, looking at the legs of a student who was beginning to go up the stairs. He heard the squeal (*a rat*, he thought) of the fat proctor: the legs became immobile, the order to come down immediately.

'But I have to get some information upstairs,' said the student.

'Come down immediately! No one's allowed up!'

'Why can't anyone go up?' asked Juan. 'If I feel like it, I'll go up right now. Want me to go with you?'

'No, no,' said the student, who'd turned pale. 'I'd rather stay down here.'

'Good idea,' said a male student. 'If you went up, they might not let you take the test.'

Juan stared at him. The proctors had begun to line up green-paper lists – with squares, dotted lines, and numbers telling the order of things, and footnotes. *Son of a list*, thought Juan staring at the student who was consulting mimeographed notes. *How long will he* . . . The door to the gallery was still creaking painfully.

'Christ, the wind is really blowing,' said the chronicler. 'It just can't be.'

With the gust of wind came an underlying sweet smell, barely perceptible at first – like boiled glue, wet paper, humidity, reheated stew. *Those smells from lower school*, thought Andrés, shaking himself, *that mysterious soapy smell that floated in the air of the classrooms, the playgrounds. Lost, but unforgettable. Was it the smell or our manner of smelling it? Some sounds, or colors of childhood, or substances so close to our faces, to anxiety* . . . This one was a tired smell – a compound of smells – brought in by the air that moved the doors.

Even the voices in the room, muted by the woodwork and the humidity, seemed part of the smell. Then it became clear that the smell had been there since they came in, that the gust of hot air did nothing more than bring out that lingering, super-sweet repugnance.

'I owe you one, kid,' the chronicler was saying to Andrés. 'Concerts like that just don't happen every day. I wish I could describe to you the face on Clara's Dad when the brawl started. In fact, he was great. We were, as you might say, one big, happy family. Too bad you weren't there. Even that guy from last night passed by. And I won't say a word about this one, the punches he landed. He took some good ones too.'

'The truth of the matter is I've got a bruised rib,' said Juan. 'Hey chronicler, don't you think it's my turn to enjoy the benefits of the bench a little?'

'Naturally. I'll sit on the floor and reverently listen to your university conversation. It's a shame Clarita's falling asleep.'

'A shame,' said Clara. 'But an inevitable shame.'

'Why didn't you make her rest?'

'Since she became an adult, she's tended to make her own decisions,' said Juan.

'She's in no shape for an exam – unless it's a clinical one.'

'You're wrong,' said Clara, closing her eyes. 'I've got enough phosphorescence. I know all the tables, even the one for Number Eight. And all the problems.' *Une paysanne, zanne zanne zanne* – she hummed, swinging her head back and forth.

'We didn't think everything would get so complicated,' said Juan. 'I'm just about done in myself. Just think, my father-in-law takes us to the concert to relax. And after that, the trip on the subway, the riot on Carlos Pellegrini. On the train, we heard there was a fire on the block where Trust Jewelers is; at least we heard people talking about the smoke and people not being able to take the heat.

'Just as we're pulling out of the station, the train gets stuck,' said the chronicler. 'We'd gone maybe a hundred yards. Then, we couldn't move. The heat was so brutal some women were screaming. In my presence . . .

but why bother you with all this.'

'Keep going,' said Andrés. 'When you're done I'll tell mine.'

'You wouldn't believe it. A woman started to cry. She was so crammed in, she couldn't get her arms free, and she was looking at me, crying, the tears pouring down her face, to say nothing of the sweat destroying her mascara. She had eye shadow stalactites, it was horrible. Immobile, you have to realize. She was crying. I couldn't stop looking at her; and she couldn't stop crying. It must be the same in jail or in a hospital, but at least there you can turn your face to the wall if you don't want to see or so no one will see you.'

'Twenty minutes like that,' said Juan. 'I wouldn't wish it on anyone. After a while, we all felt the earth. I don't know how to explain it to you. In a subway tunnel the depth doesn't bother you because of the movement. But suddenly there was that stillness that goes on and on, that feeling of anguish. Then you look at the ceiling of the car, and you know above it is the earth – hundreds of yards of it! I'd make a terrible miner: Geophobia, if you don't mind my calling it that.'

'That's a pretty word,' said Andrés. 'It stretches like a Chiclet and goes a long way.'

'Silence!' (It was the voice of one of the proctors.)

'We can't get any work done here.'

'Are you saying that to me?' asked Andrés.

'I'm saying it to everyone,' said the proctor. 'Jeez, how touchy everyone is. Can't you see we're making up the lists?'

'To tell you the truth,' said Andrés, 'there are so many lists I can barely see the two of you.'

'Don't say another word,' the chronicler cut him off. He pulled out his press identification and put it under the nose of the proctor who was closer to him. 'See this? Just keep on being wise guys, and I'll write a piece in the paper that will get the two of you canned.'

He winked at Juan: 'I've got lots of influence and won't tolerate abuse.'

'Nobody's abusing anybody,' said the proctor. 'Just lower your voices. Try to understand our responsibility, sir.'

'You have no responsibility whatsoever,' said Juan. 'You have nothing to do with us. Call the Secretary, or a professor.'

'Hey, man, don't make such a fuss,' said the student with the notes. 'First let's take the test, there's plenty of time to protest later.'

'Your name is Juárez, right?' asked Juan, standing up.

'No, my name is Migueletti.'

This bastard's technique for getting the guy's name, thought the chronicler.

'Ah, you're Migueletti. And you're going to take the exam with us, I guess.'

'Yes, unless the exam is suspended. I don't think there are any professors here.'

'So you're so well-informed you know if there are professors here or not.'

'Cut the crap, man,' said Migueletti. 'If you don't like things, why did you come to take the exam? Stay outside.'

Andrés grabbed Juan's arm and brought him over to Clara. *The guy said the right thing*, he thought in a cold rage. *We're always where we have no right to be.* Juan was staring avidly over toward Migueletti, but Clara made him sit down and scolded him in such a low voice that the others didn't hear a word. Some girls who'd laughed at the argument walked around the table and came over. Two of them looked like twins, the other was a redhead the chronicler liked immediately.

'The guy's an idiot,' said one of the twins in a low voice, 'but he's right that there aren't any professors. Now's the time that the exam's supposed to begin, and there isn't a single professor here. And what time do you have?'

'7:40,' said the chronicler. 'And you three are the kind that dazzle the examination committee, right?'

'But of course,' said the redhead. 'Everyone here is taking the same exam. There's only one committee.'

'If the committee shows up,' said the other twin, blowing her nose and sneaking a peek into her handkerchief. The gallery door squeaked open again, but along with the smell came an employee from the accounting office wearing an electric-blue suit. He vaguely glanced at them, and then immersed himself in a prolonged murmur with the proctors. The light in the gallery went out, came on again, oscillated, dimmed.

'Is there an exam?' asked the redhead.

The employee raised his hands as if he were being held up, then signaled maybe yes, maybe no, as if he were cleaning a window. He strode off at a quick pace, and they watched him enter the anteroom to the dean's office. A light went on, but the employee didn't go in, and closed the door.

'I'm suffocating in here,' said Clara. 'I'm going to walk in the gallery.'

'They won't let you,' said the redhead.

Andrés glanced over at Juan, who was writing something in his notebook. He walked Clara to the door, which he held open so she could pass through. They walked silently in the gallery, and when Andrés tried a classroom door, he could see that it was locked.

'It smells even worse out here,' he said. 'It's more and more unbearable, but actually we should be getting used to it. It's odd that it's getting increasingly annoying.'

'It might well be that we just don't adapt to some things, odd as it may seem.' said Clara. 'May I lean on your arm?'

As if lending her his arm was a delicate way of losing his life, he supported Clara. She was staggering.

'You're ice cold,' he said. 'You don't feel well?'

'It's nerves. All this will never end.'

Andrés used all his strength so Clara wouldn't notice the tremor in his hand. He recalled their walk the previous night, and that afterward, when he was no longer with her, he'd measured in the same way as delicately frustrated like a movement in a sonata, that appears and grows after we leave a concert and we're in a plaza, under the trees,

not even the memory of its sound can alter its beauty. But the arm was there, he felt it in his hand. The sound, necessary substance, flesh as a substitute for the unattainable idea.

'Everything lasts too long,' said Clara. 'It's so hard to be in perfect harmony with things. Last night I walked too much, dreamed too much, and today I ate too much. I was at the concert too long, I got too upset in the subway when the guard shoved the dog onto the tracks, when . . .'

'The guard shoved a dog onto the tracks?'

'It was contemptible. I can still see it.'

'Yes, those things we keep on seeing,' said Andrés. 'We're so soft. Did you know that photographic plates are made with gelatin?'

'Today I'd rather not be myself,' said Clara. 'When I think that last night I was living so happily, imagining that I was furious. Waiting for Juan at the House, making a scene because he was a half-hour late.'

'Look over there,' said Andrés, lightly squeezing her arm. 'Look.' Where the gallery turned, two individuals had appeared and were taking a portrait off the wall. One removed it from the hook and handed it to the other, who was keeping the ladder steady with his foot. They'd already taken down two other pictures and piled them in a corner.

'Moving day,' said Clara. 'What idiots.'

'No, they aren't moving men. Actually, they want to move others. Beginning with the most defenseless.'

'Who are you talking about?' asked Clara, staring at him.

'I think about us,' said Andrés. 'I guess about the portraits . . . I was thinking once about what a beautiful piece of music would think if it were given consciousness. It isn't impossible to imagine that, right?'

'It's pretty,' said Clara. 'Too bad someone's already written about it in a magazine you must not read, called *Tales of Terror*.'

'Is that true? said Andrés. 'Tell me the story.'

'It was so stupid,' smiled Clara. 'The only beautiful part was the central idea: imagining a dimension (on another planet, for example) where what we call music is a form of life.'

'Well, I'll devote myself to writing for that magazine,' said Andrés.

'I'll be your assiduous reader. And what would happen if music had consciousness?'

'Nothing. I just imagined the horror of a piece of beautiful music that feels itself lived through an unworthy voice, or whistled by some mediocrity. Mozart, for instance, played by that Migueletti. I thought it when I realized . . .

> For a long time now I've realized it, but today,
> when I was thinking about how values, those portraits
> if you like,

are defenseless in the hands of people who pile them up in a corner, of people who don't even destroy them, who simply set them aside.'

'But *people* don't let themselves be set aside, unless they're set-asideable,' said Clara, amusing herself by hissing all the s's. 'That's the horrible part. You feel cornered, even if you don't know by whom or against what. Now think about the people who no longer hang from their hook, who still go on posing as portraits without realizing they've been tossed into a corner.'

'Like someone who puts on a mask and a disguise in the middle of the night and just sits there alone in the dark.'

'I don't know,' said Clara. 'All I can tell you is that *I* feel as if I'm being chased. And don't think it's only because of Abel. It's something else. Ever since last night, when I noticed that my shoes were sinking into the mud – it's so hard to explain, Andrés. Much worse than either taking or not taking the exam.'

'At least you two have an exam,' said Andrés releasing her arm and walking up ahead, toward the open galleries.

'Sure, but what happens after that?' Clara's voice reached him.

'After you'll have to discover for yourself,' he said, turning around and facing her, hostile. Clara looked at him, prolonging the question. There was moisture on the floor and she slipped, but Andrés held her up. Now he was holding her with both hands, holding her still, opposite him. Clara had a shine of moisture on the skin of her cheeks, her nose. She was looking at him, expecting more. *What can I give you that you don't already have?* thought Andrés. *If at least you could save yourself, you and Juan* . . . He saw, thought he saw, horribly, Clara's skull under her face and hair, as if a black wind were coming out of her and striking him in the mouth.

'You're so sad,' said Clara. 'So silly, my poor Andrés.'

The skull was speaking. Her future death lived under the smoke, the stink of the city. Closing his eyes, canceling the image, Andrés measured how much further he had to go. Without knowing why, he took off his glasses and held them up in the air. Nothing was formulated. He only saw (with a gaze that doesn't define images exactly, the gaze that had contemplated Clara's skull) a decision, a step,

a blurred gesture towards completion.

'I'm both things,' he said, putting his glasses back on. 'Sad and silly. Silly because sad, but not vice versa. I'm silly because I have a particularly useless sort of lucidity. And above all, believe me, because I lack what Juan has a surplus of – enthusiasm.'

'Sometimes,' she said, leaning her face toward his, 'he seems like such a boy next to you.'

'Handsome compliment,' said Andrés, lightly touching her hair with his fingers.

'You deserve it,' said Clara.

'No, I mean, to Juan.'

'Ah.'

'But you and I are very similar. Now you're on the verge of your exam. Tomorrow you'll have finished it. We'll meet again in cafés or concerts, and out of all this will remain . . .

(*But it's a lie*, he thought, *I'm lying like* . . .)
one encounter among so many others.'

'You know very well it isn't like that,' said Clara. 'Why do you need to use those words with me?'

'Exaggeration makes me uncomfortable,' said Andrés. 'We fall into the idiotic habit of problematizing everything. Not only our moods, but also the things around us: a day like today, or a bothersome presence – Abel if you like. Don't fall into that, Clara, you who are above all that sloppiness.'

'You're almost advising me to keep my eyes shut,' said Clara. 'That's old advice in this country.'

'What I'm asking you to do is to not give up,' said Andrés. 'What I'm asking is that you always stay on the good verge of the exam.'

They went back, taking note as they passed that the workers had finished piling up the portraits. From the basement, through the elevator shaft, arose a confused noise. A black shape rapidly crossed the tile floor and dashed down the stairs before they had time to see

– it looked like a rat –

although, going down the staircase at that speed, it was probably a young cat;

but that way of slipping along so close to the tiles,

perhaps it was confused because the lights were blinking, fading; and fading again. A whitish glow entered from the corridor leading to the exterior galleries; but before they could recognize any shapes, a dim light, barely a light, came on.

'It was a rat,' said Clara with infinite disgust.

'It may have been,' said Andrés. 'We can go back if you like.'

'No, I don't want to. All those people annoy me. I don't know, I hoped I'd get to talk with you; but we really haven't said anything.'

'There's so little to say, when you get right down to it.'

'You're right. It always seems as if words and time were out of synch,

excuse me for being clever;

as if what I should be saying to you were inopportune, or will be one day, when you and I are gone and nothing can be said.'

'Sounds pretty,' said Andrés without irony. 'What's happening – among other things – is that the discredit language has fallen into strips us of meaning more and more. What can you *say*, anyway, in front of a Picasso? We've gotten so close to the sources that what people *say* about them is useless. And also if something's said that moves us, we no longer believe it.'

'But unfortunately,' said Clara, 'we haven't learned how to disregard things. If at least we knew how to look at each other, see each other . . .'

'There was a time,' said Andrés. 'But we didn't know it then. We weren't able to know what destiny expected of us, that is, what we expected of ourselves. *Now*: now, it's so easy to correct mistakes on paper, but time's already read the original. Talk about being clever, how about that metaphor?'

'It's bad,' said Clara. 'But so correct, if I'm understanding it. Look, this thing with Abel is a bit like that too. What's he looking for now? Think what he could have found right when he *wasn't* looking for it.'

'You mean you?' said Andrés.

'I don't know, really. I suppose so, but it's like in a nightmare. There's no reason for it, Andrés: no reason,

now.'

'It isn't reason that's moving him,' said Andrés.

'Look,' said Clara, and she handed him the letter. They had to stand under one of the lights because it was getting darker and darker. As if their sense of hearing became sharper in compensation, they heard a peal of laughter from the depths of the gallery and a noise of wrinkled papers. (Wasn't the door open? Yes, it was wide open, they could see the chronicler's back and the proctors' table.) Clara confusedly associated the smell

— it smelled like wet cotton —

with the forms in the room — the jackets, the heads, and white shirts against the woodwork and the walls. Without looking, she took the letter Andrés handed back to her and put in her pocket.

'I suppose,' said Andrés, 'that Juan is carrying a pistol.'

'No,' said Clara. 'He thinks it's a threat made by a lunatic.'

'For that very reason then. Well, I'm glad I put mine in my pocket. It occurred to me I have no idea why.

(*lie*)

Maybe the idea of believing that when things aren't going well . . .'

'It seems absurd to me!' said Clara. 'All I can imagine in your pockets are books and cigarettes.'

'You'll see,' he said. 'You'll see if it's absurd.'

Weapons, thought Clara. *The way he and I live, how strange, the value of certain gestures – a going back to the basic supports. From a revolver to holy water, there's so little . . .*

'You should try exorcism, or something more effective,' she said. 'Abel isn't in your path, and even if he were, what could you really do about it?'

'I'm not carrying the pistol because of Abel,' said Andrés. 'But I can always pass it to Juan if the need arises. But, you know, you're right. I couldn't do anything to defend you.'

'No one could,' said Clara. 'At least not with a gun.'

'You're right not to believe you can defend yourself,' said Andrés. 'But don't forget about the attacks.'

'Bah,' said Clara sweetly. 'All this . . .' She pointed to the piled-up portraits, the fog, the tiles along which the black shape had run. 'I don't think I could forget all this. Everything is against us, Andrés.'

Juan was waving to them, and they heard a whistle (it was the chronicler). Staring at the floor, Clara began walking along the gallery.

'It's useless and wouldn't do you any good,' she murmured in a voice that seemed of other times to Andrés, the voice she used when she never spoke to him that way. 'But I want you to know how sorry I am.'

'Clara,' said Andrés.

'You know very well how much I love him. I'm not sorry I ended up with him. What pains me in fact is that you and he aren't one man or that I can't be two women.'

'Please,' said Andrés. 'Everything's fine as it is. Don't say another word.'

'No, things aren't fine as they are,' said Clara. 'Not fine at all. They just are, as they always are.'

'Don't be sorry,' said Andrés.

'It isn't that, not precisely that. What pains me actually is being sure I've done the right thing; and just when I have that feeling, suddenly

the *disgust* of doing "the right thing," knowing that there isn't a right thing when more than two are involved.'

'Just don't be sorry,' repeated Andrés. 'Above all else, don't be sorry.'

'Well, at least let me be sorry for myself,' said Clara.

'I can't stop you. That you feel this way is more than I could want when . . .'

'Now at least you know how I feel,' said Clara. 'I never said anything more truthful than that.'

They were next to the door, which was engulfed in shouting and the vision of clothing and movement.

'I want to thank you,' said Andrés. 'But don't give in to goodness. Look, to be sorry when you've done nothing bad;

that horrible weakness – like condemning yourself, you know

losing the right to choose your suit and the tune you whistle each morning, and your book to read;

no, never that. Our eyes are in the front of our head, sweet

heart. It isn't your fault if I'm, if only slightly, your shadow, your echo.

If the ship can't sail without cleaving the water   look how

pretty . . .'

'You're good,' said Clara, and she smiled at him.

'And one more thing,' said Andrés. 'I think it really was a rat.'

The proctors folded up the lists and went to the dean's office carrying them as if . . .

but everyone knew perfectly well that the dean's office was empty.

'Amazing how culture proliferates,' said the chronicler as he made room on the bench so one of the twins could rest. 'Now there are more than thirty of us.'

'And what a *spuzza*,' said the redhead.   (The lights went
out.
The lights went
on.)

'A quarter to nine,' announced Juan, as if that fact were very important. Whereupon he went back to his notebook.

'The divine rhythm dominates him,' said the chronicler. 'Oh, Andrés, I really must be getting down to the paper. I don't think it will be too difficult to get there with . . .'

> They heard a series of low-sounding explosions off in the west, as if muffled in cotton; odd that the noise should reach them as if through the earth, the same way that the rat shortly before . . .

'Since you're already here, stay and keep me company while these guys take their famous exam,' said Andrés.

'The exam will be postponed,' said the chronicler. 'Notice how no one's studying? Wait: there you have young Migueletti – *phagocytizing* mimeographed copies,

mickey-mouse-o'graphed!

(In the dark. The redhead
smelled of pine soap, of matches.)

'*Fiat lux* – even if it's weak as a dressing table lamp,' the chronicler said to her, sniffing her neck. 'Comrade, you have the most fragrant skin. As long as the breeze keeps bringing us these mephitic vapors, don't budge from my side.'

'Mephi-who?' asked the redhead, hesitantly.

'*Je m'en foutism*,' said Andrés. 'That's what the breeze bears. But Clara usually carries cologne in that classy little bag of hers.'

'Go ahead, use some,' said Clara, digging out the bottle. *Yes, it was a rat,* she thought. *Dragging itself down; now it's probably in the basement, and there are people down there, I heard them . . .*

The proctors were gathered together, not being able to leave the office of the dean –

                but everyone knew there was no one in the dean's office.

Only the twins went to the gallery to review their notes, looking for a place where there was some light.

'Nice cologne,' the chronicler said as he doused his hair. 'Genuine Arabian myrrh.'

The light came back on little by little. Juan put his notebook in his jacket pocket and pointed to the doors of the dean's office.

'There he goes,' he said. 'He's taking off.'

The proctors came out, and between them walked a short, dark individual – his hands behind his back, he was twiddling his thumbs – as if seeking protection between the proctors,

who made their way shouting, 'Excuse us, please!' in bombastic tones – with young Migueletti greeting the professor and the professor not greeting young Migueletti –

until the three of them reached the gallery and slammed the door behind them.

'That little sycophant must be in charge of the preliminaries for convening the committee,' said Juan. 'It won't be long now.'

'Waiting really is death,' said Stella, pulling some dust out of her mouth. 'I think I fell asleep. What a hard bench.'

'Poor thing,' said Andrés, caressing her. 'You really shouldn't have come.'

'Why not? If you were going, so was I.'

He looked at her smiling, without saying a word. The door creaked, and the proctors reappeared. They glanced furtively at Juan's group and began to fill in some receipts. To do this, they consulted different notebooks with oilcloth covers, along with the telephone book and a book with a blue binding and golden shield emblazoned on its cover. One of the employees who had taken down the pictures in the gallery came in to tell them something; the fatter proctor made a gesture saying that he knew nothing, suggesting, with a round flutter of his hand, all the students.

'Here comes the prof again,' said the chronicler. 'What a curious way he has of slithering along – this . . .

what did you call him, Juan? Right, this little sycophant. But the guy's green.'

'He's Nile green,' said Clara. 'He's seen a ghost.'

The rat, she thought. *He ran into the rat!* They watched him pass by the group of students (some were playing cards in a corner, using a portfolio as a table) and enter the dean's rooms. It was dark inside, and the professor retreated, shouting to the proctors to turn on the lights. The fatter one didn't even look up, but the other went to the door gesturing angrily. He went in, followed by the professor.

'Nothing doing, his voltage isn't working,' said Juan. He took off his jacket, slipping it between two bars on the staircase, and rolled up his sleeves. Other students imitated him; and the chronicler pointed out to the redhead that she would be much more comfortable if she took off her blouse, warning her, should she decide not to, about the dangers of spontaneous combustion. Then he spoke to her about psychic hybrids, immediately arousing her interest. No one saw the professor leave the dean's rooms, but suddenly he was standing next to the proctors' table, escorted by the less fat proctor, who was carrying piles of rolls of paperboard. He'd put them in a wastebasket made of woven wire so they wouldn't fall.

'It looks like a bouquet of calla lilies,' said Andrés to Clara. 'Just look at that brilliant simplification of forms. Observe how bureaucracy imitates art.'

'Extremely successful – great intonation, and very elegant plastic play,' said Clara looking at Andrés with

yes, it was gratitude, a desire to extend affection to him
to be near him – but so far away in her fatigue, her eyes
drooping, overwhelmed.

'Don't use that vocabulary,' Juan said. 'Unless you're speaking for *The Voice of the Proctor*, which is what they should call the magazine of this University. So what's going on?' he shouted standing on top of the bench.

The proctors (enraged) took note of Juan, but the professor went on giving instructions in a low voice, staring fearfully toward the gallery, where the light had just definitively gone out. One of the twins was sitting on the floor not looking well at the chronicler's feet, and the other asked Clara for her cologne. *This one's going to faint*, thought the chronicler. *Unless she starts vomiting.* In a low voice, he said something to Andrés, who began to push the nearest students, who in turn started pushing the ones on the periphery –

if in fact it was possible to talk about a periphery in this mass, where the surface of the table stood out like a pit, a blemish in the general configuration of . . .

they pushed so the ill student could get a bit more air.

'No, she isn't going to vomit,' said Andrés to the chronicler. 'That bothers you a lot?'

'Man, one thing I can't stand is when people vomit.'

'I suppose,' said Andrés, 'that's because it's a reversion. Vomit is associated with Satan's sin, or the Battle of the Titans. The mythology of rebellion is vomiting on a cosmic scale. When we vomit what we've eaten, we're carrying out an organic act that obscurely coincides with our most secret human ambition – which is to tell nature to go to hell and take her T-bone steak and salad with her.'

'You're really something,' said the chronicler.

'I'm going to let you in on a big secret,' said Andrés. 'The sin wasn't that Eve ate the apple; the sin was that she vomited it.'

'Get down off that bench!' the fatter proctor shouted to Juan.

'I don't feel like it,' said Juan. 'Andrés, get a load of these characters.'

'And you listen to what's going on in the street,' said the chronicler, raising his voice because all the students were excited and moving around, swarming all over; and it was hard to hear in the cottony air

although what the chronicler was referring to was
an ambulance or fire-truck siren, followed by strident
whistles from the dock area.

'This is bad,' said Juan. 'The huns are at the gate, and, of course, the lights have to go out. Blackout!'

No one moved, but in the darkness, the heat was thicker, and everyone noticed, pointing out that whatever was floating in the air smelled more intensely. The twin on the floor whimpered weakly. In the shadow, her head weighed enormously on Clara's hand, as Clara knelt beside her, holding out a handkerchief doused with cologne. The rumors spread in shouts – half jokingly, but louder and louder. A slap, a groan –

you son of a bitch, asshole.

Hey, I didn't step on your foot, it was someone else. A match laughter filled with tickling of the redhead as the chronicler slipped his hand in her blouse and kissed the back of her neck, hugging her close and feeling the breath of hot scent in her hair, her skin . . .

Matches.

The pilgrims of Emmaus.

'Dracula! Stop screwing around, there are ladies present.'

The twin on the floor was crying. Andrés was afraid that she'd be trampled in the confusion so he stood in front of her with his arms stretched forward. Juan's laughter came from above, and when someone lit a match, he could be seen halfway up the staircase, his hair a mess and his shirt wide open. The lights in the dean's office suddenly came on; in the distance someone was knocking at a door, three, four times. The light reflected weakly on the nearest group, allowing a glimpse of the proctors' table, and the rolls of paperboard in the wastebasket. The telephone in the dean's office rang, and the fatter proctor made his way through shouts and curses. When the ringing stopped, there was a huge silence; but it was broken simultaneously by the crying of the twin on the floor, and a burst of laughter from Juan on the stairs. The proctor's voice was faint but audible:

Yes, sir.

>Hello. Yes, sir.
>No, sir.
>I think so.
>Sir, it seems to me . . .
>Hello?
>It's a supposition sir.
>Then,
>whatever you say, sir.
>Yes, sir.

'*The Voice of the Proctor!*' shouted Juan imitating a bird. An orange ray of light appeared somewhere from high above — it grew, and then stopped, oscillating.

The light.

'I feel better,' said the twin. 'The cologne was good for me, thank-you.'

The light

>*Right away, sir.*

the light in the fog   (it wasn't smoke) the vapor surrounds the
   bodies, but thick.   'It is smoke,' said the chronicler, staring at the redhead, who was straightening herself up and laughing. 'The ceiling is full of smoke.'

The card players dealt out another hand — three slaps in succession and the challenging shouts of one of them were heard and the purring of a contented cat which came from the twin on the floor now getting up, leaning on her sister and on Clara. No one expected the proctor to return from the office so quickly
   not even the other proctor, who was looking at the lights and scratching his head.

'The human sea,' Juan was saying from the balustrade. 'Andrés, the hair on your occiput is thin. Chronicler, you've got dandruff. But Clara, oh how beautiful you look, how I idolize you.'

'Enough,' said Clara. 'Come down here and be still.'

'I incuadore you!' shouted Juan at the top of his lungs. 'I pyramate you! I florimund you, I reconsider you!'

'Incredible,' said one of the twins. 'It's 9:30. Coca, go call Mom.'

'Where? With the policeman at the door and then the street, I . . .'

'Okay, I'll go.'

'No. We'll go together.'

With dialogue like that, people write notable books, thought the chronicler, looking at Juan, who was coming down but stopping on each step to study the scene, with the air of someone who pretends that he's not being seen. And the proctor who'd returned was whispering things nervously into the ear of the other. Few people were distressed when a thin girl with large squirrel eyes suddenly fainted next to the table, her hand hitting the lists and dragging them down as she fell. To get over there – that two feet of rage and sweat – was a useless task; Clara sat down on the bench next to Andrés, who seemed asleep.

'We're all sleepy,' said Clara. 'That is . . .'

'And the smoke. Look at the floor, that piece of floor under the table,' said Stella.

'I can't see it. It's impossible to see it.'

Stella smiled, happy. Chance had opened a space for her between trousers and skirts. She could clearly see that area of floor under the table. Really, she saw it quite well.

'Look, they're carrying her to the dean's office,' Juan informed them. 'Not a good idea. In a place like that, she might pass from a faint to a heart attack. Well, Clarita, I think this thing is coming to an end. Take a good look –'

and he pointed to the table with a trembling finger that several people followed with their eyes, even Andrés, who was opening them, waking from his vertiginous stroll. *Nearness*, he thought, *so longed for*. He looked at Clara's profile, her slim shoulder. *Now the necessity to invent distance, how nauseating . . .*

'This is incredible!'

'They're insulting us.'

It all follows, thought Andrés, almost surprised. *That hand was in mine, with a gesture that's been repeated since . . .*

'They're crazy, this is a mess!'
'What's it to you? Join in,
there's room for everybody!'

... that tub of pure water. It's odd that in reverse of triumph is the beauty we love. This is so beautiful. To die this way – all finished. To seek death because you have nothing seems so strange ... That dead man had something. At least he collapsed in action, without desiring it ...

The chronicler was laughing so hard. Andrés looked at him, and even Juan stopped pointing at the table to observe him. *He's crazy*, he thought. *He lives in the morning.* And the chronicler was laughing at all the chaos around the table, and the redhead with her arms stretched out, waving her hands to grab one of the rolls distributed by the proctors.

'Get out of my way, this can't be!'

The student Migueletti already had his; now the redhead got her roll and started unrolling it, holding it up high.

It's better to be here, thought Andrés. *Who knows how we'll finish off the night. Going back means taking refuge in our holes, you know. Although maybe new spaces await us out there ...* The explosion of Juan's laughter made him stop. New spaces. Here was a new space, a new time: 9:30.

(Didn't one of the twins say it?

but the poor things weren't around anymore they'd be left without diplomas.)

'Take a good look, a good look,' Juan was crying with laughter on the stairs. 'Chronicler, chronicler, you've got to write about this! This is finally perfection, the Seventh day!'

But the chronicler was holding the redhead's roll and suggesting dinner at *The Hunter's Horn*.

Clara stared at the proctor,

because there were spaces now, the students were leaving,

but when the proctor handed her her roll, she had turned around and found herself face-to-face with Juan. He was looking right at her

having jumped down to the floor,

and at Andrés, who smiled at him, thinking *Poor kids, they're taking it rather badly*; because Clara's eyes were filled with tears, she was crying now, her eyes wide open, and staring at Juan, at Andrés, at the foot of the stairs; her back was to the proctor handing her her diploma

    the space for the student's name blank below

    so pretty, in India ink;

        and the emphatic seals:

with the air of a final chord of the symphony contained in all good diplomas.

    UNIVERSITY OF BUENOS AIRES
  IN REGARD:

    And now pay ten pesos to a teacher who has good English penmanship.

IN REGARD: *(I'll grab one,* thought the chronicler, doubling over with laughter. *I'll hang it in the office, I'll bring it to the paper . . .)*

Juan hugged Clara close. Over his wife's shoulder, he looked at the proctors as they finished their task, hurrying because the lights were dimming again. A delicate creaking was heard, a breakable substance separating bit by bit from another substance. One of the lower sheets of veneer on the table was coming unstuck; genuine cedar veneer protection against . . . This humidity was greater than that foreseen when . . . An extremely fine creak, like a dialogue of dry, agile insects arguing in some point in space. Juan couldn't see clearly (and it irritated him not to see, he ran the back of his hand over his eyes like a little boy); but he could hear very well a diminutive debate in the coming apart of the table.

They accepted (and Clara went on crying) when Andrés walked between them, hooking his arms into theirs taking them, along with Stella behind, asking why not wait their turn. The chronicler praised the redhead's hairdo and how fresh she was: a real rose at this late hour of the sunset. The furniture they could see in the dark: a clothes rack, an umbrella holder, and a portrait of

San Martín. The policeman at the entrance (now the policeman at the exit)
— relativity of things —
he didn't keep them from exiting, to the contrary. But he was astonished and stared at their hands, their pockets, really, quite astonished to see them leave that way with empty hands.

7

> *Know whattsa matter,*
> *ya pie-faced dork?*
> *Yer mout's fulla chatter*
> *yer nose is too short!*

IT WAS A FRECKLED KID SHOUTING, IRRITATED. The other kid was farther off, near the *Letras* bookstore. Then he in turn shouted something unintelligible.

Ya pie faced dork!

Halfway down the flight of stairs, Andrés looked toward the river. It was strange that the houses blocked all sight of it. He confusedly remembered an image where there were no obstacles between the city, as it inclined downward, and the shore. As they silently walked down toward the water, the fog was drowning out the street light at Viamonte and Reconquista. They were certain that it made no sense to stay there, but there was no reason for them to leave. From the center of town there descended an even thicker fog, mixed with something that smelled like scorched clothes. Stella screamed when they walked by the street light because a *cascarudo* landed on her neck, scratching her with its sharp little feet. Juan pulled it off and studied it, while the insect stupidly rowed the air. Then he let it go with a soft toss of his hand. No one was speaking, but Andrés (not wanting to look at her) heard Clara's muffled crying as she struggled to contain herself.

'Look,' said Juan, pointing to a little sign for streetcars hanging under the cable. It wasn't easy to read it: Andrés shaded his eyes.

MOVE FORWARD AND CONTINUE THE DESCENT OF
THE HILL SLOWLY

'You can't tell,' said Juan, 'if it's a warning or an encouragement.'

'Not bad,' said Andrés. 'But I'm hungry.'

'Me, too,' said Clara, blowing her nose like a little girl. 'I'd eat the chronicler, I'd eat Andrés . . .'

'A praying mantis,' said Juan. 'How about that bar called *Suizo?*'

'No. I aspire to eat in those elegant places where there's a napkin for each one of us, as César Bruto says.' She grabbed Andrés' arm, and he let her lean on him as they stood on the corner. 'Actually, I'm thirsty. Inside the University . . . But you understand that everything . . .'

'No,' said Andrés, 'I don't understand it. I merely witnessed it. Poor kids, you didn't deserve that.'

'Who knows?' said Juan, pushing them so they would
MOVE FORWARD AND CONTINUE THE DESCENT OF
THE HILL SLOWLY.

'Right, who knows?' said the chronicler, sighing. 'And with this heat;

listen to the thunder over in the south   if it is thunder.'

'They'll analyze it in your laboratory,' said Juan. 'But really, I'm not sure I didn't deserve it. We were late for the wedding, and the cake was rotten.'

'I knew the entire curriculum,' murmured Clara childishly.

'It has nothing to do with that, old girl. You understand perfectly well that it has nothing to do with knowing anything. Look, let's all go to the *First and Last* and drink until the day is done, as a poet I know would put it. But, Andrés, look at that.'

Out of the bar on the corner he came

with his old habit of raising his collar (against what? the fog?)

– there were still distant explosions –

burdened, as if he were filthy   and rapid lights; cars
                                                            on Leandro Alem.

'The professor,' whispered Andrés. 'What the hell was he doing in that café, when you all . . . Better he doesn't see us.'

THE HILL.

'No way out,' said Juan. 'Good evening, professor.'

'Good evening, young man,' said the professor, who then

extended the greeting to Clara, with a slow nod of his head. When he smiled, he raised half his mouth, the rest remaining like papier-mâché. They saw his face was covered with perspiration, that he was drying the palms of his hands on his trousers.

'What a night,' he said, peering attentively at Andrés and then at the chronicler. 'There are these things in the air that you swallow and ...'

'Dust balls,' said the chronicler. 'And some little mushrooms that fly around, which we've studied at my newspaper.'

'Mushrooms?'

'Yes, the eutrapelic tri-martins,' said the chronicler.

'Ah. The government communiques ...'

'Look,' said Andrés, and he pointed to the eastern sky where reddish bands were trembling like reflectors in the clouds. 'I don't think that was in the government communiques.'

'It's that ...' The professor was going to say something more but held back, and it seemed he bent over, became smaller. *His courses on the Hittites*, thought Clara, staring at him in hatred. *His eight-page bibliographies. The big coward* ... Then the professor took Juan's arm, and came closer, demanding attention.

'I spent the whole afternoon over there.' He pointed at the *Suizo*. 'I was supposed to meet the dean and ... at seven, and ... from my table over there, see it?

you can keep an eye on the front of the University – I mean if you lean your body over a bit; and I can tell all of you

because it is rigorously ...   *Idiotic*, thought Andrés,
true

that the dean's car never appeared any time during the evening. And when night came, and that fog ...'

(he moved his hand like a spatula in the air, stirring up the yellow substance)

'then I became so frightened of ... You who are young should understand that ...'

Juan softly pushed him away. The professor wanted to go on talking, making signs they should listen to him; but Juan took

Clara by the arm and they walked down the hill. Andrés stayed behind, with a word to the chronicler to let Juan and Clara go on ahead a bit, and told Stella to follow them.

'Leave them alone a minute. They're so desperate.'

'You're right,' said the chronicler. 'Man, this . . .'

The professor followed them, muttering, twisting his hands. The chronicler turned around and looked at him: 'Go to your doctor and get a checkup,' he said politely.

'I . . .' said the professor; but he stopped, and the fog ate him up like an acid.

Andrés and the chronicler enthusiastically embraced the idea of a cigarette, stopping to light up opposite an apartment house with a small garden in front that smelled of grass and recently trodden clover. They couldn't believe it, so they went into the garden walking on the moist flagstones. The chronicler tore off a leaf and put it in his mouth. He smoked and chewed the leaf. When they left, Juan was waving from the corner.

'He looks like a ghost,' said the chronicler. 'This fog deforms images. That's the first time that . . .'

Andrés swatted him to hit away a flying insect hanging on his hair. They looked toward Reconquista, but the professor was gone.

'He's probably at his table in the *Suizo*,' said the chronicler, 'where you can keep an eye on the front of the University. And the dean's car, look . . .'

'Let's drop it,' said Andrés. 'At least we got close to that clover, and saw Juan's shadow. Don't go back to what we've already vomited up.'

'Juan's calling us.'

'Let's go, they must have calmed down a little. Hear that piano?'

'From a high floor,' murmured the chronicler, sniffing the air. 'How great that someone still . . . A little tango! "The Butterfly," of all things.'

They caught up to Stella, who was waiting for them silently and sleepily.

It's not that I'm sorry
for having loved you so, sang the chronicler. 'The tango, Andrés. Not official communiques. I feel like writing a history from 1900 until today using only tangos.'

'It would be amusing,' said Andrés, who wasn't listening to him.
If you went away for your own good
for your own good
I'll have to forgive you . . .   The Soria Pharmacy.

'The decision was taken in our corporate state to migrate to the *First and Last*,' said Juan, leaning against the window, where Clara was staring at perfumes and talcum powder. 'No dinner; just drinks and prosciutto.'

'And later on . . . ,' said Stella, excitedly.   (*Later on we go home.*)

'Later on nothing,' Andrés interrupted her. 'Forget that word for a while, and look at the firemen, what tough guys.'

They heard the sirens, the rest was a rolling and a confused color. Near the river, the heat was even more humid, and it was drizzling softly.

'Explain to me how there can be rain and fog at the same time,' said Juan. 'Does the water pass through the fog? Or do they happen in different spaces?'

'He's trying to show off,' said Clara crossing the street. 'Don't explain anything to him. It's better . . .' She fell silent, staring from the door into the interior of the corner café. Andrés, who was behind her, saw them almost at the same time. The younger man, who had been near them in the vestibule of the University; the other was one of the card players and had argued quite a bit with the proctors. They were seated at a table in the center of the main room with their diplomas unfolded;

they looked up at them,

the bottle of grappa was between the diplomas and the french fries

(a good fan swirled the air around,
 ruffling their hair;   Satisfactory.).

Juan stood at the door and cupped his hand in the shape of a megaphone.

'Assholes!'

Andrés and the chronicler grabbed him by the arm and pulled him away,

Move forward and continue the descent

while Stella laughed, shocked, and Clara went on ahead, cold and silent, as if she were indifferent. The students didn't bother to come to the door.

'It's hard to believe you did that, boy,' complained the chronicler. 'Don't you think we've had enough trouble – and then on top of everything you have to curse those guys out in a place like that? You think I came along just so I could get the shit kicked out of me?'

'*Va bene*,' said Juan. 'You're right. There's a proper time and place for everything. To see punches, you can pay fifteen pesos ring side. And have a great time watching other guys slug it out.'

'Give me a break,' the chronicler complained, expecting some help from Clara and Andrés, but no one spoke. They came into the area of the local street market and suddenly ran into some men running from the direction of Córdoba. Whistling (from Córdoba or maybe further up), and one of the men, coming along on the outside of the market, along the edge of the street. He crossed Viamonte like a whip, and as he passed alongside, Clara panted out something like 'Get out of here while you can,' or perhaps 'Get out, it bites.' Stumbling, he hesitated, leaning on one foot, then took off; and behind him other shapes came running as if herded by the police whistles. The chronicler ordered everyone to get up against the wall of the market until they could see better; they gathered together in the shadow watching the men run for their lives – there was no light in the street, and the corner café and the cigarette kiosk were closed.

'Some demonstration,' said the chronicler. 'They're giving them a beating.'

'I don't think so,' said Clara. 'At this distance they wouldn't have to be running that quickly. They're afraid, but not of the cossacks.'

'Look at those men in the market, they're carrying someone who's hurt,' said Andrés.

'He's really hurt,' said the chronicler, who'd seen the arms of the wounded man dangling among the legs of the men carrying him. They moved along in silence and very slowly, protected by the market. Then, following the order of a tall man wearing a gray jacket and a beret, they stopped right next to the group. *Nice present*, thought the chronicler when they deposited the wounded man practically at their feet, amid distrustful mutterings and whispered arguments about if

it'd be better if we went to Plaza Mayo and scattered. So young . . . Stop it, you didn't know it burned

Ma, what's gonna burn, *paviola*?

I'm telling you . . .

'Use my jacket as a pillow for him,' said a blond boy, who was trembling from – perhaps – excitement. 'It looks to me

that . . .' He looked suspiciously at Andrés then at Clara. The wounded man was taking big gasping breaths of air, and his moist lips were covered with dust balls and spittle. He was leaning against the wall, and someone put the folded jacket under the nape of his neck. Then he screamed: a dry, short scream, almost a bark; and raising a hand, he squeezed his stomach. In the darkness, it wasn't possible to see much, but Andrés noticed that the man's legs disappeared for moments at a time in the yellow vapor hovering over the ground. Only his head, his black curls, stood out from the fog.

'What happened?' the chronicler asked the man next to him.

'Whad'ya think happened? We were on our way to Retiro Park, and . . .'

'*Siamo fregati*,' said another, pushing him. '*Andiamo via súbito, Enzo*.'

'*Ma sí*, wait a minute. Anyway, now . . .'

But Andrés had already seen the furtive retreat, how one by one they melted into the fog. He tried to convince the man next to him to go on explaining, but suddenly he didn't see him anymore, he'd turned toward one of the columns in the market, and the darkness swallowed him up. Only the wounded man and the blond boy who'd taken off his jacket were left. Others passed down the middle of the street in groups, or alone, running around the few cars coming down from Retiro;

and the chronicler noted that no cars were going in the opposite direction. 'Pale grumbling,' the words came to him mechanically. 'Pale grumbling. Pale.' He repeated – 'Pale, pale' – until he drained all meaning from the word, until it was stripped of everything accessory and he discovered its sound, its form – 'pale' – its sonorousness, its nothingness – 'pale' – the hole where that other resided really without color, the opposite of a ruddy glow, opposite of something else that in turn . . .

'He's dying.'

Andrés' voice. Bark, complaint. The guy with the beret disappeared into the market. Soria Pharmacy. Clara?

Trucks.

'Carlitos, Carlitos!' the blond boy was saying, kneeling down, looking at the pasty gray face of the wounded man. 'Carlitos!'

Andrés and Juan brought Clara to the edge of the sidewalk, and Stella came back from the corner where she'd gone in order not to see and took hold of Andrés' arm.

'You all stay here or go on down,' said Andrés. 'I'm going over to that restaurant to call an ambulance.'

'I'll go with you and bring back some water,' said the chronicler. 'Pale grumbling.'

'Hurry up,' said Juan. 'The other guy's leaving him alone.'

When they crossed the street, the blond boy ran up Viamonte. Clara covered her face, screaming something no one understood and went back to the man on the ground even though Juan tried to stop her. Stella was holding her by an arm, and found herself dragged to the shadow with both Clara and Juan – all of them together now with the man flat on his back and silent.

'But don't you see he took his jacket back!' Clara was screaming. 'He took . . .!'

'Wait,' said Juan, stopping her. 'Let me.'

She was groaning, hesitant, and then kneeled down so her face would be at the same level of the wounded man's. With a shriek, she stood up and reeled back. Stella fled without understanding, looking for the area on the corner with more light. Juan clapped his hands hard on Clara's back, shaking her shoulders, and bent down in turn in the darkness. The chronicler came running over with a glass of water.

'The telephones don't work,' he said. 'Here, give him . . .'

'He's dead,' said Juan. 'I'd advise you not to look at him. Give the water to Clara. That's right, to Clara.'

'Okay,' said the chronicler. 'Drink this, Clara.' And he added the magic words: 'This will do you good.'

Arm in arm with the women, they reached Andrés on the sidewalk outside the restaurant and crossed Leandro Alem seeing only two cars and a few people on the traffic islands. Andrés told them that the restaurant wasn't open and that people had wanted to loot it at nightfall. The owner, a tough guy with a Colt revolver in his hand, was holding the fort, sipping *barbera* and eating pork sausages. A terrific guy. But the telephone was dead.

'Now what am I going to do with this glass?' said the chronicler when Clara handed it back to him. A few drops remained, which he drank slowly, peering through the bottom at a low, reddish sky. He saw a plane over in the district of the Post Office flying heavily into the distance.

'Who'd want to leave like that?' muttered Juan. 'Planes are robbery, always. Lean on me, come on. That's it.' Clara yielded, walking as if she were asleep, and Andrés came from the other direction to help him hold her up, signaling to the chronicler to take care of Stella, who was furtively looking back, deathly afraid.

'I really don't understand,' said Stella. The chronicler shrugged his shoulders, and when they started walking on the narrow sidewalk made of boards, alongside the fence around the construction site to their left, he delicately placed the glass on the ground, up against the planks.

With all that whiskey, all that grappa, all that *caña*; the *First and Last*, a little shed a nose in the wind, washed up from the river, filthy from nothing, from nothing's having happened; filthy from empty . . . from liquor falling into other people's mouths.

The first and Last: everything that happens here happens to others:

regulars (but here they say *customers*)

so a little shed for no reason, a bar for men from the river, where they don't even leave their thirst, they just use the river as you see and then they take off.

'The morality of taverns,' said Andrés stretching his legs. 'Their emptiness is my plenitude, and vice versa.'

'As obscure as the south wind,' said the chronicler, 'which also definitely applies to roulette, movies, to various and sundry objects.'

'To us,' said Juan, drying his face, 'who suck the lives of others to replenish our own. Am I speaking with you? No, I'm not speaking with you. I take speech from you and keep it for myself. I take away that smile, that look.'

'He took away the jacket,' said Clara, sighing. 'Excuse me, I'm very tired. No one should . . . '

Take away, thought Andrés. Again, he was seeing *El Ateneo*, the pair of eyeglasses swinging in the hand of the salesman. *That's right, it's less than what you might want to lose. That's for sure.* He smiled, mocking himself. Sentimental.

'And as long as we're talking about taking away or taking off jackets,' the chronicler was saying, bringing over a chair on which he could hang his own. Andrés and Juan followed suit, with that relief that any change in clothing brings. Because, as Juan said, clothing forms part of our psyche and feels things on its own, so the sooner you hang it up, the better. They were served bottles of beer

                    'it isn't too cold because . . .'
                      (something about the electricity)
and thick sandwiches of salami and prosciutto. They'd taken a table on the right, against the wall, almost all by themselves, as if the half-light had scared away the customers. A boy with mestizo features watched them from the counter, occasionally turning his head to check the time on an old wall clock between the price list and an air conditioner (which wasn't working).

'I came here,' said the chronicler, 'with a girl the night Roosevelt died. Since she was crying a lot, I had her drown her sorrow in Catamarca grappa. I think that made her resent me a bit.'

'We've come here so many times,' said Clara. 'It's so far from downtown and really only a short walk. That's why we liked it. Andrés, remember the night of the strike?'

'Poor Juan,' said Andrés. 'What a punch he took.'

'Look who's talking! It cost you a new suit. Drink up, Stella, please. I don't want any of you to be depressed any more.'

'I'm looking at that man,' said Stella, timidly pointing to a customer sitting at a center table, under one of the ceiling fans (which didn't work), sweating. He looked identical to ex-President Agustín P. Justo, but with an inflamed eye, bright red, and a stogey, in his mouth. Another four stogies, like a picket fence, peeked out of his jacket pocket which should have held (and didn't) a handkerchief.

'The complete outfit,' said Juan. 'Look at his ring: Ford Trimotor model. Glasses and short hair, black tie. Perfect. Now he's going to get up and try to sell us some fabric.'

'But he's drinking coffee,' said the chronicler. 'It's scandalous, because what he should be drinking is orangeade. Waiter!'

'Yes sir,' said the waiter glancing over at the door through which three men entered on the run. One of the men turned around and looked out at the street, the others fumbled their way confusedly around, until they chose a table in a corner. The first one waved his hand and sat with them: his face was covered with soot, his hair matted down on his temples sweat brilliantine.

'More sandwiches,' said the chronicler. 'Unless you all want to leave. Drink something Clara, you're whiter than Grock in the funny papers.'

'What I am is an idiot,' said Clara. '*Animula vagula blandula*. But it was so . . .'

'Enough, Clara,' said Juan, smiling. 'All this is slightly foul, and you behaved very well. If you don't loosen up from time to time . . . Look at that girl with the yellow blouse, she's scared out of her wits. Hey, the guy's threatening her.'

'Of course,' said Andrés. 'Hysteria's a Hellenic word. Wouldn't it be better if you were to get Clara out of here? I mean, out of Buenos Aires.'

'Killjoy,' said Juan, bitterly. 'What for? This can't last more than . . .' He made a puerile gesture and sat back to look at the stogey smoker. A good cry alone. A good cry under the sheets. A shower, a . . . He looked at the man in the small booth next to them, his knee seeking out the woman's knee. She in turn was laughing like a rat. *He's afraid too*, thought Juan, exploring Andrés' eyes and seeing something that surprised him. Then, absurdly, he thought he would have liked to have his cauliflower. They didn't speak for a while, but hearing the distant explosions was almost worse. And the halo of mist around the lights, the stalled air conditioner, the price list next to the portrait of the president: Old Smuggler, Ombú *caña*, Amaro

Pagliotti.

'It's incredible,' the chronicler said suddenly. 'Are you looking at the guy with the cigar? It's as if nothing's happening. I should write a piece about him.'

'Write it,' said Juan. 'You'll have fun. *Contrasting with the general tumult occasioned by perturbing elements . . .*

– that should be your style –

we are pleased to provide our readers with the profile of the sensible man, who at his table in the First and Last . . .'

'Shit,' said the chronicler. 'If my articles were like that, I'd already be famous.'

'Stick to it,' said Juan. 'Remember Bernard Palissy.'

Stella stirred when she heard the name but said nothing:

Children's Encyclopedia

perhaps expecting Juan to go on. But Juan was looking at Clara, who was diligently eating her sandwich. He began to imitate her, putting his head next to hers and chewing in time with her, making Andrés, who was watching them, smile.

'You probably know best,' said Andrés, as if the matter were of no importance. 'But the two of you should get out of here.'

'Why us specifically?' asked Clara. 'What do we gain by leaving? Tell him your cute ontological cachet, Juan: To go, to stay . . .'

'Listen,' said Juan. *To go, to stay,*
is the being's game.
Barely is it
after and it's before.

'I wasn't talking about ontology, I was talking about leaving this joint,' muttered Andrés. 'Don't pull those Elizabethan tricks on me.'

'This joint,' Juan repeated. 'But my dear boy, they're the same thing.'

Nevertheless, we were prepared, we knew the themes . . . Juan brewed on it, bending his head forward, concentrating on the vision of the bread and the little tongues of prosciutto hanging between his fingers. *That horrible face . . . He pulled the jacket away from him the same way he put it under him for support.* He tried to swallow his sandwich, made a movement to pick up his glass. Maybe drinking it down with beer . . . But the taste would be horrible; curious that if it was first beer and then sandwich, everything went fine. But like burning your mouth with a spoonful of stew and drinking wine to cool it, the mixture in his mouth was something disgusting that . . .

Juan tossed Clara's hair back, blowing on her forehead. He smiled at her.

'Better better old bed wetter,' he chanted. 'Better better with a change in the weather.'

Clara dropped her sandwich onto the plate and put her face on Juan's chest. He put his arm around her, blocking the immediate setting from her view.

'Come get a breath of air with me,' said Andrés to the chronicler. 'Stella, you stay here.'

Outside there was still some light, which seemed to fall from high above. The port was disappearing in the fog, from which emerged people crossing toward the market or gathering on the corner. One group was speaking in low voices. One man, on the side that led by way of Bouchard to the plaza, was parsimoniously lighting a cigarette. The chronicler looked at him a while, without paying attention. A gummy film of humidity stuck to their faces and hands. They felt dirty.

'Look,' said Andrés. 'We've got to get these two out of here somehow.'

A moth

'Okay,' said the chronicler. 'But how?'

'How, how . . . Hey, Look at that bug.' searched for

'Yeah.' the entrance

to the bar.

'The poor thing is smashing itself against the wall, and the door is right in front of its nose. Incredible how moths are always at the service of practical philosophy.'

'My sympathies are totally on the side of the moth,' said the chronicler.

'The two of them are stubborn as mules,' said Andrés. 'Even I can't figure out why it's so hard to convince them.'

'Of course.'

'After all is said and done, you and I are going to stay. And Stella too. I mean, what's going to happen to us?'

'Nothing. Nothing ever happens here.'

'But it's different for them. I don't know, it just looks that way to me.'

'It is different for them,' said the chronicler, smashing a bug running over his shoe which burst with a happy, dry noise. Looking toward the end of the block there – on the ground, he'd left the glass against the fence – he saw a vague phosphorescence over the boards being used as a sidewalk (it was eaten up by the fog; but amid the yellow tatters, bluish lights were visible).

'Look at that evil light,' he said. 'Humidity, rot – but the by-product is always a beautiful blue.'

'The sky is the gut of the dead past,' said Juan's voice. He came to them, as they walked slowly. 'Beautiful things are being said this evening . . .'

Andrés was about to answer when they heard two whistles and a hoarse scream from the direction of downtown; in the distance along Viamonte, a reddish glow grew, coloring the fog and the air as far as they could see.

'Ca chauffe,' said the chronicler, and he whistled softly. The group speaking quietly on the corner dissolved in a quick escape – with half-finished phrases. Only a few remained. The man was calmly smoking on the corner of Bouchard, and a filthy black dog was barking at the air.

'Let me speak to him,' said Andrés to the chronicler. 'Come on, Juan, let's take a little walk.'

'Well now,' said Juan, glancing back at the chronicler, who was returning to the bar. 'Better he stay with the girls. Did you hear some shouts just now?'

'Look over there,' said Andrés. From the corner it was possible to see the glow getting more and more intense. 'The funny thing is that it doesn't look like fires.'

'It's the fog,' said Juan. 'It's really starting to be a pain in the ass. What explosions those . . .'

A truck loaded with people sped up to them from the port, made a sweeping turn in the parking lot on the other side of the bar in an attempt to orient itself, and then headed for the river. The headlights sliced the fog.

'That,' said Andrés, 'is exactly what you have to do now.'

'Not that again.'

'Of course that again. Get her out of here now, Juan; without thinking twice about it.'

'Nice conditions you set. *Don't think twice.* I guess that's about right.'

'Please,' said Andrés. 'If everything is always a matter of words . . .'

'Okay, sorry. I'm not questioning your motives. But it's absurd. It's easy to talk about my leaving with her. But first of all I don't see why . . .'

'If there's anything to see in all this it's that you should leave,' said Andrés. 'Don't make it a question of pride.'

'But you're going to stay,' said Juan, stopping.

'How do I know? I'm going to bring Stella over to her mother's place in Caseros. Don't think I'm going to stick around downtown.'

'Caseros,' said Juan. 'Personally, I don't think you can get to Caseros any more.'

Andrés shrugged his shoulders. It hadn't occurred to him to think about himself, about what he was going to do. He had put off deciding – it was something to do when he felt like it. Everything decided, but still free. He'd lied randomly. Juan was looking at him and waiting for a response. He had spurred him on with his friendly accusation.

'Maybe,' said Andrés. 'But I'm asking you to get out of here with her now. I'm asking you to do it.'

'Why?' asked Juan, with the petulance of a sick child.

'No reason, I'm afraid. Clara. You can see what condition she's in.'

'Well, after the kind of schedule we've been on.'

'You've got to get her out of here right away,' said Andrés.

Since Stella was hungry, they ordered another sandwich.

'Please eat it quickly, let's get going,' said Clara. 'Don't you thing that this place is blazing hot?'

'It's the zinc roof,' said the chronicler. 'But at this hour *Apollo's heat should be diminishing*. Hmm, this place is getting crowded. My god, what faces. I wouldn't be surprised if . . .'

(and at that moment he was surprised to find himself thinking about the back of that man he'd seen outside lighting a cigarette)

'. . . if that famous professor of yours walked in.'

'Unlikely,' said Clara. 'The stinker's probably sitting at his table in the *Suizo*.'

'Waiting for the dean's car, right?' said Stella, and the chronicler congratulated her enthusiastically, at the same time helping her to get rid of a gigantic moth that kept walking over her face. Some of those drifting in were in shirtsleeves, most of them sailors. One was already drunk and went to a table;

> *Sometimes I wonder why I spend*
> *the lonely nights*
> *dreaming of a song . . .*

'Great voice,' said the chronicler, who was on his fifth glass of beer. 'He really sings what he drinks. What were you saying, honey?'

A thin man, wearing a blue pajama top, came and leaned over him.

'Excuse me,' he said, looking all around. 'It would cost you a hundred pesos.'

'Really?' said the chronicler. 'That's pretty cheap.'

'It's easy now because it's dark,' said the man. 'The river's really low. It's way back from the shore.'

'Uh-huh.'

'The thing is to get to the canal. See, I know the way . . .'

(*Now he's going to say: like the back of my hand*, thought Clara.)

'. . . like the back of my hand. The thing is to get to the canal.'

'For a hundred pesos,' said the chronicler, who was beginning to understand.

'For four. Right now.'

'Hey, Calimano!' called a voice from the back of the bar. 'Come'ere!'

'I'm coming,' said Calimano. 'So what do you think?'

'What I want to know,' said the chronicler, 'is if you think I'm running away from the law.'

Calimano smiled and went on waiting even though the voice called him again.

'Okay, I'll be hanging around,' he said finally. 'You think about it and just whistle if you want me.'

'I'll whistle,' said the chronicler, opening another bottle. 'This beer is hot. Drink up, girls.'

'No, no more for me.' Clara saw that Calimano was watching them from his table in the rear, waiting.

('But I know that guy,' the chronicler said to himself. 'When he lit that cigarette – but of course . . .')

And at times he twisted around to talk with two men, who answered him between sips of

possibly, because of the shape of the bottle and the glasses, they're drinking white wine.

'Well, well,' said the chronicler, pouring more beer.' It *was* him. This is becoming as repetitive as the theme of Siegfried's horn. 'Hey Juan, you're back, listen a minute.'

'Drink your beer and leave me in peace,' said Juan returning to his seat not looking at Clara – who looked up and began observing Andrés' face, the tic that soon made him raise his right eyebrow. A wink in reverse, how strange. He had a layer of soot on his hair, on his forehead. Clara blew on it, and the soot landed on another table, next to a plate. A carbon moth. The night's filled with – A phrase from Bruckner's Ninth Symphony passed through her head. The word ocelot. El Dorado . . . A poem by Juan: with the words, 'a golden ocelot.'

'Recite the Marcopolo for me, Juan,' she asked. 'When I'm tired, I like the Marcopolo.'

'I don't want to. Besides, it would be better if we left.'

'Where would you go?' said Andrés. 'Didn't you see what was going on up the street?'

'Recite the Marcopolo,' Clara was saying, and Stella echoed her: 'Recite the Marcopolo.'

'This is blackmail,' muttered Juan, looking furiously at Andrés. 'First you, and then these two and the Marcopolo, and . . .'

'And one hundred pesos,' said the chronicler. 'That gentleman over there is named Calimano, and he's offering you a boat for one hundred pesos.'

'What's that?' shouted Andrés.

'Just what you heard. It's the first of two news items. The other is more in the order of repetition. Don't be in such a hurry, man. What nerves!'

But Andrés was crossing the bar (and he knocked over the chronicler's glass as he got up. Luckily it was empty, so the chronicler filled it instantly.).

(*I'd like to hear the Marcopolo.*)   'Come on, Juan, recite it.'

'Where's he going?'

'To talk to Calimano,' said the chronicler. 'Actually, for you and Clara it would be the best thing.'

'Right,' said Juan and he took out another cigarette.

'I . . ,' said Clara, looking at Andrés bent over the table in the back, his thin body framing the boards of the wall, above the fake burlesque curtain (but was it fake?) – and also the door of the lavatory, the painted hand pointing out its location, and the bluish mist of smoke, and the fog entering through the hole for the stalled air conditioner. An individual came in on the run and said something to the boy at the cash register. When he went out again, bumping into a chair, the bartender shouted 'Wait!' seeing him pass out the door, and with a leap

(*Golden ocelot, really!*)

vaulted over the counter and went after him, running on tiptoe.

'Now who's going to bring me another beer?' complained the chronicler. 'The waiter really should have no autonomy, considering that I think he took off through the back door. But are they going to abandon the place? There's going to be a riot when the *marinai* get stirred up.'

Juan smiled at him, calmer now. *The real end of a day*, he thought. *Every night we see people leave, we say good-by to them, we hang our clothes in the closet – All without thinking much about it, without gravity. Because anyway, tomorrow we start all over again. Any way. Now those two are not coming back. This bar won't be open for us tomorrow.*

'We want the Marcopolo,' said Stella. 'It must be so pretty.'

'Produce the Marcopolo,' said the chronicler. 'That way we break the monotony, which is the only thing left to break by now.'

'I can't remember it,' said Juan. 'It's a dumb poem, written for another time.'

'For that very reason,' said Clara, putting her face on his shoulder. 'For that very reason, Juan.'

'Okay, okay, I'll recite it,' murmured Juan. 'This is from a time when I liked words. Poetic caviar. Sit down, Andrés, join the audience. Taillefer once again crosses the fields of Hastings, and instead of battle he regales us with an aubade or an apricot madrigal.

See? Everything comes back. Words *dont je fus dupe* – Yes indeed, my dear, we deserve the Marcopolo, and it is thus that

Marco Polo Remembers:

Your minuscule country, inhospitable and violent!
There, dwarf trees hoist their annoyance
while the moles dig and dig their conveyance,
and bold shrews rise up to the firmament.

If I reached the border of your evasive land,
how many green customs offices, how many liquid seals!
My bags hold medals and shields
for your mint-eating customs man.

Your language – that of men who stare at clouds –
arose in the barge at the breath of night,

and the dagger of danger and the golden ocelot,
and waiting for you beyond the heights without repose.

Doors of obsidian warp with age
and you were in the time behind obsidian!
With my name — that greenish gong of ancient elegance —
I tossed the open parchment over the doors.

Thirteen nights of red ablutions — insects
with crystal feet, blinded music —
Oh, the heat under the sky, pools with moon,
and you more beautiful than ever, so delayed and distant!

Your servants decipher the route of my name,
I saw the doors half close for my solo step.
My footsteps were lost for months along roads:
the caravan returned with bronze rings.

I remember and remember the moonlit terrace,
the silk you gave me and the drum of your nights.
The caravan returned with bronze rings —
I had a galley with emerald sails!

'Notable,' said the chronicler. 'A poem in radiant technicolor.'

'Shut up,' said Clara. 'It's mine, I like it; and besides it's from other days. It's like an earring for me, a little remembrance ring.'

'It really sounds like another world,' said Juan. 'After all, Clara, so few years ...'

Kaleidoscope heart
just a little distance, and you've already changed!

'You were right,' said Andrés having returned, leaning toward the chronicler, who was staring fixedly at his glass. 'The guy repeated the offer to me.'

'But these folks don't want to leave.'

'Of course we don't want to,' said Juan, thinking strangely enough about the apartment, the vase in the house with the cauliflower alone, the cauliflower in the lonely apartment.

'You're so mistaken,' said the chronicler. 'For one, the guy who's been following you is outside there.'

'What?' said Juan, and he stood up   a grab by Andrés the chair fallen over, Clara.   One hand grabbing his jacket. Abel.

'Sit still,' said Andrés. 'I don't see that you'd accomplish much by running out into the street.'

'It's odd, but I just realized it a moment ago,' the chronicler was saying to Stella. 'It's the hot beer

– this disgusting stuff urinated by an orangutan in a linen suit, by a woman full of false hopes –

this beer circulating inside my face.'

'We can see that you're quite drunk,' said Andrés. 'But you did see him, right?'

'Cigarette,' said the chronicler. 'Bouchard.'

'Let me go out for a minute,' said Juan, very calmly. 'You have no idea how much I'd like to talk to Abelito.'

'The guy to talk to is Calimano,' said Andrés. 'Please Clara, at least you can understand . . .' Stella shrieked. The moth (or another moth) was clinging to her hair. A sailor in the back of the bar mimicked her shriek, and another imitated him. A woman who'd come in a moment before quickly turned around, looked at their table, had a hand up as if to protect herself.

'Poor example of lepidopteron,' the chronicler was saying. 'Here it is – look what a silky tummy he's got.'

'Horrible,' said Stella. 'It's as if it has letters on its wings.'

'Ads,' said the chronicler. 'Disgusting slogans. Look Juanacito, look at the trouble starting. Let's get out of here. This is getting a bit thick.'

Outside, someone threw a stone that landed on the zinc roof with a hollow crash. In back, someone shouted; then a high-pitched giggle when a half-drunk sailor,

So I dream in vain
but in my heart it always will remain,

with his arms loaded with bottles removed confusedly from the shelves behind the counter –

My stardust melody Whoopee!

and one bottle (grappa) smashed, opening into a white flower, filling the air with a sweet smell overpowering the tobacco smoke and fog.

The memory of love refrained . . .

Why go on with this, thought Andrés, releasing him. 'Go ahead, man. It's time every fox headed for his own hole.'

'Since you've decided to leave my jacket in peace,' said Juan, 'you probably won't object to my going out to see if Abelito's there.'

'There are choices and there are choices,' said Andrés in a tone of fatigue. 'Some are better than others. Your best choice has a name, and it's Calimano.'

'But we don't want to go,' said Clara, looking at him sweetly.

'To stay means Abel,' said Andrés. 'Look, guys, what sense does it make to stay? That rock on the roof wasn't for the chronicler, or for Stella, or for me. It was for you two.' There was such an uproar in the bar that he had to raise his voice. 'Man, this heat. Look at your hands, Clara. Touch your face. You'll need different air than this to dry your skin.'

'It isn't that I want to stay around,' said Clara. 'It's just I don't see why we have to go.'

'Let's all three of us go outside,' murmured Andrés. 'Maybe you'll see him.'

'Abelito?' said Juan getting up

'Maybe,' said Andrés. 'Stella, stay with the chronicler, he fell asleep.'

'Sure,' said the chronicler, who was dozing off. *My name is Ozymandias, king of kings.* 'I translated it . . . Well, a single column. In what size type . . . ?'

'Many columns, for Ozymandias,' said Juan. 'Go to sleep, chronicler, the genteel Stella will watch over your hangover.'

'I,' said the chronicler, 'am not sleeping.'

Andrés stepped back, letting Clara and Juan go first. He put his wallet in Stella's hands, but then took it back to get out some money.

'It's better if . . .'

Stella looked at him, squeezed the wallet and put it in her handbag.

'Go on, it's okay,' she said. 'I can take care of myself.'

'This may take a while,' said Andrés. 'But it's better I do it alone. If you're not comfortable here or if those guys bother you, let the chronicler sleep and . . .'

'Go on, it's okay,' said Stella.

'But if not, wait for me a while.' He brushed her cheek with the back of his hand, went to the door, turned around and whistled with two fingers in his mouth for Calimano. In the back there was a clatter of chairs – square dancing with broken bottles and no music. Calimano extricated himself and came slowly, taking decisive steps.

'Stay here,' said Andrés, putting a bank note in his hand. 'When I whistle again, come over and join us.'

'You're the boss,' said Calimano. 'In the meantime, I'll have a *pineral*, which is good when you don't want to sweat.'

Juan looked at the corner of Bouchard, but between the fog and the growing glow, it was difficult to recognize silhouettes or buildings. Suddenly they realized that it was cooler inside than it was on the street – there wasn't this reverberation, this vibration in the air; that smell of scorched rubber and moist grass *even on that street*   because for moments at a time you felt . . .

A few groups were passing without speaking, taking deep breaths. There were almost no individuals, but couples or groups of five or six coming down Viamonte toward the port. Without warning, one of them would detour to go into the *First and Last*. No sign of Abel.

'As Paul Gilson says,' whispered Juan,

'Abel et Cain

> *tout le monde a bel et bien*
> *disparu.'*

'Look,' murmured Clara, clinging to him. 'Look over there.'

Despite the fog   Flames?   (Or only a reflection in the atmosphere, of   but explanations were needed); and the boards at the construction site as if moving in the mist, were entirely blue, phosphorescent —

'Pretty,' said Juan. 'Look, now they're coming on the run.'

'Soon, there will be no one else,' said Andrés. 'The people over here are talking about the street collapsing on Leandro Alem, look at them.'

A boy, holding up a woman dressed in red, said something about:

'almost . . . swallowed her up' (the red back of the woman, like a flag being carried on someone's back) and burst water pipes, and gas.

'And the city seems thus, asleep,' recited Juan, 'a nocturnal meadow carpeted

by a million white daisies.

Written at the age of fourteen in a notebook with green covers. What do you think of that, Clarita?'

She was looking at the lower levels of the sky near the ground, where she could see everything taking place. *If at least there were a bird, a sea gull*, she thought. *And there is no moon tonight*. She saw that Andrés was meandering off, as if leaving them alone. On the corner of Bouchard, he lit a cigarette, the match showed his profile bent avidly over his joined hands.

'*Tout le monde a bel*,' said Juan. '*A bel et bien disparu*. How far the Marcopolo is from this, honey.'

'And the exam,' said Clara in a tiny voice. 'Look over there, that thing is growing.'

'It is, and on the Córdoba side, just look.'

'Like a music in search of its tone. Take note.'

'Like a glove that, finger by finger, finds its hand. How about that?'

They hugged each other tight, confused, almost like the night.

'I sweat,' said Juan. 'Therefore I am. I used to write poems.'

'I used to study and study,' said Clara, 'and I killed a man who smokes and smokes.'

'Andrés?' said Juan. 'Or Abel?'

'Abel's alive. Abel's out there somewhere.'

'I don't know,' said Juan. 'I think Abel's like the city, something that *a bel et bien disparu*. So, Andrés?'

'Yes,' said Clara. 'I killed him, but neither of us knew it.'

'Killing isn't a matter of knowing. Look over there, by the plaza.'

'Yes. The tree that grows over the little hill – an ombú.'

'You can't see it.'

'But the light rises from there. It was a small, jolly ombú. What do you want?'

'Nothing,' said the man who was about to crash into them. He turned, vaguely took a few steps toward the street, cut in the direction of the *First and Last*, ended up going past it. The collar of his jacket was turned up as if it were . . .

'Now it's closer,' said Juan, pointing toward Leandro Alem.

'You're right,' said Clara. 'I don't think it will be long before . . .'

'And there, where they're digging the foundation.'

'Right, there too.'

'Poor chronicler,' said Juan. 'How fast asleep he was.'

'The chronicler is a very good man.'

'Poor guy. And Andrés . . .'

'Poor Andrés,' said Clara. 'Poor little Andrés.'

Calimano heard the whistle, put his glass on the counter, and quickly walked out. Since Andrés was looking toward downtown, Calimano saw his face illuminated by a reddish glow. Behind him, near the corner, the shapes of Clara and Juan embracing looked a little like the trunk of a tree that's been pruned, something mutilated and downcast.

'Okay,' said Andrés. 'Get ready, 'cause we're going.' He walked toward the corner without hurrying, savoring a taste that had just been born in his mouth, some soot swallowed with the air. *A cinerary taste*, he thought. '*The dove on the ark.*' *Most beautiful words. The last sound on earth will be a word — probably a personal pronoun.*

'Let's be on our way,' he said, making his body into a soft wedge, taking them by the arms without their resistance.

'Let's go,' said Juan. 'What difference does it make?'

'Careful with that cable,' said Andrés. 'My teacher taught me that electricity is a pernicious fluid.'

'Where are we going?' asked Clara, and her arm began to hold back. 'First explain to me why . . .'

'We're simply going,' said Andrés. 'That's enough.'

'It's not enough for me. We were just doing fine in the bar and . . .'

'Walk honey,' said Juan. 'Don't play the part of the immovable object, because we don't have these options.'

Knowing how to be appropriately cruel, thought Andrés. *I'll die without having learned the technique.* He whistled to Calimano, who came over and began to walk ahead. Juan separated from Andrés and going around took Clara's other arm. With their backs toward downtown, the fog confronted them like a movie screen when the camera's started and there runs before the first words a pulverulent substance with rapid sparks, a crackling of space. The wide street was empty, as was the police kiosk in the customs area.

The empty lots were on the right, with train tracks stuck in the grass (but Calimano went on, without looking right or left).

'I remember the scorpion,' said Clara. 'As you see, I don't intend to make a scene. I understand you're both dragging me along, and it all seems idiotic,

and finally

I remember the scorpion.'

'Keep talking,' said Juan, leaning over to kiss her on the hair. 'Sometimes it does a lot of good. Remember the scorpion.'

'About that scorpion,' said Clara. 'Someone said things about the scorpion, about its destiny. About its destiny to be a scorpion, and how it was necessary for it to carry out its destiny of being a scorpion.'

'You're paraphrasing the destiny of Judas, and Satan's too,' said Juan. 'Stepping back, you can see that even God . . . But it's too hot to . . .'

'I'll stick to the scorpion,' said Clara. 'And I say: is it necessary, is it really necessary for the scorpion to know it's a scorpion?'

'Yes,' said Andrés. 'So that being a scorpion has some meaning.'

'But only for the scorpion,' said Juan.

'Well, that's what matters. The rest is pure contingency, or accident.'

'I ask,' said Clara, 'because I'm thinking about Abelito. I'm wondering if it's necessary for him to do what he's doing.'

'Don't bother yourself with Abelito,' said Juan. 'What Abelito likes is for people to think about him. That's how we all look for a way in.'

Which I haven't found, he thought with a sudden rebelliousness, a desire to stop, turn around, go back where he came from. Maneuvering, they crossed the first beach, slipping over the cobblestones on the walkway. Despite the fog, things could be seen with enough . . .

| (the brick buildings on the right, the first docks, the canal) | Blue hat but you could say that about the sky: blue hat of Buenos Aires. |

Calimano had stopped and was waiting for them.

'The river,' Calimano said, 'has gone all to shit.'

'Oh,' said Juan. 'So . . .'

'What we've got to do is look for it. Of course . . .'

'Let's get going,' Andrés cut him off. 'Move ahead.'

'Look, there's the little plaza where they sold chocolate,' said Juan. 'Remember?'

'Yes,' said Clara. 'The ugly little chocolate plaza.'

'The money you made me spend on sweets!'

'To make the little plaza beautiful, you horrid miser. Everyone knows it's so . . . so ugly.'

'It looks like an island emerging from the fog,' said Andrés. 'You know, I never ate chocolate in that plaza.'

'Well, you've missed something beautiful,' said Clara.

'Of course I missed it,' said Andrés, simultaneously cursing himself for being so sensitive. *Right on the edge of all this, and I'm still incapable of hardening myself. Everything that is Juan, every word Juan,*

as if it shouldn't be that way, as if the scorpion . . . They passed by along the edge of the little plaza.

'Grass so they walk, dice for their hand that plays . . .'

'We would count ships,' murmured Clara. 'I knew all the names.'

'Don't start crying on me,' said Juan, sullen.

'No, no. There's one of the benches . . .'

'One of the two,' said Juan. 'And the old decrepit trees.'

'From the bench, we could see the ships at that dock. I remember the *Duquesa*, the *Toba* . . . You knew more of them, but I remembered the names.'

'Watching ships is nice,' said Juan. 'We sailed on all of them.'

'Cheap but nice,' said Clara. 'It was easy to hate Buenos Aires afterwards, when it was there, as always . . .'

'Watch your step!' shouted Calimano. 'The cobblestones!'

'Come on, we'll make a detour,' said Andrés. 'Why don't they put a red light here?'

'No one's going to put one here,' said Juan, 'because no one would see it. We're talking about the plaza as if we were seeing it, and that isn't the case.'

'I see it,' murmured Clara.

'No dear. You remember it.'

(And a light on the swing bridge
or was it on the guard box? Bluish.)

Later, without speaking, they slowly crossed the second walkway that led to a promenade. Calimano went along testing the cobbles, alarmed by the first hole, suspicious even of his own eyes.

Let it come to an end, thought Andrés. He looked back from time to time, to where the fog had seemed less thick because of the sounds, the light in the sky, and the heat – like a front that pushed them. *I think that if I were on the University stairway right now, I'd be able to see the river* . . . Clara and Juan were stumbling along, saying nothing. Once or twice, Clara said, 'It sounds like Honegger,' but she didn't explain. And Juan was mumbling disconnected verses, inventing things, amusing himself in his small, portable hell. A low and rubbery smell, no longer humidity, came from the river – like rotten hay, an ammoniac breath mixed with mud. *Stick out your tongue*, thought Juan. *Come on Mister River, stick out your tongue.*

But if I am tongue
if this
my tongue.   Oh how filthy how I don't like
you river right now.   (And *tomorrow*?)
But if I live in bed if I . . .

'Watch your step,' said Calimano. 'I think the fishing club has to be right around here.'

'Imagine,' said Clara, feeling for Andrés' hand, 'now we're going to a club.'

'Life is a club,' said Juan. 'But a second-rate one. Tell me that wasn't good, Andrés . . .'

But Andrés, who'd pulled back his hand when he felt the nearness of Clara's, swerved to talk to Calimano. *I won't talk with either one of them*, he thought. *Not too far to go. If they take off for* . . . And he didn't know where.

'Now you can see the guard box,' shouted Calimano. 'Now, if they haven't stolen the boat. Jesus, the river's gone to shit.'

'Hmm,' said Juan, 'actually it's the other way around. Or will be.'

'Hurry up,' whispered Clara. 'Please, let's hurry.
There . . .'

But there was nothing. Andrés, who'd stepped back with his hand on his pistol, saw nothing but the distant lights, like torches amid the ships. Then he remembered that they hadn't seen any ships at the docks. Maybe in the fog . . . But it wasn't that. He was sure there wasn't a single ship in the port. *Poor little thing, fear's on its way*, he thought. *That's the first time she's said hurry up* . . . '*And her pleasure at seeing the men so decided grew greater and greater*' . . . *Now I'm making up words*.

'Move along,' Calimano was saying. 'The fishing club: look.'

Juan deciphered the words at the entrance: Argentine Fishing Association. Tuna, catfish, Sundays, yachts. The doors and windows were wide open, stripped. The building was in darkness, covered with mud from the river bed, a soft caricature of the river . . . He turned around, now he was the last. *Buenos Aires* . . . *If still* . . .

'Come on,' said Clara's voice. 'Come on, Juan, hurry up.'

He joined her, and Andrés looked down so he wouldn't offend Juan by staring. They almost ran along the dock, Calimano moving like a cat, urging them to run. The fog was clearing over the river, and they saw a buoy twinkling in the channel. *Alone*, thought Andrés. *It can't be that we're the only ones* . . . He wasn't thinking the mere possibility was incredible; it was just that he couldn't quite believe it.

'The water starts over there,' said Calimano pointing to a chocolate-colored strip. 'Good thing I predicted this would happen and put the boat at the end of the dock. More than a few are going to find themselves hung up tonight.' Bent over the handrail, he was grumbling in a low voice. Andrés was looking as well, with a sudden fear that . . . But Juan and Clara seemed distracted, standing in the middle of the dock, looking at each other.

'Bitchy fly,' said Juan sweetly.

Andrés walked over to them.

'You have to go down that ladder' he said, holding out both hands to them: 'Ciao, you two. Calimano awaits.'

'What about you?' said Clara, almost in the tone of someone who says, 'But you can't think of leaving, it's so early!' Sincere, but unnecessary – not always what people liked to hear. (But it was Andrés who thought it, if he did.)

'Well, I've got to go back for Stella,' said Andrés. 'Juan, the trip's all paid for. Don't give him any more money.'

'Thanks,' said Juan, squeezing his hand until it hurt him. 'There's nothing I can say . . .'

'Nothing. Just get going.'

'It's incredible that you're staying,' murmured Juan. 'Why us?'

'Actually, I'm going, too,' said Andrés, smiling. 'Just a little later. Don't worry, and take Clara. Let's go, there's the ladder.'

Juan gestured. Then he put his hand in his pocket and took out a wrinkled notebook.

'Things I've been writing these past few days,' he said. 'It would be better if you held on to them.'

'Sure,' said Andrés. 'Now get a move on.'

'Andrés,' said Clara.

'Yes, Clara?'

'Thank-you.'

'You're welcome,' said Andrés deliberately. '*Thank-you*' — *so easy and absolving. Say thank-you and you're in peace*. Watching her step down and feeling for the first rung, he wondered, with deliberate cruelty, if Abel wasn't looking for her because of some other 'thank-you.' *So unjust, so stupid. I just ruined my last glimpse of her*, he thought, alone now on the dock. He heard talk, the splash of oars. Juan's voice shouted something to him, but instead of bending over the ladder, he turned around and began to retrace his steps, staring directly at the red curtain of fog that seemed to boil in the distance.

When he was near the swing bridge, he saw a thin, black dog. He went over to pet it, but the animal retreated, showing its teeth. The little chocolate plaza was there — a black circle in the bluish gray of the cobblestones. Andrés went toward the plaza, but before he went in, he lit a cigarette and looked to see if the dog was still there. The great silence of the little plaza was curious, and the distant clamor of the city made it even deeper. *Juan was right*, he thought as he took out his pistol, *this doesn't exist any more, only Clara's memory of it remains*. He was in the center of the plaza, walking slowly, when he saw the silhouette up against a tree. He thought that the silhouette was also part of Clara's memory.

'Hello,' said Abel. 'About time I found you.'

'What can I say? You never know when someone's looking for you.'

'I wasn't looking for you,' said Abel. 'You know that very well.'

'It's all the same.'

'But you're the one who helped them get away.'

'If you think so,' said Andrés, smoking.

'Yes, you, you son of a thousand bitches!'

'One's enough,' said Andrés. 'Don't amplify.'

He saw Abel's movement, felt he was coming at him. He lowered the safety on the pistol and raised it. *From here she would look at the ships*, he managed to think, and the rest was silence, such an enormous silence that it struck him like an explosion.

8

Stella made sure the chronicler was fast asleep, and after settling his head so he'd be comfortable, she left the bar, delighted to be moving around after a long stiffness. On Leandro Alem, she bought *El Mundo*, which the newsboys had begun to sell, and waited for the 99 streetcar, which was coming down Viamonte. Comfortable next to the window, she made the complete circuit of downtown without looking at the street because she was interested in reading the paper. Soon after the 99 began to rattle beyond Puyrredón, she fell asleep and rested a while, her face against the glass. The trolley was almost full, and the murmuring helped her sleep.

When she arrived, she energetically walked the block and a half that was left, thinking about the coffee she was going to make immediately. She drank it in bed, wondering if Andrés would make it home in time to sleep for a few hours. She had just enough time to put the cup on the night table, because her fatigue carried her off like a breeze.

It was after 10:00 when she awoke, the bed full of sunlight. The room was so beautiful with all that light. It was really like a little painting, a picture. Delightful.

Stella got up, rested and content. Andrés would be home soon to have lunch and then get lost in his papers and books.

Well then, a stew wouldn't be a bad idea. Outside, the neighborhood women were chatting. On the table, there was a sheet of paper with writing on it – the things Andrés would write – which it was necessary to put away in the desk drawer.

Stella changed the canary's water and gave him seeds. She'd

turned on the radio and was listening to a very pretty bolero with passionate lyrics, the kind Andrés didn't like. But there would be plenty of time to turn off the radio before Andrés came home.

September 21, 1950